Barbara Pym's (1913-1980) first novel, *Some Tame Gazelle*, was published in 1950, followed by thirteen more books. A writer from the age of sixteen, Barbara Pym has been acclaimed as "the most underrated writer of the century" by the late British poet laureate, Philip Larkin. It is curious that Pym could not find a publisher for her work between 1963 and 1977 despite early success. In 1977 her novel, *Quartet in Autumn*, was shortlisted for the Booker Prize.

The sparkle they [her novels] had on first acquaintance had been succeeded by the deeper brilliance of established art. —Philip Larkin

Barbara Pym. . .is a novelist to catch up with if you've been tardy to find her, like me. Her best ones. . .are sheer delight, and all of them companionable —*Eudora Welty*

There is a thrill of humanity through all her work.
—*Shirley Hazard*

This Christmas, the *New York Times Book Review* conducted a survey of what prominent people are reading, and three out of eighteen reported that they were enjoying the novels of Barbara Pym. . . . The usual remark made about her is that she is Jane Austen recreated, but. . .Barbara Pym is funnier. —*Anatole Broyard*

Other books by Barbara Pym

LESS
THAN
ANGELS

by Barbara Pym

MOYER BELL
Kingston, Rhode Island & Lancaster, England

Published by Moyer Bell

FIRST PRINTING

**LIBRARY OF CONGRESS
CATALOGING-IN-PUBLICATION DATA**

Pym, Barbara , 1913-1980.
 Less than angels / by Barbara Pym. —1st ed.
 256 p. 21.5 cm.
 ISBN 9781559213882
 I. Title.
 PR6066.Y58 L4 2008
 823'.914 19 87011931
 CIP

Printed in the United States of America
Distributed in North America by Acorn Alliance,
549 Old North Road, Kingston, Rhode Island 02881,
401-783-5480, www.moyerbellbooks.com and
in the United Kingdom, Eire, and Europe by
Gazelle Book Services Ltd.,
White Cross Mills, High Town,
Lancaster LA1 1RN England,
1-44-1524-68765, www.gazellebooks.co.uk

LESS
THAN
ANGELS

What would this man? Now, upward will he soar,
And little less than angels, would he be;
Now looking downwards, just as grieved appears
To want the strength of bulls of bears.

—ALEXANDER POPE

CHAPTER ONE

A CONFUSED impression of English tourists shuffling round a church in Ravenna, peering at mosaics, came to Catherine Oliphant as she sat brooding over her pot of tea. But then she realized that of course she wasn't in Italy, and the shuffling figures weren't tourists but men and women from nearby offices, coming away from the counter with their trays and settling down at the tables with hardly a glance at the mosaics on the walls. These were large bright peacocks with spreading tails, each one occupying a little alcove, almost like a side chapel in a cathedral. But why didn't the tray-carriers make some obeisance as they passed the peacocks, or lay offerings of buns, poached eggs and salads on the ground before them? Catherine wondered. Obviously the cult of peacock worship, if it had ever existed, had fallen into disuse.

She poured herself another cup of tea which had become dark and stewed, as she preferred it. She felt no guilt, sitting idly at her table in the window, watching the sun streaming through the amethyst and gold stained-glass borders, while everyone around her gulped and hurried to catch trains home, for she earned her living writing stories and articles for women's magazines and had to draw her inspiration from everyday life, though life itself was sometimes too strong and raw and must be made palatable by fancy, as tough meat may be made tender by mincing.

Catherine was small and thin and thought of herself, with a certain amount of complacency, as looking like Jane Eyre or a Victorian child whose head has been cropped because of scarlet fever. It was natural for her to look a little ragged and

untidy, and the fashions of the day, when women in their thirties could dress like girls of twenty in flat-heeled shoes and loose jackets, their hair apparently cut with nail scissors, suited her very well.

Looking out of the window and down into the street, she saw the rush-hour crowds beginning to move towards the bus-stops. Soon they began to take on a human look, to become separate individuals who might even be known to her. This seemed a good deal more likely, though less romantic, in London than in Paris, where it was said that if you sat long enough at a certain café on the pavement, everybody you had ever known or loved would pass by eventually. Surely though, Catherine thought, peering down, it couldn't be quite *everyone*, that would be far too emotionally exhausting.

On this spring evening she knew that she couldn't possibly see Tom, her present love, because he was in Africa studying his tribe, but it was odd that when the moment did come, the familiar faces in the crowd should be those of two senior anthropologists she had once met at a learned gathering he had taken her to. They seemed to be walking in the wrong direction, against the hurrying stream, and Catherine would hardly have remembered them if they had not been rather an unusual pair, like comics in a music-hall turn. Professor Fairfax was tall and thin with a rather shrunken-looking head; it was a strange coincidence that the particular tribe he had studied went in for head-shrinking and his students had not been slow to point it out. Dr. Vere, his companion, was small and rotund, the perfect antithesis.

Where could they be going at this time, in the wrong direction? Catherine wondered. Was it perhaps significant that two anthropologists, whose business was to study behaviour in human societies, should find themselves pushing against the stream? She hardly knew how to follow up her observation and made no attempt to do so, only asking herself again where they could be going. Curiosity has its pains as well as its

pleasures, and the bitterest of its pains must surely be the inability to follow up everything to its conclusion. Professor Fairfax and Dr. Vere continued to push their way through the crowds, then they disappeared into a side street and were lost from view. Catherine finished her tea and stood up reluctantly to go.

Down in the street a taxi slowed down opposite to where she was waiting to cross over. She could not have known that the distinguished-looking elderly man inside it, stroking his small silver beard, was Felix Byron Mainwaring, one of the older professors of anthropology, now living in retirement in the country.

The taxi turned into the side street and Professor Mainwaring leaned forward in pleasurable anticipation. He told the driver to stop before he had reached the number he really wanted, so that he could see the house from the outside. He tried to imagine how it would strike his colleagues, approaching in their shabby motor-cars or on foot, laden with the paraphernalia of their academic calling, raincoats, brief-cases, files of notes, from which they seemed so unwilling to be parted even on social occasions. Would they raise their eyes to the beautiful Georgian façade – would they even know that it was Georgian? – and envy his skill in having persuaded Minnie Foresight that some, at least, of her late husband's wealth could not be more nobly used than in founding a new anthropological library and research centre and endowing a number of fellowships for young men and women? Certainly *they* could not have done as much. He remembered the first-class railway carriage and the distant church spires of Leamington Spa seen in the greenish light of a spring evening last year, and Mrs. Foresight – it was difficult to think of her as Minnie which was surely an unworthy name – leaning back against the white lace antimacassar, her large blue eyes full of admiration and bewilderment while he talked and explained and persuaded . . . Felix was almost

9

chuckling to himself at the memory of it and gave the driver an unnecessarily large tip as he got out of his taxi.

Fairfax and Vere, trudging along on the opposite side of the street, were talking loudly as they approached the house. Each had a penetrating voice – William Vere because, as a refugee, he had been forced to build a new life in a strange country and make his impression in a foreign language, and Gervase Fairfax because he was the youngest of a large family and had always had to assert himself. Now they were discussing their students, by no means unkindly, for there was a friendly rivalry between them in getting the young people fixed up with research grants which would take them into the 'field' – Africa, Malaya, Borneo or any remote island where there remained a tribe still to be studied.

'Number twenty-three – this must be it,' said Fairfax shortly.

'Yes, I think so.'

They made no comment on the elegance of the house because they did not even glance at it, except to see the number on the door. They were curious to see the place – Felix's Folly, they called it among themselves – but they had both had a hard day and needed a drink.

'I hope everything is ready inside,' said Fairfax, glancing at his watch. 'It's a bad thing to arrive too early, you know. I hope Esther Clovis and her helpers have been cutting sandwiches, or perhaps Felix will have been wise enough to leave that side of it to a catering firm.'

'I suppose he would hardly concern himself with the domestic side of things,' said Vere. 'But we must hope for the best.' He had told his wife that he would not be needing a large meal that evening.

Inside the house there was plenty to eat and drink, but a crisis had arisen. The library had already been open to readers for some days and at this particular moment it happened to be full of young anthropologists, some of them mere students,

who had not been invited to the party, which was to take place in the library itself.

Miss Clovis and her friend Miss Lydgate, who was an expert in African languages, had been in and out of the room with plates of eatables in their hands several times, thinking that surely at the sight of food, unexpected in any kind of library, the visitors would realize that something was afoot and make a move to go. But they continued to read books and make notes.

'I shall have to take action,' said Miss Clovis firmly. 'Come, Gertrude,' she added to her friend, 'we will confront them yet again.'

Six faces glanced up from the long table as the two women entered the room. Miss Lydgate was exceptionally tall with white hair, her garments seeming to flutter round her like draperies, while Miss Clovis was of stocky build with roughly cut short hair and tweedy clothes.

'Good afternoon,' she called out in a ringing tone. 'I am so glad to see that you are taking advantage of this splendid new library so soon. There is really something quite special about it, you know.' She paused, expecting some kind of an answer.

It came from Brandon J. Pirbright, a short dapper young man, elegantly dressed in lavender grey with a spotless white nylon shirt and bow tie. 'I guess it must be, Miss Clovis,' he said. 'We haven't been offered refreshments anywhere else, have we, Melanie?'

'Why no,' said his wife, a dark fierce-looking woman, some inches taller than her husband and less elegantly dressed. 'I think it's a lovely idea.'

'It is a celebration of something?' asked another reader, Jean-Pierre le Rossignol, a good-looking young Frenchman, wearing a suit of biscuit-coloured corduroy velvet.

'Well, I suppose you might say that it is,' admitted Miss Clovis remembering that as well as the Foresight money they had also received a generous grant from the United States and a legacy from a distinguished French anthropologist. Perhaps,

after all, it would be a gracious gesture to include these young people in the party. 'A few people are coming in to drink sherry,' she said. 'I should be very pleased if you would join us.'

Miss Clovis now glanced rather doubtfully at the other three readers who had looked up expectantly on hearing her words. They were a girl of nineteen, Deirdre Swan, and two young men, Mark Penfold and Digby Fox. The last two were close friends and at first sight looked rather alike in their shabby tweed jackets and grey flannel trousers; but while Mark's hair was dark and inclined to be curly, Digby's was fairer and straighter and he was also thought to have a nicer disposition. To Miss Clovis they were just two of the many undistinguished-looking students with whom her work brought her into contact; solid, hard-working, worthy and just a little dull. But let them come too, she thought with an impulse of generosity, as representatives of the hundreds who will use this library. They certainly could not afford to dress as elegantly as the American and the Frenchman, but they were none the worse for that and she had never been one to judge too much by outward appearances. Indeed, she hardly could have been when she obviously paid so little attention to her own.

Esther Clovis had formerly been secretary of a Learned Society, which post she had recently left because of some disagreement with the President. It is often supposed that those who live and work in academic or intellectual circles are above the petty disputes that vex the rest of us, but it does sometimes seem as if the exalted nature of their work makes it necessary for them to descend occasionally and to refresh themselves, as it were, by squabbling about trivialities. The subject of Miss Clovis's quarrel with the President was known only to a privileged few and even those knew no more than that it had something to do with the making of tea. Not that the making of tea can ever really be regarded as a

petty or trivial matter and Miss Clovis did seem to have been seriously at fault. Hot water from the tap had been used, the kettle had not been quite boiling, the teapot had not been warmed . . . whatever the details, there had been words, during the course of which other things had come out, things of a darker nature. Voices had been raised and in the end Miss Clovis had felt bound to hand in her resignation. She had been very lucky to be appointed as a kind of caretaker in the new research centre, for it happened that Professor Mainwaring, in whose hands the appointment lay, disliked the President of the Learned Society. Esther Clovis might not be much of a tea-maker but she had considerable organizing ability and knew how to act in a crisis, as at this moment, confronted with the anthropologists who would not go.

'You will join us too?' she beamed, rather alarming in her geniality. 'We must have the younger generation represented. Mrs. Foresight will be interested to see what her money is likely to be spent on' she added obscurely.

'Thank you,' said Mark, who was the first to find himself capable of speech. 'We should like to very much. 'It's almost a good thing we are so very much *not* dressed for a party,' he murmured to his friend Digby, 'then Mrs. Foresight will see that our need is very real.'

Digby smoothed his hair, glanced indifferently at his grubby hands and made some slight adjustment to his tie. 'I suppose we'd better put these away then,' he said, bundling his notes into his brief-case.

Deirdre Swan, who supposed that she too must be included in Miss Clovis's invitation, wished that she had made her escape earlier. She was a tall thin girl with large brown eyes and a rather lost expression; she did not always quite understand what she was doing and was beginning to wonder if it had been a mistake to embark on the study of anthropology rather than history or English literature. Now she stood in a corner, as if trying to merge herself with the rows of books

13

behind her, watching the arrival of the guests with a kind of fearful wonder.

'Ah, Felix!' shrieked Miss Clovis, as Professor Mainwaring entered the room, 'so glad to see you nice and *early*!'

'My dear Esther, I have only just beaten the others to it. Academic toilers do not understand the art of being fashionably late. If it says six o'clock on the invitation cards you can be sure that my colleagues will arrive at that time.'

His forecast was accurate and the hands of the library clock were barely pointing to six when a mass of people seemed almost to hurl itself through the door. First came Professor Vere and Dr. Fairfax, still talking loudly. They were followed closely by Father Gemini, a missionary and linguistic expert, whose bushy beard and layers of fusty black garments seemed too much for the warm April evening. Behind him came others, too numerous to describe separately, men, and women too, who had all achieved some kind of eminence in their particular sphere. A few stood out by reason of their odd appearance, but the majority were reassuringly ordinary, the kind of people one might see any day on a bus or in the underground. Bringing up the rear were a small benevolent-looking man, bowed down by the weight of two suit-cases which appeared to be filled with lead, and a tall thin man walking with a catlike tread. After them there was a pause and a gap in the procession of guests, and then a worried-looking man in dark jacket and striped trousers, who was something in the Colonial Office, came in, peering from side to side. He disliked sherry which he thought 'livery', was rather frightened of Miss Clovis, and was most anxious to get back to his garden in North Dulwich, but he had never ignored the call of duty.

'Well, well, Comus and his rabble rout!' cried Professor Mainwaring, clapping his hands. The man from the Colonial Office dived quickly into a corner, but the Professor did not seem to expect any comment on his remark. 'What a pity

all our friends cannot be with us today,' he went on, almost in a sarcastic tone. 'My dear friend Tyrell Todd is at this very moment, perhaps, hacking his way through a Congo forest in search of the ever elusive pygmy. Apfelbaum is standing on his head in the Antipodes . . .' here his invention failed him and he drained his glass of sherry with a gesture. Then he was back at the door, welcoming the guest of honour, Mrs. Foresight.

'Ah, Minnie,' he said, bringing out the name almost as if he were savouring its comic flavour, 'this is a great occasion!'

Mrs. Foresight, a little plump fair-haired woman dressed in pale blue, entered the room, blinking at the sight of so many people. After she had been welcomed and introduced, she allowed herself to be placed in one of the small easy chairs which had been arranged at strategic points for the older and more distinguished guests. She found herself near Miss Lydgate and began to make what she hoped was suitable conversation.

'And are you just back from the – er – *field*?' she brought out, trying to remember if 'field' was the right word and what exactly it was that people did there. Of course she knew that, really. Felix had explained so clearly what it was that anthropologists did, or it had seemed clear at the time, whirling through High Wycombe in the dining-car, giggling a little over the difficulty of pouring out tea elegantly. They went out to remote places and studied the customs and languages of the peoples living there. Then they came back and wrote books and articles about what they had observed and taught others how to do the same thing. It was as simple as that. And it was a very good thing that these languages and customs should be known, firstly because they were interesting in themselves and in danger of being forgotten, and secondly because it was helpful to missionaries and government officials to know as much as possible about the people they sought to evangelize or govern.

These thoughts did not arrange themselves quite in this order in Mrs. Foresight's head, and they were interspersed with irrelevant reflections on the people round her, but she believed that she had remembered most of what Felix had told her that afternoon in the train and at their meetings afterwards. Her expression as she listened to Miss Lydgate's plans for the writing up of her linguistic researches, was one of rather strained interest. Women must so often listen to men with just this expression on their faces, but Mrs. Foresight was feminine enough to feel that it was a little hard that so much concentration should be called for when talking to a member of her own sex. It seemed, somehow, a waste of effort.

'It is nice for Miss Clovis to be able to share a flat with you,' she said politely.

'Oh, it all happened *most* conveniently. When Esther resigned from her post at the Learned Society of course she had to leave her flat there and the new one was rather too big for one person. So I filled the gap, stepped into the breach, as it were.'

'That is a good thing for both of you.'

'Yes, we jog along quite happily together. Neither of us knows much about cooking and we're both untidy people but it doesn't seem to matter.'

'I suppose common interests are the main thing,' said Mrs. Foresight doubtfully, thankful that *she* did not have to live with Esther Clovis or Gertrude Lydgate, for she was fond of her food and liked to have 'nice things' around her. 'How do you manage about cooking?'

'We live out of tins and on frozen stuff, don't we, Gertrude,' said Miss Clovis, who had now joined them. 'And we always choose the kind of meat you can fry – chops and things like that.'

'Braised meat can be delicious, and it isn't difficult to cook,' Mrs. Foresight began, but she was interrupted by Father Gemini, who came almost running up to Miss Lydgate, his

beard dipping into his sherry glass, waving a sandwich in his hand.

'Oh, Miss Lydgate, I must apologize for that vocabulary I sent you,' he wailed. 'It was *immensely* unfortunate, but the language is spoken by only five persons now, and the only informant I could find was a very old man, so old that he had no teeth.'

'I appreciate your difficulty,' said Miss Lydgate gruffly.

'Yes, and at the time he was drunk, also. It was *most* difficult.'

'I was interested in what appeared to be something *quite new*,' said Miss Lydgate, drawing Father Gemini almost by his beard into a more secluded part of the room. 'Was it *this*?' A very curious sound, which it is impossible to reproduce here, then came from her. Had she been in the company of ordinary people, it might have been supposed that something had gone down the wrong way and that she was choking, but here nobody took any particular notice of her or of Father Gemini when he cried excitedly, 'No, no, it is *this*!' and proceeded to emit a sound which would have appeared to the uninitiated exactly the same as Miss Lydgate's choking noise.

'Now they'll be happy for hours,' said Miss Clovis indulgently. 'I sometimes think what a pity it is that Gertrude and Father Gemini can't marry.'

'Oh?' said Mrs. Foresight. 'Is it so impossible?'

'Well, he is a Roman Catholic priest, and it is not usual for them to marry, is it?'

'No, of course, they are forbidden to,' Mrs. Foresight agreed. 'Still, Miss Lydgate is much taller than he is,' she added irrelevantly.

'That hardly seems to matter in the academic world,' said Miss Clovis. 'It is, of course, the marriage of true minds that counts.'

'But that beard is so untidy,' said Mrs. Foresight distastefully. 'A wife would make him trim it – I always think

17

Professor Mainwaring's is so becoming, a silver imperial, I suppose you'd call his.'

'Yes, Felix is a fine-looking man; he seems to dominate every gathering, and not only because of his height.'

He stood now in the centre of the room, sipping his sherry, and thinking as he did so that if it was not quite the best sherry it was certainly good enough for the occasion. Esther had been wise not to spend the Foresight money on the very best, he decided; the women would not have appreciated it and his colleagues would have been unworthy of it. Many of them, as he put it to himself, were 'not quite out of the top drawer', an old-fashioned expression but one that conveyed his meaning perfectly. He was wise enough not to use it indiscriminately in these enlightened days, however, and his manner to the up-and-coming young men who still gathered round him was gracious and often kindly. After all, it was not his fault that his father had been able to educate him at Eton and Balliol, or that his youth had been passed in the spacious days of the Edwardian era. Indeed, in his own way he had shown courage in defying the wishes of his parents, who had intended him for the Diplomatic Service, to take up a profession that nobody had ever heard of and that involved going to the remotest parts of the Empire not to govern, which would have been natural and proper, but to study the ways of the primitive peoples living there.

'There really is something rather splendid about him,' said Melanie Pirbright. 'I can imagine he'd have a strong appeal in the States to some of the women's clubs, you know. I wonder if he's ever thought of doing a lecture tour? Doesn't it seem odd that he's never married?'

'Yes, there seems to be no reason for it,' said her husband. 'One wonders whether there might be something between him and Minnie Foresight. Perhaps he feels the burden of his middle name, though. It might be tough to be called Byron— it would certainly take some living up to.'

'You think so?' said Jean-Pierre le Rossignol with his demure smile.

'Perhaps not so difficult for a Frenchman,' said Melanie seriously.

'The name really makes no difference – a man can have many love affairs whatever he is called.'

Did you ever hear that Professor Mainwaring had had many?' Melanie asked, in the tone of one seeking scientific information. 'These things might get around.'

Jean-Pierre shrugged his shoulders and the corners of his mouth turned down in a grimace that suggested a wealth of secret knowledge. But he said nothing.

'On the whole it seems to be English *women* who don't marry,' Melanie went on. 'It would be interesting to know just why that is.'

'Do you need to ask?' said Jean-Pierre, glancing round the room. 'To begin with, there are too many.'

'Yes, that is a problem. There is a good deal to be said in favour of polygamy, I always think.'

'But some women one would hardly want, even as secondary wives,' said Brandon.

'Aren't you using the term "secondary wife", in the wrong sense, dear?' said Melanie. 'It can have a rather specialized meaning, you know.'

'Listen to her,' said Digby, turning aside to whisper to his friend Mark. "Can't she ever relax? I was just wondering if we ought to say a word to Prof. Mainwaring.'

'Say a word to him? What could we talk about? I should have thought that no three people could have had less in common than we have.'

'Oh, I just meant social talk – making ourselves known and that kind of thing. After all we've got to get money from somewhere to do our field-work.'

'How sensible you are – let's go then.'

'You say something,' said Digby, giving Mark a sharp push forward.

'Good evening, Professor,' said Mark. 'We just wanted to tell you how much we enjoyed that last paper of yours at the Learned Society.'

'Most stimulating it was,' mumbled Digby.

'Let me see now, which paper was that – "Anthropology – what now?" Or was it "Anthropology – what-ho!",' chuckled the professor. 'One gets confused, you know. I don't remember noticing you in the audience.'

'We were sitting at the back,' said Mark quickly.

'Ah, yes, so that you could slip out easily. Those chairs by the door are always very much in demand. I hope you slipped out quietly? I cannot recollect that there was any disturbance. I often wonder why it is that people *do* slip out as much as they do. With women it is understandable, I think – a casserole to be seen to or some such thing; perhaps men have trains to catch, or young ladies to meet.'

'We have essays and seminar papers to prepare,' said Digby stolidly.

'And you hope to go out to the field?' said Felix, fixing them with a shrewd glance.

'Well, yes, we do,' said Mark.

'It is difficult . . .' Digby began, but he was interrupted by the arrival of Professor Fairfax who pushed his way into the group crying, 'Now, my dear Felix, I hope you haven't forgotten that you are lunching with me at my club to-morrow?'

'Gervase, my dear boy, certainly I have not forgotten. I am actively looking forward to it.'

'Good evening, Professor Fairfax,' said Mark and Digby, almost in unison.

'Ah, Mr. Fox and Mr. Penfold, how-do-you-do,' said Professor Fairfax in a perfunctory tone.

Even Mark and Digby, inexperienced as they were in the

subtler gradations of social meaning, were perceptive enough to realize that Professor Fairfax was not in the least desirous of knowing how they did, so they edged away and back into their corner.

'Dear boy! My *dear* Felix, my *dear* Gervase,' said Mark scornfully. 'All this bandying about of Christian names disgusts me.'

'We haven't yet acquired the status of being known by ours,' said Digby more mildly. 'It's an interesting study, when you come to consider it. The lower you are in status, the more formal the type of address used, unless you're a servant, perhaps.'

'Still, Fairfax does *know* our names, which is something.'

'But does he know which of us is which?' asked Digby anxiously.

'We can see that he does later. To get the names into their heads – that's the main thing at the moment.'

'Not the most brilliant of your ideas, picking on that paper of his,' said Digby. 'You might at least have chosen some occasion when we really had been present and he might have seen us.'

The young men began bickering among themselves until one of them picked up a decanter of sherry and boldly refilled their glasses. This encouraged them still further and they began to devour plates of sandwiches and little savouries.

They certainly know how to make themselves at home, thought Deirdre Swan, curling her hand round her empty glass and wishing that she had the courage to go home. At nineteen she was still young and sensitive enough to be conscious that she was standing alone and had nothing to drink and to mind about it. Everybody except her seemed to be talking to somebody. She knew Miss Clovis slightly and had spoken to Mark and Digby once or twice, but they were in their third year at the University and she was only in her first. Soon they would be going out to Africa or some other

suitable place and then even they, ordinary as they were, would acquire the glamour of those who had been 'in the field'.

Deirdre looked round the room at the little groups of people and the realization came to her that although she was rather too tall and too thin and her clothes were not particularly smart, she was undoubtedly the best-looking woman in the room and certainly the youngest. This comforted her a little and almost gave her the courage to approach one of the groups, until she noticed that it contained Miss Lydgate, whom she wished to avoid. For Miss Lydgate's brother Alaric had recently come to live next door to the Swans in their London suburb and they had not yet made his acquaintance, in spite of the efforts of Deirdre's mother and aunt. Alaric Lydgate was apparently a retired Colonial administrator, and Deirdre, who had met him in the road once or twice, thought she had detected that 'look' which being in Africa seemed to give to some people, a wild Ancient Mariner gleam in the eye which was usually a sign of some particularly persistent bee buzzing in the bonnet. She did not at all want him to engage her in conversation about Africa and she was afraid that if she made contact with Miss Lydgate it might lead to an introduction to her brother. So she had to go on standing there with her empty glass, praying that one of the young men might take pity on her.

At last Jean-Pierre le Rossignol moved away from his companions and came over to her.

'This is an interesting occasion, I think,' he declared in his precise voice. 'I have not been to such a party before.'

'It isn't like any other kind of party,' said Deirdre rather desperately. 'I suppose it is interesting if you can be detached about it.'

'Oh, but one must be detached about so many things! Otherwise how could a Frenchman endure the English Sunday?'

'It must be difficult. There's very little to do on Sunday, really, unless you go to church.'

'Exactly! And what a variety of churches to go to. There is so much choice – I am quite bewildered.'

'Yes, I suppose there are a lot to choose from if you live right in London. Where I live there are only two.'

'Last week I was at a Methodist Chapel – exquisite!' Jean-Pierre cast his eyes up to heaven. 'The week before at the Friends' House. Next Sunday I have been recommended to try Mattins and Sermon at a fashionable church in Mayfair.'

Deirdre felt a little out of her depth. Churchgoing was a serious matter in her family, one either went to church or one didn't; there was none of this light-hearted experimenting that Jean-Pierre seemed to indulge in.

'I suppose,' he went on, 'you would say I was a Thomist.' He shrugged his shoulders and then fell to examining his nails, so much more exquisitely manicured than Deirdre's were.

'People seem to be going,' she mumbled, thrown off her balance by not knowing what a Thomist was and not liking to ask.

'I believe it is not correct to stay till the end,' said Jean-Pierre, 'so I must be going. I like to do the correct thing where possible.'

People now began to leave as rapidly as they had arrived, and to pair off in a rather odd way. It was of course to be expected that Professor Mainwaring should escort Mrs. Foresight to her car and then drive away with her, but the man from the Colonial Office found himself walking down into the street with Father Gemini and being invited to 'take pot-luck' with Miss Clovis and Miss Lydgate. He protested feebly but it was in vain.

'You can easily get a train to Dulwich – they are very frequent,' said Miss Clovis firmly.

'But it is *North* Dulwich I want to get to,' he said weakly.

'Oh, there isn't such a place!' said Miss Lydgate with rough good humour, leading him and Father Gemini away.

Deirdre found herself alone with Mark and Digby.

'Time gentlemen, please!' said Digby, lurching slightly against a table.

'Did you enjoy the party?' asked Deirdre politely.

'Yes, it improved considerably towards the end,' said Mark. 'We found ourselves near the drink and took the liberty of helping ourselves to it.'

'We are not used to drinking much,' said Digby. 'Do you think we seem the worse for it?'

'I don't know how you usually are,' said Deirdre, disconcerted by their odd, stilted way of walking. Perhaps they *were* the worse for drink.

'We are usually rather dim and hard-working,' said Mark. 'You know,' he added, turning to Digby, 'I do feel we should have said a word to Dashwood.'

'Dashwood? Oh, that man from the Colonial Office. Yes, I suppose we ought to keep in with him.'

'Well, good-bye,' said Deirdre shyly. 'My bus goes from here.'

'I suppose we could have taken her to have a meal somewhere,' said Digby, looking after the moving bus.

'Whatever for?'

'It would have been a nice gesture.'

'We might have taken Prof. Mainwaring out – that would have been even nicer. Anyway, I expect her mother would have supper waiting for her at home.'

'Yes, probably. She seems quite a nice girl, but hardly . . .'

'Not very interesting really.'

'No.'

The two young men had stopped outside a cinema and were gazing at a poster which showed a young woman, with more obvious charms than Deirdre's, reclining seductively in a transparent negligée across what seemed to be Niagara Falls.

'I have that seminar paper to prepare,' said Mark reluctantly.

'Yes, of course,' said Digby meekly.

So they crossed the road and waited for the bus which would take them to their lodgings in Camden Town. But even on the bus they felt reluctant to return to work.

'I know,' said Digby, 'let's go and see Catherine. She'll probably have some news of Tom.'

'And she may be cooking something,' said Mark practically. 'It's so depressing cooking for one person, or so one hears. Let's go and make it worth her while to prepare a good meal.'

CHAPTER TWO

CATHERINE was still speculating about Professor Fairfax and Dr. Vere on her way home. She lived on the shabby side of Regent's Park in a flat over a newsagent's shop which she had taken cheaply at the end of the war. She sometimes felt, as she climbed the worn linoleum-covered stairs, that she was worthy of a more gracious setting, but then there are few of us who do not occasionally set a higher value on ourselves than Fate has done. Generally she was quite happy, for she was naturally of a sanguine disposition, and the flat, with its three rooms, kitchen and bathroom all self-contained, was so very 'desirable' in these days that she knew she was lucky to have it. It was furnished in a way that is sometimes described as 'bohemian' but which is just as often the result of not being able to buy quite enough furniture and carpets. Yet the general effect was comfortable, for Catherine was domesticated in a casual way and a good cook. Her small hands were often rough with housework and sometimes smelled of garlic. Tom used to tease her and say that it was a good thing the custom of hand-kissing was not much practised in England.

Catherine and Tom had met on a Channel boat, during a bad crossing from Dieppe to Newhaven. When they arrived in London it seemed that Tom had nowhere to go that night, so Catherine had offered to put him up in her spare room. After he had stayed a night or two it seemed pointless for him to look for lodgings when in a few days time he was going to stay with his parents in Shropshire, and when he returned to London he had come back to Catherine's flat as naturally as if it had been his own home. They had become fond of each

other, or perhaps used to each other; it was almost like being married except that there were no children, which Catherine felt she would have liked. The fact that she tended to regard most men, and Tom in particular, as children wasn't quite the same thing. Catherine had always imagined that her husband would be a strong character who would rule her life, but Tom, at twenty-nine, was two years younger than she was and it was always she who made the decisions and even mended the fuses. It did not seem to occur to Tom that they might get married. Catherine often wondered whether anthropologists became so absorbed in studying the ways of strange societies that they forgot what was the usual thing in their own. Yet some of them, she had observed, were so highly respectable and conventional, that it seemed to work the other way too, as if they realized the importance of conforming to the 'norm', or whatever they would have called it in their jargon.

She went into her sitting-room and noticed that the tulips in the window were nearly out. They should be at their best by the time Tom came. Now they were in bud and looking almost like hard-boiled eggs, but with more yellow than white in them. She reached for her note-book and jotted down the little simile; these odd details often came in useful. There was a page in her typewriter, half typed, and she sat down, hoping to finish the story she was writing. But the inspiration seemed to have gone and the falsely happy ending she had planned seemed unbearably trite and removed from life. She imagined women under the drier at the hairdresser's, turning the pages lazily and coming to 'The Rose Garden' by Catherine Oliphant. They would read the first page, the one that had the drawing of a girl standing with a rose in her hand and a man, handsomer than any real man could possibly be, standing behind her with an anguished expression on his face; but would they turn to the back of the magazine, where the continuation and ending were to be found? Catherine wondered gloomily. *Dear as remembered kisses after death*, she typed idly, but was it

likely that her hero would have read Tennyson or quoted the line aloud like that? Not very, she thought, getting up and walking about the room.

Her glance came to rest on the little table where she kept drink, when she had any. There was half an inch of sherry in the decanter, no gin, and a sticky bottle of orange squash, half full. The table was dusty, too. Feeling more cheerful, she went into the kitchen and got a duster and mop. She loved housework when she felt in the mood for it and was often inspired with ideas for romantic fiction when shaking the mop out of the window or polishing a table.

The sitting-room window looked out on to a row of small shops with flats above them. Almost opposite was a restaurant run by Cypriots, where Catherine often went to have a meal or to buy cheap wine. She was just wondering whether she could afford to have a meal out this evening, when she saw Digby and Mark approaching. She waved her mop at them and hurried to let them in. She would have to see whether she had anything to give them to eat, for they came like trusting animals, expecting to be fed, and she could not disappoint them.

'Does she do housework in the *evenings*?' said Mark as they came up to the house. 'She seemed to have a mop in her hand.'

'Yes, it's odd. People usually do that kind of thing in the mornings,' said Digby almost disapprovingly. 'I don't know what my mother would say.'

'Does it really worry you?'

'Well, I shouldn't like my wife to do housework in the evenings, would you?'

'No, I suppose not, but women usually have their own way.'

By this time Catherine had opened the door and welcomed them in.

'We've brought some beer,' said Digby. 'There's been a party at Felix's Folly, and it seemed a pity to stop drinking.'

His last words seemed a little out of character, Catherine thought. Digby and Mark were such sober, hard-working young men, though Mark was sometimes rather spiteful in his conversation.

'Oh, was *that* where the two anthropologists were going?' said Catherine. 'I saw them from a window when I was having tea. How nice that you were invited too.'

'We weren't exactly invited,' said Digby. 'We happened to be working there and Miss Clovis couldn't very well leave us out. The party would have gone on around us, as it were.'

They were talking in the kitchen, where Catherine had started to prepare a risotto with whatever remains she could find. She was mincing some cold meat in her mincing machine, which was called 'Beatrice', a strangely gentle and gracious name for the fierce little iron contraption whose strong teeth so ruthlessly pounded up meat and gristle. It always reminded Catherine of an African god with its square head and little short arms, and it was not at all unlike some of the crudely carved images with evil expressions and aggressively pointed breasts which Tom had brought back from Africa. When he had gone away she had shut them all up in a cupboard, but now she supposed she must bring them out again or his feelings might be hurt.

Digby was laying the table in the sitting-room, pausing to read the sheet in Catherine's typewriter. 'Oh, my darling love,' she sighed, laying her head on his shoulder, 'it's been so long.' 'I know – *dear as remembered kisses after death*,' he said gently. 'Did people *really* say things like that to each other?' Digby wondered. His life did not seem to have allowed much time so far for what he called 'amorous dalliance'. Either they said nothing, 'submitted to his embraces' he supposed Catherine might write, or pushed him away indignantly.

Catherine ran into the room and snatched the sheet out of the typewriter. 'You mustn't look,' she cried. 'It's not your kind of story.'

'Will you say that to Tom when he comes back? After all, it hasn't been so *very* long – less than two years. When do you expect him?'

'Next week – at least that's when the boat docks. He may go to see his mother first, it would be on the way.'

'We've decided to fly when we go out to the field,' said Mark, 'then there won't be any danger of our being expected to change for dinner. We consider it an outmoded custom, but I suppose Tom was brought up to it and finds it hard to shake off.'

'Surely he wouldn't take a dinner jacket into the field?' asked Digby in a shocked tone.

·'No, of course not. Tom has broken away from his up-bringing very successfully. He is even shabbier than you are,' Catherine added, not meaning to be unkind.

'I suppose you'd call him an impoverished young man of good family, wouldn't you?' said Mark. 'I heard that the Mallows have quite a big place in Shropshire which is now falling into decay.' There was a hint of satisfaction in his tone.

'Yes, but it's sad,' said Catherine. 'His brother manages the place and I believe his mother works very hard too.'

'Have you met his – er – people?' Digby asked.

'No, I suppose I couldn't expect to, really. Anyway, Tom only goes home occasionally, out of duty. You see, they think he has gone to the bad – it was a great disappointment to them when he took up anthropology. He could have entered the Colonial Service; that would have been all right; one of his uncles was a distinguished Governor somewhere in Africa in the twenties. But for Tom to 'go native', as they regard it – well, you can imagine . . .'

'I suppose his father is a broken man,' said Mark smugly.

'Oh, his father died years ago. An old uncle lives with them, though. I don't know whether he is a broken man or not, somehow one doesn't associate that kind of thing with uncles.'

'Is the uncle his mother's brother?' asked Digby.

'Yes, I think he is.'

'How ironical that is, when you consider that Tom has spent so much of his time investigating the role of the mother's brother in his tribe.'

'Oh, I don't understand these things,' said Catherine impatiently. She busied herself putting things on the table, a dish of grated cheese and a bowl of fruit. She had always envied Tom his family, having none of her own except cousins with whom she had long since lost touch. If she and Tom were to marry, she would acquire a mother, as well as a brother and sister. Tom's sister was rather formidable, she believed, and had married 'well'. Catherine imagined her in pearls and tweeds, *good* tweeds of course and real pearls, with an account at Harrods. He had two aunts in London, one living in South Kensington and the other in Belgravia, but naturally Catherine had not been taken to meet them. She sighed and began serving the risotto.

'What's the matter, Catherine?' asked Digby kindly.

'I don't know. I was just thinking that kind of life would be rather nice. Tom had a girl friend at home, you know, I suppose he could have married her and lived happily as a kind of squire of the village. She was called Elaine – I suppose she still is – and she used to breed golden retrievers.' Catherine giggled. 'It sounds funny, I don't know why. There's something comic and pathetic about doggy Englishwomen, and yet she may not be like that at all.'

'There was a girl at the party we might have brought along,' said Digby. 'We rather debated whether we should have taken her out to supper somewhere, but before we could make up our minds she had hurried away to some distant suburb on a bus.'

'We hadn't enough money, anyway,' said Mark harshly.

'Oh, I wish you'd brought her,' said Catherine. 'I should like to meet some of your girl friends.'

'Well, she isn't exactly that,' said Digby, 'though we thought she was quite nice. She didn't talk much.'

'She's rather too tall for me,' said Mark.

'Yes, if it were a question of her having to lay her head on somebody's shoulder, I suppose I should have to offer mine,' said Digby with a malicious glance at Catherine. 'Though Tom's would be even better.'

CHAPTER THREE

'THE rugs are all out on the lawn,' said Mabel Swan. 'I suppose Mrs. Skinner is going to beat them.'

'The morning is really the time to do that,' said Rhoda Wellcome, her sister. 'Mr. Lydgate must realize that he isn't living in the African jungle now. One doesn't want to be narrow and suburban, goodness knows, but if everybody were to beat their rugs in the evening, just think of the noise!'

'It would be like native drums, I suppose,' said Mabel mildly.

'Poor Mrs. Skinner, I think she has a difficult time,' said Rhoda. 'Probably Mr. Lydgate won't let her do things when he's in the house. I suppose he may have gone out now and she's making the most of the opportunity.'

Why couldn't Rhoda say right out that she knew he had? thought Mabel with a flash of irritation. During the afternoon she herself had heard the click of the next door gate and she knew that her sister had been standing in the dining-room window. So she must have seen him go out. What was the point of living in a suburb if one couldn't show a healthy curiosity about one's neighbours?

'Deirdre will be in soon,' Mabel said. 'I suppose I ought to go and see about supper.'

'Shall I help you?'

'No, no, I have everything planned, thank you.'

The sisters had been sitting in Rhoda's bed-sitting-room, which commanded an excellent view of the next door back garden. They often did this on the lengthening spring evenings between tea and supper, for they were both at home all day

and their household duties were not particularly arduous. It was natural that they should find the unmarried and apparently rather eccentric Alaric Lydgate more interesting than their neighbours on the other side, a married couple with three young children, whose lives followed a pattern which was now familiar, though they had once considered them unconventional. Mr. Lydgate was not often to be seen in the garden, but there was always the hope that he might appear, especially when the weather got warmer. There was a good deal about him that was promising. He was tall and thin and looked rather ill; indeed it was said that he had retired from the Colonial Service because of ill health and come to live in this suburb where a house had been left to him by a relative. He was apparently to do 'light work', whatever that expression, usually associated with gentlewomen unwilling to soil their hands with 'rough', might imply for men. There did not seem to be any trace of a Mrs. Lydgate, but he had a housekeeper, Mrs. Skinner, a little grey-haired woman with a curiously indignant expression who usually wore large artificial pearl ear-rings.

Mabel Swan went downstairs. She was glad that her sister was not helping her with the supper, for she liked to do things in her own way and Rhoda was apt to suggest different ways which, she had to admit, were often more efficient, but after all it was her house and she couldn't be expected to change after nearly thirty years of running it. She pottered round now, a tall vague woman in her early fifties, with a long pale face and brown eyes which her daughter Deirdre had inherited. As she pottered she murmured to herself, 'large knives, small knives, pudding spoons, will they need forks too? Oh, *large* forks, serving spoons, mats, glasses, well *two* glasses in case Deirdre and Malcolm want to drink beer, Rhoda probably won't . . . and now, wash the lettuce . . .' It was nice when the warm weather came and they could have salads for supper, she thought, though why it was nice she didn't really know.

34

Washing a lettuce and cutting up the things to go with it was really almost as much trouble as cooking a hot meal, and she herself had never got over an old-fashioned dislike of eating raw green leaves. When her husband had been alive they had always had a hot meal in the evenings, winter and summer alike. He needed it after a day in the City. But now he was gone and Rhoda had been living with them for nearly ten years now and everyone said how nice it was for them both, to have each other, though of course she had the children too. Malcolm was a good solid young man, very much like his father, reliable and, although of course she never admitted it, a little dull. He did not seem to mind about the hot meal in the evenings. But Deirdre was different, clever and moody, rather like she herself had been at the same age, before marriage to a good dull man and life in a suburb had steadied her.

'Shall I lay the table?' Rhoda asked, appearing in the kitchen doorway.

'Oh, thank you, that would be a help. I've put the things out on the trolley.'

'You've forgotten side plates,' said Rhoda evenly, taking four from the plate-rack.

'Have I? Well, I hadn't really finished putting out the things. I just put out some to be getting on with. Then I thought it would be better to start washing the lettuce.'

Rhoda wheeled the trolley into the dining-room and began to lay the table. It irritated her to see Mabel in the kitchen, doing things so vaguely and inefficiently. Sometimes it was all she could do not to interfere, but they had had 'words' about this when Rhoda first came to live with the Swans and Rhoda was sensible enough to realize that it was Mabel's house and she must be allowed to do things as she liked. For, after all, they got on so well together. They both liked church work, bridge and listening to the wireless in the evenings. And then they looked so alike, both tall and dark with brown eyes; it was difficult to believe that Rhoda was

the elder, for she was neater and better dressed, better preserved, one might almost have said. But then she had not been married and had two children. She had always lived very comfortably, keeping house for her parents, living alone for a short time after their deaths, and then coming to live here with Mabel and the children. It was a very satisfactory arrangement and Rhoda was not in the least envious of her sister's fuller life, for now that they were both in their fifties there seemed to be very little difference between them. She would perhaps have liked what she called 'the experience of marriage', a vague phrase which seemed to cover all those aspects which one didn't talk about, but she would not have liked to have had it with poor Gregory Swan. She was still sometimes faintly interested in men, as she was now in Alaric Lydgate, but in what way she hardly knew. She certainly did not think of marriage any more.

Every evening there was the arrival of Malcolm and Deirdre to look forward to. After a day at work they were, or should have been, full of interesting little scraps of gossip and information about this and that, and if they sometimes seemed uncommunicative and withdrawn it was quite easy to draw them out with a little tactful questioning and perseverence.

Malcolm came in now as she was laying the table. He was a pleasant-looking young man of twenty-five with brownish hair and eyes and nothing particularly distinctive about him. He put his bowler hat and neat flat brief-case down on the hall table and went into the downstairs cloakroom to wash his hands.

'Had a good day?' Rhoda called out.

'Not too bad, thanks,' he replied, as always, and then went through to the kitchen to get his usual glass of beer.

Rhoda went into the hall and took up his evening paper which was lying neatly folded on top of his brief-case. There had been a nasty murder, or series of murders; bodies of women had been discovered in a house in a not very nice

36

part of London, and Rhoda, in common with a great many people in all walks of life, was anxious to read about the latest developments. It was dark in the hall, for the stained-glass windows on either side of the door did not let in much light, but she sat down and began to read avidly.

'Deirdre's rather late tonight,' said Mabel, passing through to the dining-room with a dish of salad in her hand.

'Mm, yes,' murmured Rhoda, turning a page of the newspaper. 'They noticed a strong smell, it says, no wonder.'

'As we are just having salad, I think we had better start without her,' Mabel went on. 'I expect she'll be in soon.'

Deirdre was at that moment sitting on top of a bus which was moving very slowly along a suburban road. The drinks she had had seemed to have sharpened her perceptions and she looked about her in a detached way, noticing her surroundings as if she were a stranger visiting the neighbourhood for the first time. But she was not yet detached enough to appreciate any of the beauties of the scene. The houses seemed to her ugly and their well-kept gardens conventional and uninteresting. The wallflowers and tulips were the same every year and the lilacs and laburnums obviously could not grow in real country gardens. Even the magnolias were not the right kind, with shiny leaves and huge creamy flowers, which one saw growing against Georgian houses in country villages.

She got off the bus and hurried along her own road. Mr. Dulke who lived opposite, was cutting his hedge, but she pretended not to see him, walking along with her head bent, fearful of the facetious greeting or comment that might come. Towards the end of the road the houses became larger and there was the church, a modern red brick building with a vicarage to match. The Swans' house stood back from the road and the front garden was overgrown with trees and shrubs. Just inside the gate was a guelder rose bush; Deirdre had loved the greenish-white flower balls when she was a child, but now the bush seemed to need pruning and the flowers, when they

came, were full of green fly. Ah, my childhood, my innocent childhood, she thought, remembering a Tchekov play which she had recently seen. In the middle of the garden path lay a headless doll, no doubt left there by one of the Lovell children from next door. Deirdre pushed it aside with her foot.

'Is that you, dear?' Her mother's voice greeted her as she opened the front door.

'Yes. I hope you haven't waited supper?'

'No, we were just going to start.'

In the dining-room Rhoda and Malcolm were already sitting at the table contemplating their salads.

'I had salad for lunch,' said Deirdre.

'Oh, did you, dear? I hope you don't mind having it again.'

'Well, it's not madly exciting, is it.'

'You could have an egg,' her aunt suggested.

'I don't feel like an egg,' said Deirdre unhelpfully. 'I'd like something *different*.'

There was an expectant silence round the table.

'Some rice, all oily and saffron yellow, with aubergines and red peppers and lots of garlic,' went on Deirdre extravagantly.

'Oh, well, dear, it's no good wishing for that sort of thing *here*,' said her mother with an air of relief.

'You look rather pink in the face, dear sister,' said Malcolm in a jocular tone. 'Almost as if you'd been drinking.'

'I've had three glasses of sherry,' said Deirdre rather defiantly. 'I was at the new Library place – Felix's Folly we call it – and there was a sort of party there.'

'I suppose it was for anthropologists,' said Rhoda, bringing out the word with difficulty.

'Yes, there were quite a lot there.'

'What about the one you rather like – was he there?' Mabel asked.

'The one I like?' said Deirdre coldly. 'I can't think who you can mean. I don't like any of them particularly.'

'I thought there was one who lent you some notes or some-

thing,' floundered Mrs. Swan. 'I'm sure you said something about it.'

'One of them may once have been a little more polite than the others,' said Deirdre, 'but I don't think I particularly liked him for it.'

'I expect the right one will come along one of these days,' said Rhoda with an aunt's confidence. She liked to think of her niece as being courted by suitable young men, though, from what she had heard of them, she rather doubted whether anthropologists could be so regarded. There was something disquieting about all this going out to Africa to study the natives, she felt. She would have preferred to see Deirdre married to one of Malcolm's friends and comfortably settled in a nice little house nearby.

'You must make us some of this rice you were talking about,' said Mabel quickly. 'I dare say it is delicious and if we weren't going out to bridge or seeing Father Tulliver about anything it wouldn't really matter about the garlic, would it, Rhoda?' she turned to her sister, anxious to prevent her from making any more remarks about the right young man coming along. Spinsters didn't really know how to deal with young people, and even mothers said the wrong thing often enough.

'All right, I'll get the things in Soho one day,' said Deirdre quite graciously.

'Do you happen to know whether Mr. Lydgate's sister lives rent free with that Miss Clovis?' Rhoda asked.

'Why ever should I? You'd better ask Mr. Lydgate,' said Deirdre. 'Though somehow I can't imagine Miss Clovis letting anyone have anything for nothing.'

'It's a wonder she doesn't live with her brother,' mused Rhoda. 'Of course the house is smaller than this one, but there would certainly be room.'

The older woman speculated on this, while Malcolm finished his meal and left the room. He usually spent the evenings pottering about with his car or at the local club, where the

young men of the neighbourhood gathered for mysterious manly purposes. Deirdre was reminded of the African men's associations which she had read about in the course of her studies. But the object of many of these seemed to be to intimidate the women, whereas here women were allowed to belong to some sections of the club and might almost be considered as one of its amenities. Perhaps they intimidated the men. Certainly they often led them captive in marriage and Malcolm had recently become engaged to a girl he had met when playing tennis. Deirdre almost spoke her thoughts aloud, but then she realized that neither her mother nor her aunt would appreciate her points and would think she was trying to be 'cynical', which they thought a pity in a young woman of nineteen with a happy home and all her life before her.

When they had finished the meal Deirdre offered to help her mother with the washing-up.

'No, dear, don't you bother,' said Mabel. 'You've been working all day, Rhoda and I can manage it.'

'You always say that, Mabel,' Rhoda reminded her when they were alone together at the sink. 'What will she do when she has a home of her own?'

'I expect she'll leave everything until she has no more clean crockery left,' said Mabel, who sometimes felt as if she would like to do this herself.

'I can't settle down to listen to the wireless when I know there's washing-up to be done,' said Rhoda. 'It really worries me.'

'But there are worse things to worry about,' said her sister.

'Worse things?'

'Yes, things going on in the world, bigger things.'

Rhoda's face looked grave for a moment. She knew that there were worse things, but she also knew that her sister did not really worry about them. It was the same with books and programmes on the wireless. There were the books they

felt they ought to read and which they sometimes put down on their library lists; but they were secretly relieved when each time they went to get a book the librarian handed out yet another novel. For if by any chance she should produce that heavy work of politics or literary criticism it never happened to be the right time for reading it; it was not suitable for a week-end or a holiday or a hot summer or cold winter afternoon. And so it came about that, like many other well-meaning people, they worried not so much about the dreadful things themselves as about their own inability to worry about them.

When they had finished in the kitchen they took their seats by the wireless in the drawing-room, each with some sewing or knitting.

'There's a talk on the Third Programme,' said Rhoda, as if to make amends for worrying about such a trivial thing as unwashed dishes, 'something about the betrayal of freedom. It might be . . . she stopped and began tuning the wireless set, for she had been going to say 'interesting', but the word seemed inadequate. 'I think it's already started, but I expect we'll soon get the thread.'

They sat back in their chairs and a torrent of words rushed at them. A man seemed to be talking, at phenomenal speed, about tables and why they did not rise up into the air.

'I suppose this *is* the right programme,' said Rhoda doubt-fully. 'He must be thirsty, talking so fast and for an hour, too. Still, I suppose he would have a glass of water by him.'

'It is a recording,' said Mabel, consulting the *Radio Times*. 'Perhaps they have put it on too fast.'

They listened for a little longer and then Mabel said tenta-tively, 'It would be a pity to miss the beginning of the play.'

Without a word her sister altered the tuning of the set. 'I dare say Malcolm and Deirdre might have understood some of it,' she said. '*We* cannot hope to now.'

There was a certain tragic dignity in her utterance. What

had freedom to do with tables? she wondered helplessly. And yet, they were *not* free to rise up into the air of their own accord, so there might be *some* connection there.

They were soon absorbed in the play, for it was about people like themselves, being an adaptation of a well-known stage success. After a while both the sisters realized that they had heard it before, but neither could remember exactly how it ended. So life seemed to go round in a circle, with tables hurtling through the air.

Up in her room, which was over the drawing-room, Deirdre could hear the booming of the wireless voices, which prevented her from concentrating on the anthropological book she was trying to read. 'A ritual monster called *mbusia*' she read aloud in a serious tone. This was tough going and one could not afford to let one's attention wander for an instant; it was disconcerting the way it seemed to want to. She had often wondered why the atmosphere of her own room was so much less conducive to study than that of a library. Perhaps it was because of the bed, which was not a real divan and could not hope to look like anything but a bed, even when it was covered with a folk-weave spread and heaped with cushions. She had always been meaning to get Malcolm to saw off the ends for her, but he was generally too busy with his own odd jobs when he wasn't at the club. There were a few books in the room and the pictures reflected Deirdre's changing tastes from adolescence to young womanhood; wild duck flew in over an estuary, seemingly unconscious of the Braque still-life beside them. Most of the furniture had been painted turquoise blue when she was sixteen and had wanted an unusual colour scheme, but the curtains and carpet had become so faded that they would have gone with anything. Deirdre had lost interest in the room now and did not really care or notice how it looked, for somehow it had not fulfilled its promise. The work that was to have been done up here, the poems written, even the little informal parties that were to have been held,

had not come to anything after all. As she sat at her desk in the window, her book open before her, Deirdre was conscious only of the booming of the wireless beneath her and Mr. Dulke watching her from his front garden opposite. Or if he was not actually watching her, he was *there* and she could hear the snip of his shears. Would he never go in to have his supper? Surely it was time for Mrs. Dulke to appear and summon him in? Deirdre looked up from her book and caught his eye. He waved up at her with an almost roguish gesture. He had known her since childhood and was one of the oldest residents in the road. He had lived in the same house for over forty years, as he never tired of telling people – he and Mrs. Dulke, their two sons and three daughters, all grown up and married now. He could remember when the district was little more than a village and there were fields opposite his house. Then more houses had been built and finally the church and the vicarage. There was something depressing, Deirdre felt, in a place that had grown up within living memory. She would have liked to live in the heart of London or deep in the country. There could be no dignity or beauty or even interesting squalor in a place that was no more and no less than a nine-penny bus-ride from Piccadilly Circus.

At last Mrs. Dulke appeared in the garden opposite, wearing a flowered smock, to summon her husband to his evening meal. They usually had some simple dish, scrambled eggs or macaroni cheese, Mrs. Dulke would explain to anyone who cared to listen; Edgar liked the big meal in the middle of the day, he couldn't take anything heavy at night.

Deirdre closed her book, marking the place carefully, for it was not the kind of book which one could pick up casually and remember exactly what point had been reached, and went downstairs to the drawing-room. The play had finished and Rhoda had just made a cup of tea. There was something reassuring about the scene, her mother and aunt sewing and knitting in the pleasant chintzy room cluttered with photo-

graphs and ornaments, the silver tea-tray and the gay tartan tin of shortbread on the little oak table. Deirdre felt comforted without realizing that she had been in need of it.

A muffled sound came from outside. It was like the cutting down of the trees in *The Cherry Orchard*, Deirdre thought, except that the sound wasn't quite sharp enough for an axe.

'That can't be Mrs. Skinner beating the rugs *now*,' said Rhoda. 'She must be mad.'

'It might be Mr. Lydgate himself,' suggested her sister. 'In some ways, you know, he is rather strange.'

It must be his life in Africa, Rhoda thought later, as she stood in the dark uncurtained window of her room, looking down into the next door garden. She could just make out his shadowy figure in some long garment; if he had been a clergyman it could have been a cassock, but as he was not she was forced to the rather shocking conclusion that it must be a dressing-gown. He seemed to be moving about on the lawn, picking up the rugs which had been lying on the grass. When he had gone into the house she drew the curtains and put on the light, and began to get ready for her bath. She made her preparations slowly and efficiently, following a careful routine. She left the bathroom as she would wish to find it, folding her own towels and everyone else's in a special way that pleased her. It worried her a little that Malcolm was not yet in, for he would spoil the symmetrical arrangement of the towels and might splash water on the floor, in the way that men did when they had a bath. Still, if he was very late he might decide not to have one, there was always that.

Before going back to her own room, Rhoda went quietly downstairs to see if her sister had laid the breakfast satisfactorily. She saw that Mabel had made an effort, but there were one or two things missing, the marmalade spoon and the mats for the coffee; she put right these omissions and then returned quietly to her room.

What is she doing, creeping about like that? Mabel

wondered, lying in bed listening to Rhoda's careful footsteps. Then she heard Malcolm's key in the door and relaxed herself for sleep. He too crept quietly in. No raucous voice or drunken shout disturbed the peace of the suburban road; the occasional screech of an owl made it seem as if one were in the country. The moon shone through the stained-glass window on the landing as Malcolm took off his shoes and started to creep upstairs.

CHAPTER FOUR

DEIRDRE seemed to have been awakened by the sound of organ music and voices singing a hymn. At first she thought she must be still dreaming, but then she realized that it was probably some Festival or Day of Obligation and that Father Tulliver must be having an early morning Sung Mass. It gave her an uneasy feeling to have the church so near her bed and she felt almost guilty that others should be up and singing, such very high hymns too, the voices did not seem able to reach the top notes. They were, of course, predominantly women's voices.

'I do hope the vicar will be having a good breakfast,' said Mabel Swan, as they sat having theirs. 'Something hot, I should imagine; even cereal would be hardly enough.'

'What funny things you hope for, mother,' said Malcolm looking up from his paper.

'Well, dear, he ought to have a good breakfast after taking such a very early service.'

'And I think *I* ought to have something hot too,' said Rhoda, coming in wearing her hat and coat.

'Why, have you been to church? I didn't know there was anything today.' Mabel looked a little annoyed, for there was a certain amount of rivalry between the sisters about church-going, and Father Tulliver was so much higher than the former vicar that it was sometimes difficult to keep up with him. 'It wasn't a Day of Obligation, was it?' she asked rather self-consciously, for these new expressions did not come easily as yet.

'No, not of Obligation, but of Devotion,' said Rhoda, unable to help sounding a little smug.

'Well I never,' said Mabel, rather ruffled. 'I suppose you didn't have a cup of tea before you went out?'

'Well, hardly,' said Rhoda, but she too remembered the old Low Church days of their girlhood, when a tray of tea and even a plate of thin bread-and-butter was put out for the early church-goers. 'I will fry myself an egg,' she declared. She felt slightly resentful, as if her sister should have offered to fry it for her, but Mabel, piqued at what seemed to be Rhoda's deceit, sat firmly reading the *Daily Graphic*.

Malcolm and Deirdre finished their breakfast and got ready to go to their work. Malcolm always travelled to the City by Underground, but Deirdre preferred the bus ride although it was much slower. She sat in a kind of dream, an anthropological book open on her lap, realizing that it was a lovely morning but not thinking about anything in particular. She was conscious of little vague longings and a slight feeling of discontent, but these were not unusual. She wished she were cleverer and had a flat of her own and she would have liked to be in love. She remembered that she was going out to the theatre that evening with a friend of Malcolm's, who was rather fond of her in a dull sort of way, but the prospect did not fill her with any particular excitement. Bernard Springe was the kind of young man her mother and aunt regarded as 'suitable', which was enough to damn him in Deirdre's eyes. Still, it might be a fitting occasion to wear her new dress, which had a strapless bodice.

When she arrived at the school of anthropology, or rather the corner of some other building which was all that the college authorities could allow to the study of this new and daring subject, she found two third-year students, Vanessa Eaves and Primrose Cutbush, preparing to go to a seminar. This barbarous ceremony, possibly a throwback to the days when Christians were flung to the lions, took place every week.

Somebody prepared and read a paper on a given subject, after which everybody else took great pleasure in tearing it and its author to pieces and contributed their own views on various matters not always entirely relevant.

Deirdre listened with a certain amount of awe to the conversation of the two girls. Primrose, a tall fair Amazon, had strong political views, while Vanessa, who was dark and languorous, was generally in the throes of some desperate love affair. Today, it seemed, she had a hangover and was due to read a paper at the seminar.

'I feel *exquisitely* brittle,' she moaned, 'as if I were spun out of Venetian glass and the merest *breath* would shatter me.'

'If you really haven't finished your paper you can expect some rough handling from Fairfax,' said Primrose brusquely.

'I know – just think of the exquisite agony of it! The heavy sarcasm of that special voice he puts on – do you suppose he *practises* it? I wonder if he'll be wearing his rough tweedy suit – so *manly*, isn't it.'

'I can't think what you see in Professor Fairfax,' said Primrose sensibly. 'He isn't even good-looking.'

'I know, bless him,' murmured Vanessa in a fond silly tone, 'but ugly people can be so *desperately* attractive, I always think.'

Deirdre listened scornfully now. She had thought that only female undergraduates at Oxford talked in this affected way, but then she remembered that Vanessa lived in Kensington from which anything might come. She settled herself down to work in the dark depressing room, which had many tattered books in shelves round the walls and some moth-eaten African masks, put there either to inspire the students in their work or because no museum really wanted them. There was even the skeleton of a small animal, a relic of the days when the room had been used for the study of Zoology.

As the morning went on, Deirdre was not alone in her work, for the room, as well as being a general dumping-ground for

unwanted anthropological specimens, was also regarded as a kind of no-man's land, where former students of the department, who had nowhere else to go, might find a corner in which to write up their field-notes. There were one or two tables spread with papers and these were spasmodically occupied by these shabby hangers-on. They lived in the meaner districts of London or in impossibly remote suburbs on grants which were always miserably inadequate, their creative powers stifled by poverty and family troubles. It would need the pen of a Dostoievsky to do justice to their dreadful lives, but they were by no means inarticulate themselves, often gathering in this room or in a nearby pub to talk of their neuroses and the pyschological difficulties which prevented them from writing up their material. Some of them had been fortunate enough to win the love of devoted women – women who might one day become their wives, but who, if they were thrown aside, would accept their fate cheerfully and without bitterness. They had learned early in life what it is to bear love's burdens, listening patiently to their men's troubles and ever ready at their typewriters, should a manuscript or even a short article get to the stage of being written down.

On this particular morning one pale wretched-looking young man sat in a corner, murmuring a strange language into a kind of recording machine, while another banged furiously at a typewriter for a quarter of an hour, then tore out the sheet of paper, crumpled it up on the floor and hurried out of the room, his hand to his brow in a stricken gesture. Nobody took any notice of Deirdre, but she found it hard to concentrate and was glad when lunch-time came. She was just gathering her books together when the door opened yet again and another young man came in. He was of about the age of the desperate ones – twenty-eight or nine – but Deirdre could not remember that she had ever seen him before. He was tall and dark, with thin aristocratic features and brilliant

grey eyes – or this was how Deirdre always described him afterwards. Perhaps at the time she was conscious only of the shabby raincoat and the battered brief-case, and the fact that he stood over her rather disconcertingly, as if he expected a welcome.

'I suppose we don't know each other,' he said at last, smiling at her. 'I've been away nearly two years and feel like Rip Van Winkle.'

Deirdre was so astonished that he should take notice of her that she could think of nothing to say and at the best of times she was always too shy to have a quick reply ready. 'I think most people are at the seminar,' she ventured.

'Of course – the Friday seminar! One might just as well come back on the Judgment Day and expect to find things normal and I believe one would. I'm Tom Mallow, by the way.' He began walking about the room, taking books out of the shelves and making derogatory comments on them, as if he could not decide whether to go or stay. 'And what's your name?' he asked.

'Deirdre Swan,' she mumbled, thinking what a silly name it was.

'Deirdre of the Sorrows,' he said, but somehow she did not mind the old joke from him. 'And you do look rather sad sitting here all by yourself. Shall we go and have a drink?'

'Oh, thank you, that would be nice . . .' She hardly knew what to say, being unused to drinking in general and in the middle of the day in particular. She hoped she hadn't appeared too eager to go with him; the male students in her year never asked her to drink with them, though there were one or two of her contemporaries who were more favoured as they were thought to be 'good value', whatever that rather sinister phrase might imply.

'Drinking alone is rather depressing, I always think.'

So he had been going to have a drink anyway, she noted.

But of course he had. He had expected to find a crowd of people he knew. She supposed it might be some kind of a compliment to herself that he had not waited for them to come out of the seminar. Unless, of course, he had been so eager for a drink that he just couldn't wait.

'I don't think I've ever tried drinking alone,' she said. The idea of it made her want to laugh. She imagined herself in her room at home with a bottle of gin and her mother or aunt calling out, 'What are you doing, dear?' Or Mr. Dulke watching her from his front garden.

Tom smiled at her and said, 'No, I suppose you're too young to have done much drinking of any kind.'

'I'm nineteen,' she said rather coldly.

'Oh, much too young,' he mocked. 'This is the usual place, I believe, unless you prefer one of the others?'

They had stopped outside one of the many pubs in the area. Deirdre didn't know whether it was the usual place or not. One pub seemed very much like another to her, except that some were of the old cosy type, while others, like the one by the river at home, all new and gleaming. This was of the cosy kind, with round tables and shabby horsehair benches. The bar was crowded with what Deirdre thought of vaguely as 'business men', all laughing excessively loudly at what must have been a joke made by the fat elderly woman who was serving them. Though perhaps it did not always need a joke to make a group of men laugh loudly in a pub.

'We shall have to drink beer,' said Tom rather apologetically. 'I hope that's all right?'

'Oh, lovely,' she said, taking a large brave gulp of the tepid bitter. 'I simply adore it.'

There was a silence and Tom began to wonder why he had asked this strange girl to drink with him instead of waiting for Mark and Digby or somebody else that he knew to come out of the seminar. He had left Catherine busy finishing a story and seeming to have no time for him, so it was both soothing

and gratifying to have Deirdre beside him, her great brown eyes fixed on his face, an occasional interested or sympathetic murmur her only interruption to his account of himself and his work. Tom had never had to make much effort with women, who took a natural and immediate liking to him, so he did not lay himself out to be particularly interesting to Deirdre or to ask her anything about herself.

Love at first sight can hardly ever be mutual, though it may seem to have been when discussed and remembered later. Tom was certainly not aware of Deirdre as anything much more than a satisfactory audience, but with her it was very different. She felt such a rush of happiness that she could have listened for ever to his voice going gently on about the complications of lineage segmentation. Something of what she felt must have shown itself in her face, for when she turned towards him with a smile on her lips and an uncomprehending starry-eyed look, he smiled too, said something about being a bore and went to get another drink.

With the second bitter they looked at his photographs. Dark-skinned figures, dressed in white robes, bits of cloth or nothing, crowded together in various unidentifiable activities, mostly seen from a distance. Sometimes, for a change, there was a close-up of a menacing figure in a mask or a dress of leaves, or a beautiful girl, naked to the waist and wearing a lot of beads, which Deirdre stared at dutifully but with some embarrassment, not quite knowing what to say. The last photograph seemed to be of Tom himself, standing outside a hut with a pointed thatched roof.

'I think I like that one best,' she said shyly, hoping that he might give it to her, but he just laughed and said that it was in the worst possible taste to show photographs of oneself in the field, and then gathered them back into their wallet.

Deirdre looked at the clock. She saw to her amazement that it was after two. 'I must go,' she said. 'I told my mother I'd be home early this afternoon.'

'Oh, I hope she won't worry, then. Mothers do tend to, I find.'

Could it be that he too had a mother? thought Deirdre in wonder. 'Does your mother worry?' she asked, emboldened by the bitter.

'She certainly does. She's bought herself a book about tropical diseases and has rather a horrid time reading about everything I might get. I hope you aren't awfully hungry,' he went on, as they walked along the street. 'I should have bought a sandwich for you, but I've had a meal myself so I'm afraid I forgot.'

Deirdre wondered what meal it could have been. An early lunch seemed unlikely, so perhaps it was a very late breakfast? She was able to ponder about this on the bus home, remembering the whole wonderful experience and his friendly, if too casual, 'see you again, sometime.' But *when*, she had wanted to ask, wondering how she was going to endure her evening with Bernard Springe and all the days ahead with the uncertainty of her next meeting with Tom lying over them.

There are few experiences more boring and painful for a woman than an evening spent in the company of one man when she is longing to be with another, and that evening Bernard's dullness seemed to have a positive quality about it so that it was almost a physical agony, like the dentist's drill pressing on a sensitive tooth. And yet Bernard was tall and well-dressed, better-looking than Tom Mallow, and his conversation, if one were to analyse it, was perhaps more interesting than Tom's had been. He took Deirdre to a play she had been wanting to see and gave her a good supper afterwards. What was more, he had a car, which meant that the ride home to the suburb was done in comfort, with no anxiety about the last bus or tiring journey in crowded stuffy tube.

The wine she had drunk had put Deirdre into a silent brooding mood and they drove without speaking for some time. She was trying to imagine what an evening with Tom

would have been like. Of course he hadn't any money, so they would just have gone somewhere cheap to eat or perhaps just sat in a pub drinking beer and talking about his work. Segmentation of the lineage, fission and accretion, she thought, desolately and without humour.

'What are you thinking about?' Bernard asked gently.

They could have ridden on top of a bus together, but of course she didn't yet know where he lived. Perhaps somebody at college would know – surely she could bring the conversation round to Tom Mallow somehow without it seeming too obvious?

'You *are* in a dreamy mood,' Bernard persisted. 'I feel as if you were miles away.'

'Oh, I'm sorry,' she said. 'I was thinking about the play. It was so sad.'

'Shall we stop and look at the river for a minute?' he suggested in a rather shaky voice.

'All right,' said Deirdre indifferently. People who didn't live here always thought the river looked so beautiful at night, but to her it was just the place where Mr. Dulke and Mr. Lovell took their dogs and the young men from the club walked with their girl friends. Looking out of the car she could see Mr. Lovell now, walking rather too briskly for Snowball, his old sealyham, who lolloped along like a little rocking-horse in his efforts to keep up with his master.

'Not unhappy about anything, are you, dear?' Bernard asked.

'Oh, no, thank you, just not very gregarious, I'm afraid,' said Deirdre. She hated to be called 'dear' and Bernard's arm had now crept round her shoulders and his hand was straying further than she wished. But suddenly it stopped and withdrew quickly as if it had touched an asp or a scorpion. He must have come upon the bone of her strapless bodice which made her such an odd shape. He would hardly have expected to find a bone *there*, she thought, stifling her laughter.

'I'm not really that shape you know,' she said suddenly in a gay tone. 'It must feel like a chicken's carcase – so unexpected!'

Bernard was perhaps a little embarrassed for he had no ready answer, so she went on in the same uncharacteristic way 'A chicken's carcase is all hollow inside and domed like the roof of a cathedral, so noble!'

'What strange things you think of,' he said reverently. 'I suppose I ought to take you home now – it's after midnight.'

After midnight – then it was tomorrow! And she might see Tom. She turned to Bernard, her eyes shining, and thanked him for a lovely evening. Greatly relieved, for he had been disturbed by her strange talk, he kissed her and she did not seem to object, as she so often did. A funny girl, that was how he summed her up in his own mind. Next time they might go and see a musical show which would have been his own choice rather than the gloomy problem plays she seemed to prefer.

'Look, there's a light next door,' she said, as they approached her house. 'I wonder what Mr. Lydgate's doing?'

'Having a sundowner?' Bernard suggested, for he did not know much about colonial administrators and his ideas about what they might be doing were limited and conventional.

'Oh, *no*, he's performing some ghastly rite to propitiate his ancestors,' said Deirdre wildly

'Good heavens! Do you see that?' Bernard pointed to the lighted window where a grotesque silhouette appeared, lingered for a moment, and then moved away.

'It looks as if he's wearing an African mask,' said Deirdre. 'It seems a strange thing to be doing at this time of night – probably the neighbours will complain.'

She said good-night to Bernard and crept quietly up the stairs, but both her mother and her aunt were awake, and her mother called out 'Is that you, dear?' as she always did.

Deirdre reassured her and then went to her own room and

stood in front of the looking-glass, contemplating herself in the bony-bosomed dress from all angles. Then she took off the dress, flung it carelessly over the back of a chair and knelt by the bookcase in her petticoat. She had remembered a poem, cherished by many schoolgirls for many different kinds of love, the sonnet by Dante Gabriel Rossetti, beginning,

When do I see thee most, beloved one?

She read it through and then got ready for bed. *African Political Systems*, her current bedside book, was unopened that night.

CHAPTER FIVE

THE ugly black marble clock on the mantelpiece in Alaric
Lydgate's study struck one. It had been his father's, a
present from his colleagues at the Mission. It had kept good
time for over forty years under the most difficult conditions,
being shaken about by his carriers bearing his loads over
rough country, and later, when Alaric had inherited it, ticking
its way through the hot steamy days and nights of Africa.

At the thought of Africa the expression on Alaric's face
might have been seen to soften, had his face been visible, but
it was concealed under a mask of red beans and palm fibre,
giving him the alarming appearance which had startled
Bernard and Deirdre. He often sat like this in the evenings,
withdrawing himself from the world, feeling in the stuffy
darkness of the mask that he was back again in his native-
built house, listening to the rain falling outside. He often
thought what a good thing it would be if the wearing of
masks or animals' heads could become customary for persons
over a certain age. How restful social intercourse would be
if the face did not have to assume any expression – the strained
look of interest, the simulated delight or surprise, the anxious
concern one didn't really feel. Alaric often avoided looking
into people's eyes when he spoke to them, fearful of what he
might see there, for life was very terrible whatever sort of
front we might put on it, and only the eyes of the very young
or the very old and wise could look out on it with a clear
untroubled gaze.

Alaric Lydgate regarded himself as a failure. He had been
invalided out of the Colonial Service, where he had not been

awarded the promotion he felt he had earned. He had achieved nothing in the fields of anthropology or linguistics, and the trunks of notes up in his attic, which he had never even sorted out, were a constant reproach to him. He felt also that he was disliked by most of his acquaintances because he found himself unable to make small talk or even to bring out the pleasant harmless little insincerities which help everyday life to run smoothly.

In one field, however, Alaric had achieved a mild though limited fame. He was well-known as a writer of sarcastic reviews, and he was engaged this night in completing one for a learned journal. The fact that he had not been able to produce an original work himself was perhaps responsible for his harsh treatment of those who had.

He had been pacing about the room, seeking fresh inspiration, but now he flung off his mask and returned to his desk.

'It is a pity,' he wrote, 'that the author did not take the trouble to inform himself of some of the elementary facts underlying the social structure of these peoples. He would then have been less likely to perpetrate such howlers as "the clan-head" (when there are, in fact, no clans), "the part played by the mother's brother in marriage transactions" (when it is the *father's* brother who plays the chief role here) . . .' He searched the pages of the book to find more howlers, incensed at the idea of 'these anthropologists' – he gave the words heavy scornful quotation marks in his own mind – thinking they could study a tribe in three weeks when his own eleven years of life and work among them had produced nothing more than a few articles on such minor aspects of their culture as incised calabashes and enigmatic iron objects.

In his search he came upon a native word wrongly spelt. His pen gathered speed. 'It is a pity,' he went on, 'that the proofs were not read by somebody with even a slight knowledge of the language, so that the consistent misspellings of vernacular terms in everyday use might have been avoided.'

In unfavourable reviews it is sometimes customary for the reviewer to relent towards the end, to throw some crumb of consolation to the author, but this was not Alaric Lydgate's practice. His last paragraph was no less harsh. 'It is a pity,' he concluded, 'that such a reputable institution should have allowed a work of this nature to appear under its auspices. Its reputation will certainly not be enhanced by unscholarly rubbish of this kind, and it can hardly be gratified to learn that its funds, which are known to be limited, have been squandered to no purpose.'

He drew a heavy line on the paper, folded the sheets and put them into an envelope. In a day or two the editor of the journal, who was a gentle patient man, would set to work to improve the English and tone it down a little. 'It is a pity,' he would say to himself, 'to have three consecutive paragraphs beginning "It is a pity".' He might even remember that Alaric Lydgate had once been refused a grant from the reputable institution whose limited funds had been squandered to no purpose. He might then go on to ask himself whether funds can be *squandered* to no purpose, whether indeed they can be squandered to *any* purpose. Certainly, as editor, he would feel none of the exhilaration which Alaric felt on finishing his review.

He leapt up from his desk and hurried from the room. His housekeeper Mrs. Skinner, who was a light sleeper, woke suddenly and turned on her bedside lamp. Then she realized that it was only Mr. Lydgate going up to the attic, and although this seemed an odd thing to be doing in the middle of the night, she was used to him by now and composed herself for sleep again.

Alaric pushed open the door and turned on the light. The room was filled with tea-chests, containing masks and pottery and other relics of his life in Africa; there were also several black tin trunks and wooden boxes, filled with his tropical kit and the accumulation of eleven years' note-taking. He

pulled at the lock of one of the tin trunks. It was rusty and came away in his hand. The hinges too were eaten away with rust and it was not difficult to open the box. Inside were piles of note-books and loose papers which gave off a dank musty smell. He picked up a wad of foolscap; the corners had been eaten away. Mice or white ants had been more diligent than he had. One day, he thought, I'll get somebody to type all this stuff and then it will be manageable. But now it was nearly two o'clock. The exhilaration he had felt on finishing his review had given way to an intense weariness. He went rather sadly to bed and, although there was no particular reason for it, set his alarm clock for six o'clock.

'Do you know,' said Rhoda at breakfast next morning, 'I almost thought I heard Mr. Lydgate's alarm clock going off this morning. About six o'clock, it must have been. I had been awake some time.'

'Did you have a good evening with Bernard, dear?' Mabel asked Deirdre.

'Oh, not bad. He's rather a dull old thing but I enjoyed the play.'

'Well, I'm glad about that,' said Mabel, 'though when I was your age I think I should have felt embarrassed at going to see that kind of play with a man. It doesn't sound at all nice. Still perhaps it's a good thing really, being able to see plays like that, I mean.'

But why was it a good thing? she wondered, unable to answer her own question. People did not seem to be any better or happier now than they had ever been, nor were the relations between men and women any more satisfactory. Of course in the early nineteen-twenties, when she had been Deirdre's age, there had been some very daring plays but she had not known the kind of young men who would have taken her to see them. Gregory Swan had liked *Rose Marie* and *No, No, Nanette*, and in her circle it was the men who

formed the women's tastes. Now, perhaps, it was the other way round.

'I suppose Bernard would have preferred a musical, like that thing at Drury Lane,' went on Deirdre, answering her mother's question, 'but musicals are so boring. I doubt if I could sit through it.'

'The Dulkes enjoyed it very much,' said Rhoda, 'and Malcolm is going to take Phyllis for her birthday.'

'There you are,' said Deirdre, 'it just isn't my kind of thing, I'm afraid.'

'I should think Bernard is a high-principled young man,' said Mabel, continuing in her own line of thought.

'He hasn't had much opportunity to be anything else as far as I'm concerned,' said Deirdre rather pertly.

'No, dear, but he is a good type,' said Mabel. One of the minor public schools, then he had done well in the army and now had a very safe position with his father's firm . . . 'I mean, he always sees you home and in good time.'

'Oh, yes, and only the mildest of good-night kisses. He's not so bad really. I must go now.' Deirdre stood up. 'All this talk about Bernard's high principles has delayed me.'

'Have you many lectures today?' asked Rhoda.

'Not till the afternoon. I thought I'd spend the morning at Felix's Folly.' And perhaps she might see Mark and Digby there and they might be able to tell her something about Tom Mallow. She hardly dared to hope that she might see Tom himself.

On the bus she wondered whether Tom had high principles, like Bernard. She was sure, somehow, that he had a delightful lack of them.

When she arrived at the research centre she found nobody there and settled down rather grimly with a pile of books. She had been working for about an hour when the door opened and Professor Mainwaring came in.

'Miss Clovis not here?' he asked of nobody in particular.

'Ah, then she has hidden herself away in her sanctum, far from the madding crowd's ignoble strife.'

Deirdre, who was sitting alone at a table, while one of the library assistants worked at a card index, thought the implication a little unfair, but she did not think any answer was required from her and she certainly would not have felt capable of providing one.

'I hope I may have arrived in time for a cup of tea?' continued Professor Mainwaring, addressing the library assistant.

She assured him that it was just made. He then went to Miss Clovis's room, where a young woman presented him with a cup.

'Ah, a fair tea-maker!' he exclaimed. 'Wasn't it De Quincey who described her thus?' He plucked at his beard and glanced at her quizzically, making her giggle and leave the room hastily.

'Young men nowadays cannot afford to take opium,' said Miss Clovis briskly, perhaps anxious not to dwell on the subject of tea, which had once nearly proved disastrous for her.

'No, even the Foresight grants will hardly be generous enough for that,' laughed Professor Mainwaring. 'Have you received many applications yet?' Miss Clovis was acting as secretary to the selection committee and enjoyed the work which was congenial to her natural curiosity about people and her desire to arrange their lives for them. The revelations of age, background and education were sometimes most surprising. Who would ever have thought, for instance . . . she smiled at some reminiscence.

'They are coming in,' she said. 'Have the committee decided yet when they will hold the interviews?'

. Professor Mainwaring tweaked at his beard with an almost pizzicato gesture. 'Ah, *that*! I have a new plan this year and one which I think Fairfax and Vere should approve. I will reveal it to you in due course.'

'It seems difficult to introduce any novelty into the ways of

selecting holders for the grants. Are the young people to be made to sing for their supper, or entertain the board in some unacademic way?' suggested Miss Clovis, hoping to draw out some details.

But the Professor would not give anything away, and soon afterwards he left her, brooding among her collection of off-prints which she was sorting out.

These single articles, detached from the learned journals in which they have appeared, have a peculiar significance in the academic world. Indeed, the giving and receiving of an off-print can often bring about a special relationship between the parties concerned in the transaction. The young author, bewildered and delighted at being presented with perhaps twenty-five copies of his article, may at first waste them on his aunts and girl friends, but when he is older and wiser he realizes that a more carefully planned distribution may bring him definite advantages. It was thought by many to be 'good policy' to send an offprint to Esther Clovis, though it was not always known exactly why this should be. In most cases she had done nothing more than express a polite interest in the author's work, but in others the gift was prompted by a sort of undefined fear, as a primitive tribesman might leave pro-pitiatory gifts of food before a deity or ancestral shrine in the hope of receiving some benefit.

Most of the offprints bore inscriptions of some kind – 'with best wishes', grateful thanks', 'cordial greetings', 'warmest regards' – every degree of respect and esteem short of the highest emotion was represented. Love itself had not been inspired; perhaps it was hardly likely that it would have been or that the author would have thought it fitting to express it even if it had. Some of the inscriptions were in foreign languages and one even had a photograph of its African author pinned to it.

Each article, and some were now yellowed with age, had its memories, and Esther turned the pages thoughtfully, some-

times half smiling at the persons and incidents they recalled. *Mit bestem Grüssen*, Hermann Obst . . . This offprint, in heavy German script, was one of the first she had ever received and its auther was dead. Poor Dr. Obst . . . once, many years ago, at some learned conference abroad, they had been walking together one evening after dinner and he had taken hold of her in a most suggestive way. Not to put too fine a point on it, he had made a pass at her. Miss Clovis smiled; she was older and more tolerant now, and wondered if she need have slapped his face with quite such outraged dignity. Why had she done it? Had she been thinking of her rights as a woman, the equal of man and not to be treated as his plaything, or had it been because she had not found Dr. Obst particularly attractive? Would she have slapped Felix Mainwaring's face if it had been he who had made the pass? The question hung in the air, unanswered. Her German was rusty now, but she could make out the title – *Blutfreundschaft*, Blood brotherhood – and perhaps it was pathetically appropriate. She was back in the warm velvety darkness, hearing the soft splash of fountains and seeing dimly the broad sword-shaped leaves of some exotic plant with huge red flowers – 'It is canna, I sink', in Dr. Obst's gentle foreign voice – and then the 'incident'. Madrid, 1928 or 1929, she couldn't remember the exact year. Such a thing had not happened to her since and it would not again. She put the offprint back into its folder and turned to the next one.

'With all good wishes from Helena Napier and Everard Bone'. That had been a most promising partnership which had never come to anything. Two gifted young people, who had worked together, but Helena Napier had a husband and Miss Clovis's efforts in the cause of anthropology had been in vain. After a short estrangement the Napiers had been reunited and Helena had retired to the country. Everard had married a rather dull woman who was nevertheless a great help to him in his work; as a clergyman's daughter she naturally got on

64

very well with the missionaries they were meeting now that they were in Africa again.

'Esther Clovis from Alaric S. Lydgate.' The next offprint bore this curt and characteristic inscription. Esther could not like her friend Gertrude's brother, especially when she thought of those trunks full of notes which he would not let anybody else make use of. Dog in the manger, she thought angrily, *most* unChristian. She was not herself a Christian, and she doubted whether Alaric was either, in spite of being the son and brother of missionaries, but it seemed a useful standard to judge people by, though perhaps it hardly applied in rationalist circles. Most unethical, was perhaps what she should have said. Her hand moved over to the telephone and she dialled Alaric's number. The bell went on ringing but there was no answer. Surely that ineffectual Mrs. Skinner could at least answer the telephone? No wonder Gertrude was not particularly anxious to live in his house, but he should certainly have asked her to. Esther let the bell go on ringing a little longer and then slammed down the instrument in disgust. She had been feeling in just the mood for an angry little talk, perhaps as an antidote to the slightly disturbing memories aroused by Hermann Obst's offprint. Frustrated, she stumped off into the library to see if she could disturb any of the readers.

She was disappointed to find only two people there, and at first sight they looked unpromising, a lanky dark young man in a shabby corduroy velvet jacket and a young girl, making what Esther scornfully described as 'sheep's eyes' at him. Then she looked more closely and saw that the girl was Deirdre Swan, who lived next door to Alaric Lydgate, and the young man Tom Mallow, one of the most promising of the younger anthropologists, who had been working among the tribe which Alaric had administered for so many years.

'Ah, Miss Swan and Mr. Mallow!' she called out in her terrifying genial voice. 'You are just the two people who should get together. I wonder if you know why?'

Because I love Tom? Deirdre thought, but obviously that couldn't be the answer. The wonderful surprise of meeting him here now seemed to be enhanced and the whole thing made respectable by Miss Clovis's apparent approval.

Tom looked puzzled and was unable to supply any answer even of a superficially gallant nature, so Miss Clovis triumphantly enlightened him.

'Miss Swan lives next door to Alaric Lydgate,' she said meaningly.

'Oh, you know him, then?' said Tom, turning to Deirdre.

'Well, not really. I mean, he's only just come to live next door.'

'Oh, but you must have spoken over the garden fence,' said Miss Clovis confidently. 'Borrowing a lawn-mower and that kind of thing.' She knew life in the suburbs even if only at secondhand, people were always talking over garden fences and borrowing things from each other.

'He doesn't seem to bother much about cutting his lawn,' said Deirdre, feeling that they were getting off the point whatever it might be.

'Do you know what he has hidden away in his attic?' Miss Clovis asked.

'His African girl friend?' suggested Tom quickly, without thinking.

'Oh, you naughty young man!' Miss Clovis let out a bark of laughter. 'No, I was of course referring to his eleven years work on *your tribe*. He has this silly idea about not letting anyone see his notes till he's written his book, but I know he'll never write it. He might have some material that would be useful to *you*.'

'Well, he might,' said Tom doubtfully. 'But these people are usually rather weak on social structure, you know. They haven't had the proper grounding.'

'You mean Professor Fairfax's seminars,' said Miss Clovis in what might have been a sarcastic tone. 'Well, that may be so,

but I do know Alaric was a glutton for land tenure. You must ask Miss Swan to make love to him for you.' And with that rather horrifying suggestion she stumped out of the room in high good humour.

Deirdre turned to Tom with an expression of dismay on her face. 'But he wouldn't listen to anything *I* said,' she protested.

'Don't worry,' he reassured her. 'Esther Clovis always has these little plots. And now,' he looked at his watch, 'I really must go.'

'Good-bye, then.' Deirdre could think of nothing to say that might detain him. There seemed no reason why they should ever meet again unless Tom wished it; perhaps she would have to do something about Alaric Lydgate after all.

Tom stood up and gathered his books together. In her eyes he had read the unspoken question, that was so often in women's eyes, 'When shall I see you again?' His first impulse had been to ask 'Are you any good at typing?' for Catherine seemed to have so much work of her own to do at the moment, but his country upbringing had made him kind-hearted and fond of animals, and Deirdre was rather sweet, really, like a puppy or a colt. So what he did say was rather different.

'Are you free on Saturday evening?' he asked. 'A friend of mine is giving a party – perhaps you'd like to come?'

CHAPTER SIX

CATHERINE poured herself rather a large glass of gin. 'I need some inspiration in the kitchen,' she explained, 'and cooks in literature are always drunken, aren't they?'

Tom looked up from the desk where he sat at his typewriter. 'Where did this gin come from?' he asked. 'We usually have beer and cider at these parties, don't we? It might create a precedent if we offered gin.'

'Yes, of course. This is only for private drinking, so that we shall be able to face our guests. I had a cheque for a story today, so I went out and cashed some of it and then I suddenly found myself in St. James's Street, standing in front of one of those very grand wine merchants with no bottles in the window. I was quite astonished to find that they sold low ordinary things like gin. And the man was so nice – he gave me another little wine book.'

Catherine collected wine lists and booklets and was liable to read aloud from them to anybody who would listen.

Tom, feeling that such a reading might be imminent, turned quickly again to his work, but he could think of nothing to type, and so was forced to listen to her babbling away about something, port he supposed, 'very old in wood and of great delicacy'.

'It sounds like something out of the Psalms, doesn't it,' she said. 'Long-suffering and of great goodness, is that what I mean? And when you've finished your thesis, Tom, we'll have a bottle of Pouilly Fuissé.'

'A bottle of *what*?' he asked, amused but exasperated, for

Catherine was sometimes very trying and, for an intelligent woman, remarkably frivolous at times.

'Oh, I can't say it again! Anyway, it's only twelve shillings a bottle. Now what shall I make to eat? They're always hungry, unfortunately. I sometimes wish we moved in the kind of circles where people just nibble at salted almonds and potato crisps. . . .' Catherine was standing in the kitchen now, for it led out of the sitting-room and she was able to carry on a conversation while she worked. Or rather she talked while Tom sat at the desk, brooding over his typewriter, as if by looking at it long enough he could make it write words that would turn themselves into a thesis.

We're just like an old married couple, Catherine thought, a little depressed, for she meant it in the worst sense, where dullness rather than cosiness seemed to be the keynote of the relationship. Not much rapture now, but it was nice to have him about the place again, the bathroom all untidy and pages of typescript lying on the floor in the sitting-room.

'I can only make a really *smooth* sauce when I'm a little drunk,' she called out gaily. 'I can stir it more like a madman then, less inhibited.'

'I shouldn't have thought you were ever that,' said Tom rather dryly, giving up his attempt to work and coming into the kitchen. He stood behind her and leaned his cheek against hers. She seemed very small because she was wearing flat shoes, slopping about in espadrilles like an old Frenchwoman – so bad for the feet, she had often written articles on this subject for her magazines. Even when she was dressed up there was usually some detail of her appearance that was not quite right, but although she was often conscious of this it did not disturb her unduly. She was too much aware of herself as a personality to make much effort to change, and she had become so used to writing about such things that she could have summed herself up very quickly in her bright, magazine style – 'red skirt and black top (could be velvet), long jet

ear-rings (*not* if you're five feet two or under), and (oh dear!) those shabby blue espadrilles bought in the market in Perigueux on a fine June morning.'

'I suppose I'll do for the party except for my feet,' she said.

'What's wrong with your feet?'

'Well, I ought to wear high-heeled shoes and stockings.'

'Those black dangling ear-rings,' said Tom doubtfully, 'will you be wearing those?'

'Why not? Don't you like them?'

'They seem so very black.'

'Of course! And men don't always like women in black, do they? Does it foreshadow death, or are they afraid that it has some depressing significance, like Masha in *The Seagull*, in mourning for her life? Or Thurber,' Catherine laughed, 'the unfolding of some dreary tale about a past love affair that went wrong that makes a man want to reach for his hat?'

'I don't know exactly,' said Tom, frowning. He sat down on the kitchen table. Catherine had told him once that somebody she loved had been killed in the war, and he was sensitive to other people's unhappiness, especially when they made light of it. Then a memory of his grandmother, cutting grapes in the conservatory at home, came to him. There had been a feeling of oppression in the house – it must have been just after his grandfather's death. 'Didn't people wear jet for mourning,' he said, 'I seem to remember my grandmother . . .'

'So I remind you of your grandmother!' said Catherine lightly. 'I wonder what the psychoanalysts would make of that?'

'It was just the feeling of them, so heavy and black-looking and when you touch them, so light.'

'I shouldn't have thought she'd wear jet in those days. It could only have been about twenty-five years ago.'

'Ah, but she was old, you know, and it was in the country.'

'Yes, of course.' Tom's childhood in the house in Shrop-

shire with his brother and sister had always seemed so enviable to Catherine who had lost both her parents when young and been brought up by an aunt who was now dead. 'We aren't getting on very fast with your welcome-home party,' she said, disengaging herself from his arms.

'I wish we weren't having it now.'

'Oh, you'll enjoy it once it gets going.'

'By the way, I asked a little girl anthropologist to come along, her name's Deirdre. I found her sitting all alone.'

'Good. What pretty names your girl friends have,' said Catherine, busily grating cheese. 'Did you see Elaine when you were at home?'

'No, she was away.'

'Had she taken the dogs with her?'

'I don't know – I shouldn't think so. I suppose one of her sisters could look after them.'

'But are the sisters as fond of them? And think of the dogs, too. I always imagine them as being so *very* devoted to their mistress, and they might pine. Are they loose-limbed bounding dogs, or heavy solid ones with broad backs, the kind you see with money boxes strapped on to them, collecting for charity?'

'Catty, I really don't know and I *don't care!*'

'All right, go and see what the room looks like, will you? Tidy away all bits of your thesis, please.'

The room looked quite tidy to Tom. He pushed Catherine's work-basket under one of the arm-chairs, emptied an ash-tray into the fireplace and straightened cushions as he had seen women do. Catherine hurried in and out with plates of food and bottles and glasses. Then the bell rang, so she ran to her bedroom where she hid the bottle of gin behind her dressing-table. She sat down in front of the looking-glass, splashed scent over herself in a haphazard way, moistened her lips with the tip of her tongue, pushed up her short-cropped hair at the sides and straightened one of the jet ear-rings. But she

forgot to change her espadrilles and it was this one flaw in her appearance which reassured Deirdre when she arrived some time later to find herself in a room full of what seemed to be complete strangers and Catherine coming forward to greet her in a most friendly and charming way.

'What a lovely room!' exclaimed Deirdre, looking around her in wonder.

In daylight the sitting-room, with its pale green walls, looked rather ordinary and in need of redecoration, but the dim lights were as flattering to it as they are to most people, and to Deirdre, used to the beige walls and flowered chintz of her mother's drawing-room, it was the most attractive room she had ever seen. Large jugs filled with leaves or even branches of trees stood on bookcases obviously full of 'interesting' books, but it was really no more remarkable than many another such room in Chelsea, Hampstead, Kensington or Pimlico. Who can say, also, whether there might not be such a room in Balham, East Sheen or Paddington?

The people in the room, who had been similarly softened and improved by the dim light, now turned out not to be strangers at all. Deirdre realized with a shock of astonishment that the two almost handsome young men standing in a corner against a background of leaves were none other than Mark Penfold and Digby Fox. Here, with drinks in their hands, they had a relaxed air, and Digby, who had on entering the room cast a startled glance at Vanessa Eaves's bare shoulders and made for an opposite corner, now found himself joining the little circle she had collected round her. As for Tom, he did not need any dim flattering light or exotic background, for when a man is loved he is never more doted upon than when he appears at some slight disadvantage, in the harsh light of day. Deirdre had not been aware of this and was a little disappointed to see him moving from group to group with drinks or food in the suave way that a good host should. Whenever he passed near her he gave her a vague sweet

72

smile and once he put his hand on her arm in a reassuring sort of way.

Conversation at real life parties is not usually very witty or worth recording, and where members of the same profession are gathered together it is likely to be incomprehensible to all but themselves. Deirdre, from feeling herself to be on the fringe of anthropological circles, now seemed to plunge right in, and the sensation was altogether delightful to her. She found herself joining in the speculations about the Foresight research fellowships, laughing at malicious little stories about her teachers and having what seemed to be a profound discussion with the American couple, Brandon and Melanie, and Jean-Pierre le Rossignol, about the changed position of the sexes, for now, Brandon maintained, women were more likely to go off to Africa to shoot lions as a cure for unrequited love than in the old days, when this had been a man's privilege.

'But there are more wild animals left in the French territories,' declared Jean-Pierre, 'and that is a good thing, I think, for Frenchmen are so much more likely to have women hopelessly in love with them.'

Deirdre looked down at him, her eyes sparkling, almost feeling that *she* could love him at this moment.

'I have the intention of visiting your church one Sunday,' he said rather primly. 'It is a thing I have not yet studied, the Sunday morning in the English suburb. When is the best time to come?'

'I should think at Whitsuntide. There is usually a procession at the eleven o'clock service and more people are likely to be there.'

'Ah, yes, Pentecost,' declared Jean-Pierre in a superior tone. 'And afterwards there is the traditional English Sunday dinner with joint?'

'Yes, most families eat their joint on Sundays.'

'And after, the sleeping? That is a custom too, I think?'

'Well, with the older people, perhaps.'

'Lovely!' said Catherine, joining them. 'I adore sleeping on Sunday afternoons. Where do you live?' she asked Deirdre.

Deirdre told her.

'With your family, I suppose?'

'Yes, my mother and brother and aunt.'

'How lucky you are to have relations! I haven't any now,' said Catherine sadly.

'They're rather a nuisance, really,' Deirdre mumbled. 'I should like to live in a flat on my own.'

'But they *care* about you,' said Catherine. 'They fuss when you're home late. I expect your mother lies awake till you get in and then calls out when she hears you creeping up the stairs.'

Deirdre laughed. 'Yes, she does do that.'

'And on Sundays you all have a big tea together. Sunday afternoon is horrid in the middle of London. The flat's all littered with crumpled Sunday papers, and after tea there's the sad sound of church bells.'

'You must come and have tea with us on a Sunday,' said Deirdre shyly. 'If you can face the journey, that is. I'm afraid it's rather a long bus ride.'

'Oh, I should like that! May I really come one Sunday?'

'Of course, my mother would love to meet you. Do you think I dare ask Tom to come as well?' Deirdre burst out, encouraged by Catherine's friendly manner.

'Why, yes! He's so busy with his wretched thesis all the time, it would do him good to get away from it.'

Somebody had now put a record on the radiogram and a few people began to dance. When Vanessa stood up it was seen that she wore tight-fitting leopardskin trousers; these, with her long silver ear-rings and bare-shoulder black jersey, made a striking effect.

Jean-Pierre leaned back in an arm-chair, eyes closed and finger-tips joined in a prayer-like attitude, listening to the jazz as if it had been Bach.

74

Deirdre found Tom beside her, asking her to dance. 'Not like Vanessa and her Ethiopian boy friend,' he said reassuringly. 'I can only do ordinary dancing, going round the room and turning at the corners. *We* prefer dancing like this, don't we.' He took hold of her right hand and laid it against his heart.

'We haven't ever danced together before,' said Deirdre, feeling rather gauche but happy that he should have singled her out in this rather unusual way. She closed her eyes, trying to hold the moment, but it would not stay. Soon the record came to an end and although another was immediately started that came to an end too, and at last people began to go home.

After the good-byes and thanks had been said, Deirdre was outside in the street with Mark and Digby, who seemed to be going in her direction.

'Quite a good party, wasn't it,' said Mark dispassionately. 'Plenty to eat and drink.'

'Yes, Catherine usually has good parties,' said Digby. 'A woman who can cook *and* type – what more could a man want, really?'

'I think she's awfully nice,' said Deirdre, in the warm tone a woman unconsciously uses when praising another woman to a man.

'Trust Tom to get himself well looked after,' said Mark. 'I suppose it must be his ruling-class upbringing asserting itself. A Coppersmith's research fellowship, and they're about the best one can get, and a nice cosy place to live.'

'Does he live in the same house then?' Deirdre asked.

'He lives in the same flat,' said Digby.

'With Catherine,' Mark added.

'He *lives* with Catherine?' Deirdre's voice faltered a little, for she could not believe that Mark and Digby could mean what they seemed to. 'You mean, he is her lover?' she went on, in a high unnatural voice.

'Well, we haven't actually asked him, but one presumes that is the arrangement.'

'It would be a reciprocal relationship – the woman giving the food and shelter and doing some typing for him and the man giving the priceless gift of himself,' said Mark, swaying a little and bumping into a tree. 'It is commoner in our society than many people would suppose.'

'I wonder if we could find anyone to look after *us*?' asked Digby. 'Perhaps if we were to advertise in one of the learned journals. "Two personable young anthropologists, early twenties, would like to meet sympathetic woman under thirty-five with flat and private income – object subsistence."'

'Miss Clovis and Miss Lydgate might take us on,' suggested Mark. 'I believe they are quite kind, really, but I suppose we should have to give "help with rough", as they say in advertisements.'

'All the same, Catherine is quite attractive,' said Digby. 'We might aim at someone a bit younger than Clovis and Lydgate.'

Deirdre walked between them in a stunned silence, their frivolous conversation passing over her head. It had never occurred to her that Tom might be attached to another woman. She had not realized that the very fact that she had immediately loved him could mean that other women would love him too.

'I suppose they will be getting married?' she asked at last.

'Who – Tom and Catherine? Oh, I shouldn't think so,' said Mark cheerfully. 'Catherine isn't keen on going to Africa with him and she isn't a trained anthropologist. He would do better to marry Primrose or Vanessa.'

'Or even you,' said Digby, squeezing her arm affectionately. 'You're still young enough to be moulded.'

'I think there will be a train still running,' said Deirdre quickly, as they approached an Underground station, 'so I'd better go down here. Good-bye!'

She had gone before they could offer to see her to the train, which they would not have done in any case.

'Did you think she seemed a bit upset about something?' asked Digby as they walked on.

'No, did you?'

'She looked as if she might be going to cry – it was when we were talking about Tom and Catherine.'

'But she hardly knows Tom, does she?'

'No, but I think she likes him. I wonder if she will be all right? Ought one of us to have seen her home – supposing there isn't a train as late as this?'

'Seen her home?' echoed Mark in astonishment. 'Has the drink or the night air gone to your head? She probably lives miles away. You really must cure yourself of these old-fashioned ideas.'

'Yes, of course, one's apt to forget that women consider themselves our equals now. But just occasionally one remembers that men were once the stronger sex,' said Digby almost sadly.

'Of course, if she really wants Tom,' said Mark, his eyes brightening as they did when there was the prospect of some interesting piece of gossip, 'there's no reason why she shouldn't get him. Did you notice how he seemed rather interested this evening? A few obstacles in the way will only make it more worth while for her.'

They had come to a crescent of once beautiful houses, now decayed and shabby, in one of which they shared a flat with an African student. The sound of his typewriter greeted them as they opened their front door. The kitchen was full of washing-up and there was no milk left for breakfast. Mr. Ephraim Olo liked to drink Ovaltine while he composed articles of a seditious tone for his African newspaper.

CHAPTER SEVEN

ONCE Deirdre had recovered from the shock of learning that Tom and Catherine were living together she began to feel quite cheerful again. At nineteen one's hopes do not remain blighted for very long and Deirdre was soon able to find a good deal in the situation to encourage her. Mark and Digby had not seemed to think that Tom and Catherine would marry and certainly they had not appeared to be very much in love, though it was a little difficult to know how they could have shown this at a party when they were busy looking after their guests. Anyway, Catherine was neither particularly beautiful nor even young, and it was quite likely that Tom was beginning to grow tired of her, expecially if she was not an anthropologist and therefore unable to take an intelligent interest in his work. This last was terribly important, Deirdre felt; it was really a privilege to have the opportunity, especially when the work was difficult and unrewarding in itself. Not that she wanted to deprive Catherine of Tom's love, for she had taken a liking to her in the way that a younger woman often does admire an older one who appears to have an interesting and enviable life. For Catherine seemed to Deirdre rather a splendid person – her Bohemian flat and way of living, and her writing were all very different from the suburban background which Deirdre found so stifling and from which she now felt herself struggling to break free.

The day on which Catherine and Tom were coming to tea was Whitsunday. At breakfast the question of churchgoing was discussed. Mrs. Swan was grieved that Deirdre had not been with them at Early Service. The vicar called it Low Mass,

but she could not yet bring herself to adopt this unfamiliar and somehow rather shocking terminology.

'Malcolm and Mr. Dulke took the collection,' she said. It was such a nice service – I wish you'd come, dear.'

'I didn't feel like it,' said Deirdre evasively. 'I don't really know that I believe in it all any more.'

There was silence at the table. Malcolm passed up his cup for more coffee. Rhoda took another piece of toast. Nothing was said, but Deirdre began to feel that her remark had been rather childish and in bad taste.

'What was that thing the organist played when we went up?' Malcolm asked. 'Rather a nice tune, I thought.'

'It *sounded* like Hiawatha's wedding feast,' said Rhoda in a worried tone, 'Coleridge Taylor, you know. But I don't think it could have been that.'

'Mr. Lewis was improvising,' said Mrs. Swan. 'There were nearly a hundred communicants, I should think, and I dare say his thoughts wandered. I suppose the music wasn't really so very unsuitable, in a way; many Indians are Christians, aren't they?'

'These were *Red* Indians, surely,' said Malcolm.

They seemed to be getting into rather deep water, so Mabel changed the subject by mentioning that there was to be a procession at the eleven o'clock service.

'I might come to that,' said Deirdre. 'I suppose it will be quite an interesting spectacle.'

Mabel wisely made no comment and was glad to see that Deirdre was ready to go with Rhoda and Malcolm when the time came. She herself was staying behind to cook the Sunday joint, a fine fillet of veal.

If only I lived by myself in a flat like Catherine's, thought Deirdre, as she sat in their usual pew between her brother and aunt, then I shouldn't have to worry about family peace and hurting people's feelings.

So as to make sure of their favourite seat they had arrived

rather too early, and there was nothing to do but look around the church which, like so many suburban churches, had been built at the beginning of the present century and had no ancient monuments or outstanding architectural features. Everything that could be was beautifully polished, from the altar candlesticks and lectern to the memorial tablets to late vicars, Ernest Hugh la Motte Spofford, George William Brandon, and James Edward Ferguson Law. The present incumbent, Laurence Folkes Tulliver, could not expect to be immortalized in brass for some years to come, for he was a man in vigorous early middle age who had introduced into the services many features which were new and startling to his congregation. He had been wise enough to do this gradually, so that by the time the church had won the right to have the mysterious letters DSCR after its name in Mowbray's *Church Guide*, most of the congregation were rather proud of themselves for having become High Church almost without knowing it. Only some of the older members still found the bells and incense a little alarming, for as Father Tulliver put it, rather aptly where Asperges was concerned, the young people had taken to the ritual like ducks to water.

Of course if you had to go to church at all, Deirdre told herself, this kind of service was much the most interesting and worthy to be compared with the religious ceremonies of the peoples she read about in her anthropological studies. Strangers often came to the church, which had never happened in the old days when Mr. Law was vicar. Even now a stranger was walking up the aisle looking for a seat, for Father Tulliver had done away with the old system of cards in the pews to mark the sittings of the regular worshippers and subscribers to church finances. Usually Mr. Diprose, the verger, showed strangers to a suitable pew, but this one seemed to have evaded him and when the footsteps came past Deirdre she saw that it was Jean-Pierre le Rossignol, dressed all in pale grey and carrying a pair of yellow gloves. He deliberated for a

moment and then walked into a pew near the front, which he must have judged likely to command a good view of the proceedings.

'That man's in the Dulkes' pew,' whispered Malcolm to Deirdre. 'I wonder if I ought to ask him to move?'

But before he could do anything the Dulkes themselves had approached and were seen to hesitate in the aisle at the sight of the stranger. There are few things more disconcerting or even upsetting for a regular worshipper at a church which is not normally very full than to find his usual seat occupied by somebody else. Perhaps such a thing had never happened to the Dulkes in all their forty years at the church. There was indeed an empty pew in front and another behind, but that was not quite the same thing. Their pew was exactly opposite that spot where in winter the hottest blasts of air came up out of the grating set in the encaustic tiles. Today it was summer, but that was irrelevant.

'What will they do?' whispered Rhoda to Deirdre.

For a moment there was real tension in the air, then Mrs. Dulke seemed to recover herself and made as if to enter the pew. Jean-Pierre, with a charming smile, moved up to make room and then unhooked a kneeler for Mrs. Dulke with a courteous gesture. She removed her gloves and fox fur, and knelt for a moment in flustered prayer. Mr. Dulke hardly even attempted this for at that moment the tinkling of a little bell was heard, the organist started to play some indefinite music and the procession came in.

As it was a Festival the servers were in their lace-trimmed cottas and Father Tulliver was wearing a particularly splendid cope. Jean-Pierre could hardly have chosen a better occasion to visit the church and he appeared to be following the proceedings intently. There was no sermon as such, that is, Father Tulliver did not actually enter the pulpit, but stood in the chancel and said a few words, touching on the significance of the Festival with a note on the meaning of the word

'Paraclete'. The service was beautifully conducted and there was perhaps nobody who did not feel in some way the better for having been present at it.

Deirdre had been worrying a little about Jean-Pierre, remembering her rash invitation or half-invitation to Sunday lunch when they had been talking at the party. She had never imagined that he would really turn up. Perhaps he would just slip quietly away now and there need be no embarrassment, but they all seemed to come out of church together and it was impossible to avoid talking to him.

'So you came after all,' she said lamely. 'Did you like the service?'

'I found it enchanting.' Jean-Pierre bowed.

Hardly the right word, Deirdre felt, though she saw what he meant.

'Of course I felt almost at home, though there were some interesting differences in the ritual.'

'You are a Roman Catholic, then, Mr. er . . .' Rhoda looked appealingly at Deirdre who had not so far introduced the good-looking young man.

Deirdre always forgot introductions or did them the wrong way round, but eventually it was made clear who Jean-Pierre was, and there was a perceptible brightening in Rhoda's manner.

'You must stay and have lunch with us,' she said. 'We are always so glad to meet Deirdre's friends. My sister, Deirdre's mother, that is, will be delighted. She is at home cooking the meal – of course things are not as they were,' she added obscurely.

Deirdre supposed that she must be remembering the old days when they would have had a cook.

'There has been quite a social revolution in England, I believe,' said Jean-Pierre politely. 'The dynamics of culture change.'

'Such a pity,' said Rhoda, puzzling over the end of his

sentence. 'In some ways, that is. Of course one *does* want things to be shared more equally, that is good . . .'

'Provided one gets the larger share oneself,' said Jean-Pierre, rushing forward to open the gate. 'What a delightful house!'

'It is detached, of course,' said Rhoda, 'which is an advantage.'

'Yes, detachment is a good thing. But one can be *too* detached, perhaps?'

'How about a drink?' Malcolm suggested, and Rhoda was a little relieved when the 'young people', as she thought of them, carried their gins and tonics into the garden. She herself hurried to the kitchen to break the news to her sister.

'I knew you wouldn't mind my asking him to lunch,' she said. 'It looked such a large piece of veal, and we do want to encourage Deirdre's friends here, don't we. Of course he is a Frenchman and he does seem to be rather foreign, those yellow gloves, but he speaks English perfectly and seems very charming. Now, have we done enough vegetables, do you think?' she went on rather fussily. 'I'd better see about laying the table. He sat in the Dulkes' pew by mistake, but he moved up when they came in, so it was all right. He unhooked a kneeler for Mrs. Dulke – I don't suppose you'd find an Englishman doing that. It's still only twenty past twelve – what a good thing Father Tulliver didn't give us a proper sermon, just a little talk about the meaning of Pentecost.'

'What *is* the meaning?' asked Mabel, who had been sitting at the kitchen table, listening to the happy sound of the meat sizzling in the oven. 'I've often wondered.'

'Oh, it is Jewish or Greek in origin,' said Rhoda in a flustered tone, 'and Paraclete, that is Greek too. *Come thou Holy Paraclete*, you know the hymn. I think we'd better have the *lace* mats, don't you?'

'By all means.' Mabel was thinking that Rhoda, after her morning in church, seemed more of a Martha than she herself

83

who had spent the morning quietly in the kitchen. It was nice for Deirdre to have a friend to lunch, but she hoped her sister wouldn't make too much of it. Deirdre had been so moody and difficult lately, they would have to be very tactful.

The meal was highly successful and everyone liked Jean-Pierre, who put his questions about English suburban life so charmingly that nobody could possibly have taken offence. After they had finished eating Mabel and Rhoda went to wash up while the others took coffee into the garden. It was a hot afternoon and the Sunday quiet was broken only by the sound of a distant lawnmower.

'I must not keep you from your sleeping,' said Jean-Pierre politely. 'I suppose it will be outside in the summer?'

Malcolm leaned back in his deck-chair. 'It's only elderly and middle-aged people who sleep after lunch,' he explained. 'I usually go along to the club for a game of tennis.'

'Are you going today?' Deirdre asked, wondering how she was going to sustain a conversation if she were left alone with Jean-Pierre.

'Yes, I expect I'll go along about three o'clock. Perhaps you'd like to come?' He turned to Jean-Pierre.

'Alas, I am not the type for outdoor sport,' he said simply. 'And I have another engagement at three o'clock. There is a meeting in Bayswater, a message from the Other Side. I could perhaps take a bus from here?'

'Oh, yes, of course,' said Deirdre. 'I'll show you.'

'I must say good-bye to your mother and aunt, if I am not disturbing them?'

'I expect they're still in the kitchen washing-up.'

'I see; the older female relatives work in the kitchen when there are no servants. The mother and the father's sister?'

'No, Aunt Rhoda is my mother's sister.'

'Ah, yes, I understand. Women more closely linked would work better together – they would not fight.'

After he had gone Deirdre settled down in the garden,

waiting rather apprehensively for Tom and Catherine to arrive for tea. Mabel and Rhoda were still in the house, either resting in their rooms or getting out the best tea-set. Deirdre's offer of help had been refused and she felt rather sulky. She sat in a deck-chair with an anthropological book and a volume of poetry on her knee, but she opened neither. She lay with her eyes closed thinking about Tom, trying to remember his face. After a few minutes of concentrated meditation, she had recalled all his features separately but had failed to fuse them together so that the result was like a Picasso head, the brilliant grey eyes and the sharp nose appearing in unexpected places. Then she began to have the feeling that somebody was watching her through the hedge which separated the garden from the Lovells' next door. She opened her eyes but was at first too dazzled by the sun to be able to see anything. At last she discerned what were undoubtedly two bright dark eyes peering intently through a small gap in the leaves. She realized that it was one of the Lovells' children, a little girl of about five. For a moment she returned the stare but was forced to turn away before its unwavering intensity. She picked up one of her books and opened it.

'What are you doing?' The words came in a hoarse whisper.

'Nothing,' said Deirdre in a dignified tone.

'*Why?*'

Deirdre could think of no reasonable answer to this that a child of five might appreciate and began to wish that she felt more at ease with children. Wordsworth, she thought, remembering with distaste poems she had read at school, might have made something of this situation, but it was beyond her. She turned the pages of the anthropological book, a slender green volume, rather badly written and with too many footnotes. Not the most congenial kind of reading for a fine Sunday afternoon.

'You were *asleep*!' The voice rose triumphantly now and ended in a gurgle of laughter. 'I *saw* you!'

'I wasn't asleep. I was thinking.'

'*Why?*'

This exchange could have gone on all afternoon if Rhoda had not at that moment come out into the garden carrying a wickerwork cakestand.

'I think we could have tea in the garden,' she said. 'I expect your friends would like it.'

'Yes, it would be pleasant. Shall we have it over the other side, under the apple tree?'

'Yes, I think that's the best place.'

Rhoda was glad that Deirdre had suggested it for she had secretly wanted to have tea on Mr. Lydgate's side of the garden which she felt to be more interesting than the Lovells'. Mr. and Mrs. Lovell, the children, Roy, Jenny and Peter, and Snowball, the old sealyham, were dull and familiar. Who knew what they might hear or see through the hedge on Mr. Lydgate's side?

Catherine, walking with Tom along the road from the bus stop, was delighted with the tranquil beauty of the Sunday afternoon scene, the tree-lined road, the neat colourful front gardens, some empty in the sunshine, others being vigorously tended by men in open-necked shirts or women in cotton dresses and sandals. Through it all came the pleasant sounds of children, dogs, birds, lawnmowers and hedge clippers.

'I suppose this is what you call suburbia,' said Tom. 'It seems rather pleasant.' He had lived in London himself and had occasionally visited his aunts in Kensington and Belgravia, but he was totally ignorant of that territory in which a vast number of people pass their lives.

'Oh, look!' Catherine cried out. 'This house is called Nirvana!'

'Hush, Catty, they might hear,' said Tom in a low voice. She was in what he thought of as one of her worst moods this

afternoon, the kind that he found most difficult to cope with. The less encouragement he gave her, the more wild and frivolous would her fancies become. Now, to his horror, she began to sing, something about lotus flowers and finding Nirvana within his loving arms.

'As the river flows to the ocean,
My soul, my soul shall flow to thine!'

she concluded in triumph, clinging on to him affectionately.

They walked in silence for a few seconds but then Catherine's attention was again caught by a row of houses whose gateposts were ornamented with stone lions. She stopped in front of them in delight and began to stroke their heads and bodies.

'Poor things,' she said, 'their noses and paws are all worn down, like soap lions might be after the first time of using. You know my *favourite* Shakespeare sonnet, don't you? *Devouring time, blunt thou the lion's paws* . . . do you think *he* could have seen a worn stone lion and that gave him the idea? On the gate-post of some noble house, perhaps?'

'I really don't know,' said Tom impatiently. 'Do hurry up, we mustn't be *too* late.'

'Of course he didn't really *mind* about devouring time blunting the lion's paws,' she continued thoughtfully, 'or even about the long-lived phoenix burning in her blood. The point was that time mustn't touch his *love's* fair brow. *Nor put no lines there with thine antique pen* . . . do you remember that?' She glanced up at him but he did not answer. 'You do seem to have a few little lines that I hadn't noticed before,' she said rather maliciously. 'But then so have I, oh, lots of them! They add character to a face, that's what I always say when I'm writing articles for the over-forties. If your face is smooth you can't really have experienced joy and sorrow and love. . . .'

'I think this must be the house,' said Tom rather coldly.

'Oh, yes, I'm sure it is. How much nicer the houses are at

this end of the road, larger and nobler. Do you suppose the late Mr. Swan was a prosperous merchant, something in Mincing Lane, perhaps?'

'Look, there is Deirdre in the front garden,' said Tom quickly.

'And the snowball tree you told me about,' said Catherine, hurrying forward to greet her. 'What a lovely thing it is!'

'I hope you were able to get here without too much fuss,' said Deirdre. 'I always think it's rather a bore having to uproot oneself on a Sunday afternoon.'

'Oh, the bus ride was lovely and Tom was delighted to be dragged away from his thesis writing,' said Catherine gaily. 'He's been moaning about it all day.'

'Poor Tom,' said Deirdre softly.

'Men seem to have so little will-power and concentration at times,' Catherine went on, as they sat in the garden waiting for tea. 'Why is that?'

Deirdre had never given much thought to the problem and she felt that Catherine was being rather disloyal to talk about Tom in this way. She was as yet too young and in-experienced to be quite sure that one can love and criticize at the same time. 'It must be very difficult writing a thesis,' she ventured.

'Of course it is, but he chose to do it. He shouldered the burden of his own accord.'

'Perhaps he needs . . .' Deirdre began.

'Somebody who really understands him?' Catherine laughed, flashing a glance between the two of them.

'Yes, Deirdre, that's exactly what I *do* need,' said Tom, giving her a rather special look.

'Oh, here are my mother and my aunt,' said Deirdre, jumping up from her chair.

Two middle-aged ladies in neat summer dresses, coming through french windows on to a lawn and carrying trays of

tea-things, is a most pleasing and comforting sight, Catherine thought, envying Deirdre who must see it so often.

Introductions were dealt with and they arranged themselves under the apple tree. Mabel began to pour out. The tea fell in a wide arc from the spout of the silver teapot. Rhoda looked on anxiously, for she considered herself to be a better pourer than her sister, but she managed to control her fears and turned to Catherine with a polite question.

'So you write? Stories, Deirdre told us.' Her tone was a little uncertain for she had never met a writer before. She had heard that either they hated you to mention their profession or were offended if you didn't and she could not decide which class Catherine was likely to belong to.

'Yes, trite little stories for women, generally with happy endings,' said Catherine, adopting the rather derogatory tone behind which writers sometimes hide from the scorn and mockery of the world. 'I manage to earn my living that way.'

'I'm so glad you write *happy* endings,' said Mabel. 'After all, life isn't really so unpleasant as some writers make out, is it? she added hopefully.

'No, perhaps not. It's comic and sad and indefinite – dull, sometimes, but seldom really tragic or deliriously happy, except when one's very young.'

'*Rarely, rarely comest thou, Spirit of Delight,*' murmured Deirdre with brooding intensity, for the thought of Tom and Catherine and their cosy life together had suddenly come upon her.

'We must look out for your stories,' said Rhoda politely. She was a little disturbed by Catherine's conversation which was not quite what she had expected. Catherine, as if realizing this, began to praise the home-made cakes and soon they were comparing recipes quite happily, while Deirdre and Tom began a little conversation of their own about anthropological personalities. Mabel and Rhoda were each thinking what a nice girl Catherine was, and how glad they were that Deirdre

had found a sensible woman friend who would probably do her a lot of good.

'*They* seem to be having tea out of doors too,' said Rhoda casually, with a gesture towards Alaric Lydgate's garden, and indeed a woman's voice, unusually loud and clear, was heard declaiming, almost like a station announcer, '. . . Ealing train, not stopping at South Kensington and Gloucester Road. Father Gemini was quite distracted – just think of it, he was carried right on to Earl's Court!'

'That's Miss Lydgate,' whispered Deirdre.

'He protested, but the train went on. It *would not stop* at Gloucester Road.'

'A Richmond train would have been safer,' said another loud female voice, belonging unmistakably to Miss Clovis. 'Or even Hounslow, though there is something about a Hounslow train that I don't like and I generally feel that a Wimbledon train should be avoided . . .'

'It was an experience,' said Father Gemini's milder voice, 'and I have learned a lesson by it. I shall take a bus in future.'

The men's voices were softer than the women's and the rest of the conversation was less easy to hear, especially as it was felt that the Swans could not really give themselves up to listening to all of it. Catherine asked about Alaric Lydgate and was given a rather highly coloured description by Rhoda.

'He walks in the garden at night, wearing an African mask,' she whispered, 'and nobody ever comes to see him, as far as I know, apart from his sister, that is. He seems to be a lonely kind of person.'

'I always think the loneliness of men is so sad,' said Catherine. 'Those advertisements you sometimes see from a man wanting a companion to go on holiday, in such respectable papers too, like the *Church Times*. I can't really bear them.'

'Oh, come, Catty, lots of women are lonely too, far more than men,' said Tom with a touch of complacency.

'Yes, but that isn't so bad somehow. Loneliness can often

be a kind of strength in women, possibly in men too, of course, but it doesn't seem to show itself so much.'

'Would you say that Mr. Lydgate had that kind of strength?' asked Mabel.

'It is an inner thing, really,' said Rhoda. 'One thinks of hermits . . .' she paused, for perhaps one did not think of hermits in the suburbs.

'Oh, Mr. Lydgate's just a rather bad-tempered man who writes slashing reviews of books,' said Deirdre impatiently. 'There's nothing noble or hermit-like about him.'

'Don't forget all those trunks of material he has in his attic,' said Tom. 'Wasn't that what Miss Clovis told us?'

'Yes, I suppose you ought to meet him,' said Deirdre.

'Oh, but I have met him,' said Tom. 'Europeans out there can hardly avoid running into each other.'

'And you never told me,' said Deirdre. 'I was thinkig . . .'

'That you'd have to make love to him as Clovis suggested?' said Tom laughing.

'Wouldn't it be nice for you to renew your acquaintance?' said Rhoda hopefully. 'Perhaps if Mr. Mallow were to stand up, his head might be seen over the hedge.'

Tom stood up obediently, feeling rather ridiculous.

'Why, look, it's Mr. Mallow,' shouted Miss Clovis. 'Now Alaric, you two really must get together.'

Soon everybody was standing up and talking over the hedge. Tom and Alaric were like suspicious animals, eyeing each other doubtfully. Tom said that his thesis was nearly finished anyway, and that he didn't think he would be able to use any more material. Alaric hurried to point out that his notes dealt almost entirely with religion and material culture and would therefore be of very little use to anyone writing a thesis on social and political structure. The ladies talked among themselves and Father Gemini held himself aloof, then suddenly divested himself of two layers of his fusty black garments as if he were performing a strip-tease act.

Catherine, who had been observing Alaric closely and with the frank interest and curiosity which any new male acquaintance aroused in her, thought, why, he's rather attractive! So tall and rugged, and that rough-hewn face with its grim expression reminds me of those images from Easter Island, once seen in the British Museum. Poor old Easter Island man, bullied by his sister and her masterful friend – what things men have to put up with!

Rhoda felt that they had definitely 'made progress', though it was obvious that Alaric was not a socially 'easy' person. 'I suppose we shall *really* get to know him one of these days,' she said rather wistfully, when the parties had returned to their respective tea tables. She saw again the odd scene on the other side of the hedge, the tall brother and sister, stocky Miss Clovis, and Father Gemini with his wispy beard, suddenly taking off his clothes in that disconcerting way. She had noticed too the primitive tea, the uncut loaf, the butter still in its paper, and the pot of jam. Surely Mrs. Skinner could have left things more ready than that? Later, when it was beginning to get dark, and Rhoda was sitting at the window in her room, she saw the remains of the tea still there on the little bamboo table, looking strangely forlorn. Why had nobody taken the things in? she wondered. She had heard Miss Lydgate and Miss Clovis and Father Gemini leaving earlier, but what was *he* doing now? In her imagination she entered Alaric Lydgate's study.

He sat at his desk, doing nothing. It would have been a good time to start writing up some of the material in his tin trunks, for he had no book to review at the moment, but he lacked the energy to go upstairs and do anything about it. Instead he found himself thinking about the tea-party next door, the two girls and the young man, and the older women in their pretty light dresses, so different from Esther Clovis and his sister Gertrude, dowdily dressed and full of anthropological gossip and interfering suggestions. Why had he not

asked them round to have a drink? Because he didn't do things like that – presumably that was why. It was too hot to hide in a mask this evening and he felt defenceless, as if people passing could look in through the window and see him sitting there idle. His hand strayed to the side of his desk where he had hung the publication lists of various learned societies and institutes, and also the wine-lists of one or two stores. He would read from each according to his mood, to refresh himself in different ways. At this moment, with the dusk falling, there was something distasteful and galling about the outpourings of anthropological works by others, so he turned to a wine-list and soothed himself with the magical name, *Deidesheimer Rennpfad Riesling Auslese . . . per bottle* 67/6. That seemed to go with the girls in the garden, the voices and laughter floating over the hedge. He could find no wine appropriate to his own ungracious tea, and his sister and Father Gemini demonstrating something they called 'breathy voice' to each other.

CHAPTER EIGHT

As the summer went on Esther Clovis began to feel that it was high time Professor Mainwaring did something about awarding the research grants from the Foresight fund. There was a slight air of irregularity about the whole thing and she sometimes found herself wondering whether there was really enough money for the purpose. The vagueness and untidiness of the arrangement was displeasing to her and as she sat at the research centre, waiting for the Professor to arrive, she determined to get some definite information from him. While she waited she turned over some of the application forms and began to feel an unaccustomed tenderness towards the young applicants which she found rather disturbing. The details of their education seemed pathetic, the outlines of their proposed research pitiful. She had never felt like this before; it seemed to date from that day when she had been sorting out her off-prints and remembered poor Hermann Obst and the episode in the Spanish garden. It occurred to her to wonder whether her friend Gertrude had ever experienced a tender human feeling. One evening they had squabbled about who should get supper ready, and Esther had found herself saying that she didn't care tuppence about aspirated 'k', 't', and 'b', an interesting feature of the language Gertrude happened to be studying at that moment. Of course they had made it up, in their gruff way, but it had happened and that was the surprising thing.

Professor Mainwaring came into the room waving a letter in his hand. He was elegantly dressed in a lightweight suit of American design and his beard was newly trimmed.

94

'What do you think about *this*?' he asked.

'What is it? Ah, I see, a letter from Minnie Foresight. Is she getting anxious about her money?'

'No, it isn't quite that. She has taken exception to an article Fairfax has written in one of the learned journals. I sent it to her because that number had an account of our little party in it.'

'Really?' Miss Clovis looked puzzled. 'I wonder which article it can have been? I can't *remember* anything that could have offended her.'

'Oh, it is nothing personal – it is just that she considers Fairfax's article obscene.'

'*Obscene?*' Miss Clovis spat out the word indignantly. 'But it's a perfectly straightforward account of the initiation ceremonies of the tribe he studied – the seclusion of the boys and girls in the bush – the coming forth – the dancing, and the licence allowed in certain forms of behaviour, with a rough translation of the songs they sing . . .'

'Evidently Fairfax's translation was *too* rough,' chuckled Professor Mainwaring. 'We must remember that our patroness is not an anthropologist.'

'What does she say?'

Professor Mainwaring handed over the letter, and Miss Clovis read such phrases as 'deeply distressed', 'most shocking', 'unpleasant details'.

'Well, she obviously has no idea how important it is that *every* detail should be known,' said Miss Clovis bluntly.

'Quite, but I do feel that Fairfax has perhaps been a little *over*-zealous on this occasion. And what a pity he is such a poor Latinist!'

'There seem to be some Latin phrases here,' said Miss Clovis, turning the pages of the article.

'Yes, he knows *ad hoc* and even *primus inter pares* – that much he will have imbibed at his red brick university.' Here the Balliol man in the Professor could not help coming out and showing itself for a moment. 'He is not an Oxford man,

you know, or even a Cambridge man. Everything that has offended poor Minnie could have been put into Latin and she would have been quite satisfied. Some women have a great veneration for the classical tongues. Yes,' Professor Mainwaring plucked at his beard and paced round the room, 'the Latin of Petronius Arbiter or another of the great *Silver* Latin poets . . .' He gave an extravagant sigh, as if his thoughts were back in those elegant days of decadence. 'I could have turned this very prettily into Latin if only Fairfax had consulted me, but of course he did not. I'm afraid it would not have occurred to him to do so. Gervase is a dear boy, but humility is *not* one of his virtues.'

'It does seem an odd use for Latin,' said Miss Clovis thoughtfully, 'to avoid giving offence to those who probably cannot understand it anyway. I suppose Greek could be used too.'

'Indeed, it has been. My own study of certain unusual relationships in a primitive society had a good deal of Greek in it, and I believe it *was* Greek to a good many people. Did I not give you an offprint? – 1911 or 1912 I think it was published.'

'No, you didn't.' It seemed unnecessary to point out that she would have been only eight or nine years old at the time.

'Oh, then I will – I believe I still have a few left. Now to business. I shall write to Minnie and do the best I can. Perhaps dinner and a theatre, or a box at Covent Garden; she is fond of opera, I know.'

'There is a fine production of *Aïda* in the repertoire this season,' suggested Miss Clovis.

'*Not* that, I think. Nothing with negroes or dark-skinned peoples in it; we should try to keep her mind off such things for the moment. *Madame Butterfly*, also, might suggest unsuitable behaviour on the part of anthropologists in the field . . .' Professor Mainwaring seemed to be enjoying himself now, picking out suitable and unsuitable operas and Miss Clovis had to bring him back to reality rather sharply.

'We ought to do something about the Foresight grants,' she said.

'Oh, that is all under control. You notice that Minnie wants to pay us another visit here? We must try to make a particularly good impression. Now that little room on the first floor – it seemed rather bare when I looked into it the other day, not *quite* worthy, I felt.'

'It *is* bare,' said Miss Clovis shortly. 'There is nothing in it at all except for that antler hat-stand you gave us.'

'Do you find that visitors leave their hats on it?' asked the Professor in an interested tone. 'I have noticed that many young anthropologists don't seem to wear hats. Perhaps they like to feel the breeze in their hair.

> *Rolling along*
> *On the Tongchidderongtong,'*

he sang gaily. 'There is a river of that name, somewhere in the Sudan, if I remember rightly. Now what about this horsehair sofa? You don't really need it here, it would fill up a good deal of space and no doubt you have an odd table and one or two chairs you could spare. I have a splendid mahogany sideboard at home, an ugly piece but the wood is very fine.'

'Well, I hardly think a sideboard would be suitable here.'

'No, perhaps not, visitors might expect us to fill it. It's just that we don't want dear Minnie to feel that we have squandered her money by taking a larger house than is necessary.'

'I will arrange the room somehow,' said Miss Clovis. 'And now *what* about the research grants? I have had the applications for some time now.'

'And I have been meditating on them. I thought it would be pleasant to invite the candidates down to my house one weekend, to stay, you know. I thought it might bring out something more than the conventional type of interview.'

'It might indeed,' said Miss Clovis a little doubtfully. After he had gone she decided to get the sofa moved there and then,

while she still remembered it, and went to the library to see whether there were any strong-looking young men reading there. She rejected Brandon Pirbright and Jean-Pierre le Rossignol as being too elegantly dressed to move furniture, and a small nervous-looking clergyman was obviously too fragile for the task. Those two solid young Englishmen, Mark Penfold and Digby Fox, were the obvious choice. She beckoned to them mysteriously. They looked rather startled and hesitated for a moment, but at last one pushed the other forward and they went to the door together.

'How would you like to move some furniture?' asked Miss Clovis in a jolly tone.

Fortunately the honest answer did not spring immediately to their lips, and Digby even managed to murmur that they would be delighted. So it was that they found themselves struggling with the awkward bulk of the horsehair sofa down a narrow flight of stairs.

'Do you think this will do instead of that other little scheme of ours?' panted Mark, as they rested on a difficult corner.

'What scheme?'

'You know, the lunch.'

'Oh, that. Well, it might, but I think the lunch would somehow drive it home better, don't you? When people have eaten food you've paid for they're under a certain obligation to you, after all.'

'Are they? Then it's a pity girl friends don't realize that a little more often,' said Mark bitterly.

'You sound as if you were always taking girls out and buying meals for them. I shouldn't think it's happened within living memory, has it?'

'Let's not get off the point. Will you ask Miss Clovis, or shall I?'

'Both together, that would be the thing.'

At this point, as may often happen when two people are carrying a heavy and unwieldy object, the young men dissolved

into helpless laughter, so that they were forced to sit down on the stairs with the sofa stuck between them.

'It would probably have been easier upside down,' said Digby weakly. 'Look, it's to go in this little room. I wonder why?'

'I don't think it's our business to speculate,' said Mark primly. 'Shall we tidy ourselves up a bit and then go and ask Miss Clovis?'

They approached her door rather nervously and seemed to fall through it both together.

'We were wondering if you would have lunch with us one day, Miss Clovis,' said Mark in an indistinct hurrying tone.

'Yes, we were wondering,' Digby added.

'Lunch? But how nice,' said Miss Clovis.

'When would you be free?' Digby asked.

'Why, today, and now,' she said, looking at her watch. 'No time like the present! It's nearly half past twelve.'

'Oh, that's fine,' said Mark, wondering if Digby had any money on him. They had not imagined that she would accept their invitation so promptly; indeed, they had felt that a little nearer the time of the board to decide the Foresight grants would have been more appropriate.

As they went out into the street, the tall gaunt figure of Miss Lydgate was seen approaching on the other side. She waved and called out to them so that they were forced to stop until she could cross the street.

'Come and join the party, Gertrude,' said Miss Clovis. 'We are going to have lunch.'

Mark and Digby looked at each other in consternation. This was not at all what they had planned.

'I have nearly a pound,' muttered Digby.

'I've only three shillings,' said Mark. 'I dare say we can manage between us. Where would you like to go, Miss Clovis?' he asked, raising his voice. 'Have you a favourite restaurant near here?'

'Let me see now,' Miss Clovis seemed to be considering the matter in an ominously thoughtful way, 'there are so many places. Somewhere where we shall get plenty to eat, of course. What do you think, Gertrude?'

'This place is rather good,' she said, stopping outside a reasonably modest-looking restaurant which had a menu up outside. Reading it, Digby noticed with relief that some of the prices were modest too. He hoped Mark would have the sense to order Chipolata Sausage Toad (2/2) or Braised Tripe (2/-) and not go off the deep end with Steak and Chips (5/6). He supposed Clovis and Lydgate would want that; they looked like the kind of women who would eat red meat, he thought resentfully.

Inside, the restaurant was full of business men who were joking with the waitresses. Mark cunningly chose a table served by a particularly pretty girl, in case, he thought vaguely, there was any difficulty about the bill. She might let them go away and bring the money back later. He could leave his watch as security.

'Now,' said Miss Clovis, a little too quickly for Digby, who had been going to say the same thing, 'what are we all going to have?'

'I expect you'd like some soup or hors-d'œuvres first, wouldn't you?' suggested Mark smoothly.

'Well, I don't know, really. What are you going to have?' She turned to Mark who had been studying the menu intently. He had done even better than Digby and had discovered, right at the bottom, Macaroni Cheese (1/9). 'I don't eat meat or fish,' he said, 'so my choice won't be very helpful.'

Digby looked a little surprised.

'Are you a vegetarian?' asked Miss Lydgate in an interested tone? 'I have great sympathy with those who are, though I am not one myself.'

'No, not exactly,' mumbled Mark. 'I have eaten meat. I am not what you'd call a big eater, really.'

'Oh, we are,' said Miss Clovis cheerfully. 'I think I should like the steak and chips and perhaps another vegetable too, runner beans, I think.'

'Yes, so will I,' said Miss Lydgate. 'What is the secret of making CHIPS?' Her normally loud voice seemed to have increased in volume so that it could be heard throughout the restaurant. 'Potatoes are OVAL or ROUND. Chips are RECTANGULAR. I don't see at all how it is done.'

'I think you cut the potatoes in thick slices and then into strips,' said Digby. 'I have watched my mother do it.'

'So that is it. I must remember that – first in thick slices, then in strips. Now what are *you* going to eat?'

'Oh, braised tripe for me,' said Digby hurrying over the words distastefully.

'Well, I really think you boys ought to have something more nourishing after the hard work you had moving that sofa,' said Miss Clovis, 'but I suppose you know best. Now, what about something to drink.'

'Oh, yes, what would you like?' asked Digby politely.

'Guinness is very strengthening, let's have that.'

'I think I should prefer a glass of lemon squash,' said Miss Lydgate.

This was a relief, if only a slight one, Digby felt, as he assured Miss Clovis that he and Mark never drank in the middle of the day.

'I feel one shouldn't go into learned societies or libraries smelling of drink,' said Mark, at his most prim. 'It might create the wrong impression.'

'Oh, I hadn't thought of that,' said Miss Clovis, sipping her dark foamy drink. 'I don't suppose anyone would notice. Of course it's all right for librarians to smell of drink,' she added jovially.

'Of course,' said Digby enthusiastically. 'But you see we are in a different position, more on show, as it were. We feel that we must be on our best behaviour.'

'I am sure you are always well-behaved,' said Miss Clovis with unusual warmth. 'You were most helpful to me this morning.'

The young men looked pleased. They all finished their first course and ordered the next. Miss Clovis and Miss Lydgate had Apple Pie with Ice Cream (1/6); Mark and Digby declared that they were passionately fond of Jelly (6*d*). Afterwards the ladies had coffee but the young men declined it.

'It might keep us awake in Dr. Vere's lecture,' joked Digby.

'Oh, that would never do!' chortled Miss Clovis.

The bill was brought and Digby took out his pound note, but Miss Clovis pushed it back into his hand and snatched the bill from him.

'I shouldn't dream of letting you pay,' she said indignantly. 'This is to be our treat, isn't it, Gertrude?'

'Certainly,' said Miss Lydgate. 'Young men shouldn't be expected to take middle-aged women out to lunch.'

'Well, it's very kind of you,' said Digby, not quite knowing what attitude to take.

'We have had the pleasure of your company,' said Mark with an effort. 'But we really did mean to take you out,' he added, thinking of the three shillings in his pocket.

They walked out into the street together. It appeared then that Miss Clovis and Miss Lydgate had some shopping to do, so that Mark and Digby were soon left alone.

'Quite a new side of you came out today,' said Digby, turning to his friend with a laugh. 'The abstainer from drink and flesh foods. A rather noble character, I feel.'

'Yes, things didn't go quite as we'd meant them to, did they? Still, it wasn't really our fault and I think we left quite a good general impression. I felt almost that a joking relationship had been established.'

'Yes, there could be such a thing between a young man and a middle-aged woman, but it would need careful handling. I

rather wish I had known beforehand that they were going to pay for the lunch, though.'

'Yes, I don't think I should have chosen macaroni cheese and jelly, if I'd known that.'

'Well,' said Digby, pausing outside the decorated glass door of a saloon bar, 'we've still got the money we should have spent on our lunch if we'd had any.'

They were soon swallowed up into the warm smoky atmosphere, and decided, half an hour later, that perhaps it wasn't worth going to Vere's lecture after all.

CHAPTER NINE

'Tom, the bay leaf I'm putting in this *bœuf à la mode* was plucked from a tree growing in the garden of Thomas Hardy's birthplace,' Catherine called from the kitchen. She did not really expect an answer and indeed none came from Tom, sitting hunched over his typewriter, so she went on, almost to herself, 'I wonder if it's *wrong* of me to use it for cooking? Perhaps I ought to have pressed it in *Jude the Obscure*, or the poems, that would have been more suitable. Those sad couples he writes about seem to me a bit like us, sometimes. I wonder if, when I'm old, you'll offer me the hand of friendship down life's sunless hill, or whatever it was. Will you?' she raised her voice.

'I don't know what you're talking about, sweetie,' said Tom in an abstracted tone.

Catherine turned back silently to her beef. Oh, what joy to get a real calf's foot from the butcher, she thought, and not to have to cheat by putting in gelatine. The small things of life were often so much bigger than the great things, she decided, wondering how many writers and philosophers had said this before her, the trivial pleasures like cooking, one's home, little poems especially sad ones, solitary walks, funny things seen and overheard. Tom's long absence abroad had turned her in upon herself and her own resources which had always been considerable. Their eighteen months apart had made them grow more like themselves, so that now they seemed almost more like strangers than when they had first met.

She took a glass of sherry to him. 'There's something to encourage you,' she said. 'How does it go?'

'Not very well.'

'I'm sorry. It seems like some dreadful elderly relative doesn't it, your thesis, always with us. Won't it be lovely when it's finished? We can say it's dead – Called to a Higher Sphere, perhaps – and give it a splendid funeral.'

'Catty, must you always make everything into a joke?'

'No, I'm very naughty,' she said seriously. 'I do sympathize really, you know.'

Tom got up from the desk and began to walk about the room. 'The worst of it is that I think I've lost my faith,' he said.

Immediately there sprang into Catherine's mind the picture – surely a sepia daguerrotype – of a high-collared, bewhiskered Victorian clergyman, his beliefs undermined by Darwin and the rationalists. But she tried to shut it away and said reassuringly, 'I didn't think you had any faith, at least not the kind one loses, so I shouldn't worry if I were you.'

'I mean my faith in anthropology,' he said rather impatiently.

'Oh, *that.*' The words were out before she could stop them. 'But what *is* faith in anthropology – I didn't know it was the kind of thing people had.'

'Well, perhaps not quite in the usual sense. But I just wonder sometimes what's the use of it all. Who will benefit from my work, what exactly is the *point* of my researches? Are my people out there going to be any happier because I happen to have found out that they have a double descent system? Who will be any better off for my having discovered new facts about the importance of the mother's brother?' Tom stopped in his pacing and stood over Catherine almost accusingly.

She felt then the general uselessness of women if they cannot understand or reverence a man's work, or even if they can.

'You make me feel like something in Milton,' she said defiantly. 'Towering over me like that. It's like – oh, what? – *Paradise Lost,* I suppose. Adam and Eve.'

'You've never even *tried* to understand,' he said in a detached tone, which was more hurtful than if he had sounded angry.

'Oh, Tom,' she protested. 'You know I tried to read those books, but I couldn't get through them. I suppose I was too stupid,' she added on a surprised note. 'But obviously it's the right thing for *you*.'

'I'm not so sure any more. I sometimes feel I should have stayed at home and helped Giles and my mother to run the place. That would at least have been useful.'

They sat down on the divan together and Catherine put her arms around him, wondering what Victorian wives and mothers had done with their menfolk who had lost their faith. What had they said to them? Matthew Arnold, she thought idly, the last lines of *Dover Beach* coming into her mind.

'*Ah, love, let us be true to one another*,' she said softly.

Tom looked down at her, a little startled. He had certainly been seeing a good deal of Deirdre lately but nothing had really come of it so far.

'What makes you say that?' he asked.

'I was quoting. You probably remember how it goes on, something about the world having neither joy nor love, nor peace, nor help for pain,

> *And we are here as on a darkling plain*
> *Swept with confused alarms of struggle and flight,*
> *Where ignorant armies clash by night.*'

'Oh, I see,' he said inadequately. 'But I don't think your Victorian poets are much help these days.'

'That's not a comfortable poem, though,' she said impatiently. 'It isn't meant to be. People have so many wrong ideas about the Victorians.'

'All right, then,' he smiled, 'tell me the right ones.'

'Shall we go out and have a meal?' Catherine suggested, feeling that the Victorian wives and mothers would surely

have provided a good meal for their doubting men, if nothing else 'The *bœuf à la mode* won't be ready for a few hours.'

'Yes, a good idea. A lot of food and drink.'

It was a successful and pleasant meal, eaten at the little Cypriot restaurant in the street opposite. Catherine found herself remembering it a few evenings later, when she was coming home, walking slowly because her string bag was laden with exotic foods she had bought in Soho. She decided to go into the restaurant for a bottle of wine. It was early for an evening meal and the room was nearly empty except for some dark-haired women with gold teeth talking Greek, and a couple, deep in conversation, sitting at the table she and Tom usually had.

'Good evening, Mrs. Katerina,' said the old fat waiter. 'Mr. Tom is here early tonight.'

'Yes, isn't he,' said Catherine. Now that she had recognized Tom and Deirdre over in the corner, she felt almost calm and not really surprised. She had suspected that they did sometimes have meals together, and why shouldn't they? She stood very still, waiting for her bottle of wine to be brought, noticing Tom's hand on the checked table-cloth stained with other people's meals, with Deirdre's lying comfortingly on top of it.

He is telling her about his lost faith, Catherine thought, and she, poor child, is wondering what on earth she can say to him. How awful if she too is quoting *Dover Beach* – Tom will think all women are alike. But did girls of nineteen know Matthew Arnold – was he much read nowadays?

The waiter brought a bottle of the cheap red wine Catherine usually had. She took it absent-mindedly and offered him a ten-shilling note.

Deirdre's hand still lay on Tom's; their moussaka would be getting cold, Catherine thought, and then pulled herself up, horrified at the sardonic detachment with which she had been watching them. When her change was brought, she hurried

away and back into the flat, where she put down her shopping and the wine and then ran out again with no very clear idea of where she was going. I'm not one of those *excellent* women, who can just go home and eat a boiled egg and make a cup of tea and be very splendid, she thought, but how useful it would be if I were! She thought wistfully of herself like this. But surely there was, or ought to be, some cosy woman friend, some old school contemporary to whom she could run? Somebody who lived in a bed-sitting-room, who would bustle about making scrambled eggs and coffee on the gas-ring and then sit ready to receive confidences? Catherine thought regretfully of all the people she had meant to keep in touch with, and rather shamefacedly of others whom she had rejected as being dull. Somehow the women she met in connection with her work weren't the cosy, coffee on the gas-ring type, and they were nearly all married anyway. She imagined that Deirdre's mother and aunt would be comforting sort of people, but she could hardly go there. The best she could do was to turn her steps towards a vast eating-place where people were helping themselves to a curious variety of foods, for it was really too late for tea and too early for supper. And yet how many souls – she thought of them in this hymn-like phrase – seemed to be eating here at this unusual time.

Catherine got herself a tray of oddments, welsh rarebit and bread-and-butter and a little cake shaped like a boat, and sat down at a table with two women. She allowed herself to get carried gently along on the flow of their conversation, which was unceasing.

They evidently worked in the same office, for they began by discussing the boss, how he came in and expected something to be done by half past five, which was naturally impossible. Catherine imagined that bosses were always discussed like this; she was more interested in the shortcomings of somebody who had just left and whose filing system was impossible for anybody else to understand.

'Just you guess what she's filed it under,' said one in a tone of triumphant anticipation.

'I really can't think,' said the other, pandering to her friend.

'M. M for Miscellaneous, I suppose! Did you ever hear anything so silly?'

'I always believe in plenty of cross references. When *I* leave there won't be the slightest difficulty in finding things.'

Ah, but there will, Catherine thought. Understanding somebody else's filing system is just about as easy as really getting to know another human being. Just when you think you know everything about them, there's the impossible happening, the M for Miscellaneous when you naturally assumed it would be under something else.

Now, she realized, they had gone on to another subject, an ecclesiastical matter, it seemed.

'The minister's quite a *young* man and doesn't always dress like a clergyman.' This came from the woman Catherine had christened black-beetle; the other was leopard-hat.

'Of course,' black-beetle went on, 'the *other* church, that's the Anglo-Catholic one, has an old man as vicar. It's a pity the Church of England doesn't get some of these young men, they all seem to be old, haven't you noticed.'

'Well, youth isn't everything,' said leopard-hat. 'The young ones are sometimes a bit awkward. And even the old ones must have been young once.'

'Oh, yes, I'll grant you that. They must have *been* young. What I want to know is, what happens to the ones who've just been ordained? Who gets *them*?' Black-beetle's voice had risen indignantly.

An electric organ, which Catherine had not noticed before, now began to be played by a capable-looking woman in a tailored suit. The sounds which came out of it, purring, treacly and at the same time bouncy, mingled with the flat voices of black-beetle and leopard-hat in a nightmarish way.

Catherine could bear it no longer and she seemed to have no coffee either. 'Do we get coffee brought to us?' she asked black-beetle.

'Oh, yes, they bring it round. But it won't be *coffee* till seven o'clock.'

Catherine pondered over the strangeness of this for a moment. So it wasn't even seven o'clock yet. What was she going to do with the evening? Would Tom and Deirdre go to her flat? she wondered. It might seem to be the obvious place to go if they wanted to go on quietly holding hands. Men appeared to be so unsubtle, but perhaps it was only by contrast with the tortuous delicacy of women, who smothered their men under a cloud of sentimental associations – *our* song, *our* poem, *our* restaurant – till at last they struggled to break free, like birds trapped under the heavy black meshes of the strawberry net, she thought, changing her metaphor. Yet she *had* regarded that little restaurant as being hers and Tom's, and it only now occurred to her that it had happened to be near and cheap and that perhaps that was all there was to it.

A young man in a white coat was pouring some rich fragrant liquid into her cup. She accepted it with gratitude and resignation, for it was strong and bitter, almost medicinal, and as she drank she was conscious that it was doing her good. Tea is more healthy than alcohol and much cheaper, she reflected, and there must be thousands of people who know this.

'A nice cup you get here,' said black-beetle in a rather friendly tone.

'Yes, it's good and strong,' said Catherine. 'One needs that sometimes.'

'Excuse me for asking,' leopard-hat began, 'but is there – have you – er – recently suffered a bereavement?' she brought out in a rush.

'I? Oh, no, not exactly,' said Catherine, feeling rather flustered and unsure of herself.

'It was your black dress and those jet ear-rings – excuse me for mentioning it.'

'Oh, that's quite all right. I easily might have done, after all.'

'Yes, we must be prepared,' said leopard-hat. 'My friend here has just lost her mother.'

'Oh, I'm so sorry . . .' Catherine looked at black-beetle in a kind of wonder and thought how strange it was that anybody who looked as old as she did should have had a mother recently living.

'Now that mother's gone I'll be able to go to the Congregational church,' said black-beetle confidingly. 'The minister's quite a *young* man and doesn't always dress like a clergyman. Of course the other church, the Anglo-Catholic one, has an *old* vicar. . . .'

Catherine stood up rather abruptly. The nightmare, which the strong tea had temporarily dispelled, seemed to be coming back. She wondered how long they would sit there discussing the ages of clergymen, and whether they would ever discover who got the young ones just ordained.

'Please excuse me,' she said, 'I have to go now – good night!'

Now that mother's gone . . . it would have been a sad loss, certainly, but at least she could now go to the place of worship she preferred. If Tom went, she would be free too, but there wasn't the comfortable certainty of the Congregational church and the young minister waiting for her. She imagined him standing at the door, shaking hands after the Sunday evening service, perhaps with a special word for those who had recently suffered a bereavement. . . .

There was no sign of life when she looked up at the window of the flat, though she hardly knew whether she had expected to see any. In the sitting-room the desk was littered with pages of Tom's bad typing. She took one up and read a sentence, 'prior to the commencement of my second field trip . . .' it

began. She remembered suggesting some simplification of this phrase, but he had not heeded her. I suppose we love people for what they are and not for what we hope to make them, she thought, holding the page against her cheek. She wandered aimlessly about the room, watching the darkness come outside and wondering if Tom and Deirdre were still in the restaurant. They might well be, since it was still not very late, and with all that holding of hands they must be making very slow progress with their eating. Perhaps they would go for a walk in the park. Tom was not as a rule fond of Nature, but Catherine knew that in the early stages of a love affair it was not at all unusual for people to act out of character.

She now remembered that she had not been able to have any coffee with her supper, so she made some and then settled down at her typewriter at the table in the window. There was, as usual, a half-written page in it, stopped in the middle of a sentence, so she was able to go straight on, filling in the French background of the story she was writing, where two strangers, soon to become hero and heroine, found themselves with three hours to wait between trains in the middle of a hot afternoon and wandered into the square of the little French town. They sat on a seat and looked at the pink and white oleanders, making conversation to the strains of a distant military band . . . Catherine became so absorbed that nearly two hours went by, until she heard a step on the stairs and found Tom standing, looking over her shoulder.

'Hullo,' she smiled up at him, absently, for she was still far away. 'Had a good evening?'

'Yes, thank you. I'm rather hungry, though.'

'I suppose you had an early meal,' said Catherine lightly. 'As a matter of fact I did too – we'll have an omelette, shall we?'

While she was cooking, Tom took a piece of paper from his pocket and read it, then he called out, 'Do you know who Scheherezade was, Catty?'

'What a funny question! Some sort of Arabian slave girl, I think, who kept on telling stories to the Sultan and she had to go on and on because if she failed to hold his interest he would have her beheaded the next day.'

'I see. The kind of thing you might do rather well, but not everybody.'

Catherine could feel that he was smiling as he spoke. She made the omelettes and brought them to the table, pushing her typewriter to one side of it.

They ate in silence for a time, then Tom said in a rather stilted tone, 'Being married to somebody must be rather cosy, in a way.'

'In what sort of way?' asked Catherine, deliberately unhelpful, for she felt disinclined for a talk about marriage in the abstract.

'Oh, having a person there all the time, you know – the same face on the pillow, and at breakfast and then still there when you got home in the evening.'

'I think you make it sound horribly depressing, if it's just a question of having the same face around all the time.'

'Yes, that's what I feel too, in a way,' said Tom almost eagerly. 'I mean, there might come a time . . .'

'When you wanted a different face,' said Catherine promptly.

'Well, not all the time perhaps, but sometimes.'

'Unfortunately we can't yet cope with that very well,' said Catherine. 'Two wives or even two girl friends need a good deal of time and skill and even money to manage successfully, and you've got your thesis to finish, don't forget.'

'Oh, Catty, you're really *too* responsive – you understand things almost too well.'

'There isn't all that much to understand, is there?'

'She seems so unhappy, perhaps that's it,' said Tom in a puzzled tone. 'In a way, I feel that she needs me and a man likes to feel that sometimes.'

'Of course he does,' Catherine agreed. 'That's what seems

wrong with so many relationships now, the women feeling that *they* are the strong ones and that men couldn't get on without them. In the olden days,' she smiled at the phrase, 'it was quite different – or so we always imagine. Or were women more diplomatic then?'

'She lives in that rather depressing suburban house, where nobody really understands her,' Tom went on. 'Oh, yes, I know it was very pleasant going to tea there. . . .'

'So it *is* Deirdre we're talking about.'

Tom looked startled. 'But of course. Who else did you think it could be?'

'I don't know, but you seem to meet so many girls in the course of your studies. How do I know which ones are likely to hold your hand in restaurants? I hope it was one of the *better* meals this evening, by the way? We know how the food can vary there.' She darted an amused look at him, and he thought how different her merry sardonic grey eyes were from Deirdre's intense brown ones with their spaniel-like look of devotion. The trouble was that he liked – perhaps even loved – both of them. He began to form a sentence about polygamy and how primitive societies were really rather better arranged than our own civilization, but another glance from Catherine stopped him.

'Yes, I *did* see you,' she said. 'Now, Tom, what *practical* arrangements will this involve? You can't bring her to live here, you know. Her mother and aunt wouldn't like it and there isn't room, anyway.'

'No, I suppose there isn't,' said Tom, as if he had been seriously considering bringing Deirdre to live in Catherine's flat. 'Perhaps I could take a room with Mark and Digby.'

'Oh, Tom, in that depressing mouldering house by the railway, and with that dreadful geyser in the bathroom!'

'I can finish my thesis there as well as anywhere,' said Tom rather stiffly.

'And anywhere will do for love, won't it. Now I can see what Donne meant when he wrote about love making one little room an everywhere. And it will be such a *very* little room, quite *poky*, you might say . . .' she began to laugh in an uncertain way.

Catty, please don't.' He came and sat beside her. 'I don't have to go, you know. I didn't mean to start all this, and I don't think I did. It seems to be all your idea.'

'But it's a good idea, and you'll be able to finish your thesis much better away from me,' She looked up at him, apparently recovered.

'I believe I could have Ephraim Olo's room in a week or two,' said Tom thoughtfully. 'He's going back soon.'

'Has he finished his studies then?'

'Yes, he's going to be a Cabinet Minister.'

'Of course, they've got their own sort of government now, haven't they. It's comforting to know you'll occupy the room a Cabinet Minister once had. It's a bit like Marx and Lenin living in London and then going back to Russia. It would be even more comforting if it were somebody like Mr. Gladstone, wouldn't it?'

'Yes, darling,' he said, humouring her.

'I suppose we can see to your packing in the morning?'

'Good heavens, yes. I shan't be going for a week or two.'

'It seems rather cold-blooded, doesn't it, not going for a week or two? In books and films and even in life, too, people go and pack suit-cases there and then and hurry out of the house.'

'Catty, please, I don't want to go *now*.' Tom suddenly realized that he was very tired. The long and unaccustomed walk with Deirdre in the park must have taken it out of him. He hadn't really meant to start anything; perhaps in the morning they would realize that it had all been a mistake.

CHAPTER TEN

THAT same evening Rhoda Wellcome sat writing a letter to the Electricity Board. The bill for the last quarter had just arrived, and it was preposterously large, more than if they had left all the electric lights and fires on in the house all day and all night. Round her on the table were strewn the bills for past quarters, which she was studying and comparing, reading out extracts to her sister, who sat knitting and trying to listen to a popular humorous programme on the wireless.

'There *must* be a mistake,' Rhoda repeated for the fifth or sixth time. 'And now that I come to think of it, the man couldn't get in to read the meter last time, or *said* he couldn't, though I'm sure there must have been *somebody* in, so I filled in the card myself.'

'Perhaps you did it wrong,' said Mabel Swan mildly.

'Well, I'm going to look now.'

'All right, dear. I'll come and make a cup of tea, that would be nice, wouldn't it. Perhaps Deirdre will be in soon and would like some when she comes in.'

Rhoda crouched among the metres, holding a torch to read the little clocks, but whatever she saw there did not seem to solve the mystery. Finally she wrote a sharp note, being as rude as one can only be to an impersonal body, and flinging at them a kind of challenge, which was perhaps irrelevant but which relieved her feelings. 'I have also noticed,' she concluded, 'that the light has become much dimmer lately and should be glad to know how you would explain this. Yours truly, Rhoda Wellcome.'

She sealed up the envelope and addressed it, but her remark

about the dimming light had left her with a faint sense of disquiet, as if it might have a wider and more disturbing significance. Though perhaps it could be put right by some comparatively simple means, such as the buying of more powerful electric light bulbs.

'Let me see now,' said Mabel, 'who is Deirdre out with tonight?' There was an undertone of pride in her voice, which Rhoda did not fail to notice for she said quickly and with an air of inner knowledge, 'Oh, Tom, of course! He's definitely the one now.'

'Poor Bernard,' sighed Mabel. 'Still, men must put up with these things and I never thought she was really very keen on him.'

'Oh, certainly not! She endured his attentions,' said Rhoda, feeling that she had read the phrase somewhere in a novel, 'but that was all. She and Tom have so much more in common.'

'Yes, and he is older than Bernard. I feel she's been needing an older man, someone she can respect and look up to. From what she says Tom seems to be just that kind of person.'

'And his people have an old place in Shropshire, so I dare say there will be some money there,' said Rhoda in a full tone. 'Of course he is a brilliant anthropologist.'

The sisters were silent for a moment, either in tribute to Tom's brilliance, or because there seemed nothing to say about a profession of which they were almost totally ignorant. If Mabel thought rather wistfully of Bernard's steady position with his father's firm, she did not mention it.

'Of course there is Catherine,' she said uncertainly. 'One doesn't quite know if there is any attachment there.'

'You mean Miss Oliphant?' said Rhoda in a surprised tone. 'Oh, surely she is just a friend. I thought her very nice but rather an odd little thing, not the kind of girl to attract a man.'

'All the same, I shouldn't like to feel that Deirdre was – well, causing any unhappiness there.'

'I should think Catherine is well able to look after herself,' said Rhoda positively, 'and after all, women must put up with these things too, as you said about Bernard. That's life, isn't it.' She spoke with an almost callous detachment, for although she knew that it might be life for other people it had not been so for her. An aunt can if necessary fight as tenaciously for a niece's rights as a mother can for a daughter's.

'There's Deirdre now,' said Mabel, her sharper mother's ear having heard the key in the lock. 'But she seems to be going straight upstairs.' She lifted the lid of the teapot and peered inside it. 'There is some tea here if she'd like it – it hasn't been made long.'

'I expect she'll come down if she wants any,' said Rhoda sensibly.

Upstairs in her room, Deirdre combed her hair and put on more powder and lipstick to compose herself for meeting the searching glances of her mother and aunt. She would have preferred to go straight to bed, to go over in her mind the dinner at the little Greek restaurant, the walk in Regent's Park and the things they had said to each other which, for a girl of nineteen, are full of the magical freshness of never having been said before. This evening she could almost have believed that Tom loved her as much as she loved him; only the thought of Catherine, so sweet to her at the party and altogether such a nice person, cast a slight cloud over her happiness. Naturally they had not spoken of Catherine during dinner and certainly not when they were stumbling over the grass in Regent's Park. Deirdre salved her conscience by remembering that Catherine had laughed about Tom and his thesis, and this seemed such a very dreadful thing that perhaps she deserved to lose him.

When Deirdre came into the drawing-room she could feel her mother and aunt consciously restraining their curiosity, asking her if it had been raining outside, if she would like some tea or anything to eat.

'No, thank you,' Deirdre said. 'I couldn't eat. Tom gave me a very nice meal at a Greek restaurant and then we went for a walk in Regent's Park.'

'Regent's Park!' Rhoda exclaimed, unable to hold herself in check any longer. 'How lovely that must have been! Queen Mary's garden,' she added, hardly conscious of the slight incongruity of her words.

'We didn't go there,' Deirdre smiled.

'You must bring Tom here again some time,' said Mabel, encouraged by her daughter's friendliness. 'We could ask Malcolm to ask Phyllis, or you could invite that nice girl Catherine who came to tea and that young Frenchman. We could have quite a jolly party.'

'Yes, I'll ask Tom to come to supper one evening,' said Deirdre absently. But not Catherine, of course, her mother and aunt did not know about Tom and Catherine and she herself did not want to think about them now.

'I dare say Father Tulliver would come too, and of course if we could get Mr. Lydgate as well...' Rhoda's ambition was driving her almost into the realms of fantasy. 'It would be a cold meal, as it's summer, a fork supper, and perhaps a wine cup of some kind.' She could see it all laid out on the table like one of those lovely coloured pictures in *Good House-keeping*.

Deirdre, like Tom, was tired after the long walk and was glad when the time came to go to bed and dream about him. But dreams can seldom be arranged as we wish them, and Deirdre's were of Digby Fox, of all people. They were walking in a garden full of flowers and he kissed her. She woke up feeling disappointed and cross, and was quite rude to him when she met him the next morning. And yet he was very kind to her, offering to lend her some notes he had made on a long and difficult book, which would save her the trouble of reading it.

'How refreshing to meet a feminine and unscholarly girl,' he

119

said to Mark, 'not too proud to accept my humble offering of a few notes. Most girls would throw them back in your face.' He wondered if he should ask her out to lunch with him but then thought better of it. No amorous dalliance until the Foresight Fellowships were settled, but then, ah *then* . . . he promised himself.

Deirdre and Tom had arranged to meet in the afternoon at Felix's Folly, where they could sit quietly side by side reading their books. They had been doing this for about ten minutes, when Tom began to talk to Deirdre in a low voice. Opposite them sat Miss Lydgate, surrounded by sheets of paper covered with lists of words and charts in brightly coloured chalks. Her white hair stood up on end, for she had been running her fingers through it. The expression on her face was almost one of anguish, her eyes glared through her spectacles and seemed to fix themselves on Tom and Deirdre.

'Come outside a minute,' he whispered. 'I've got something to tell you. We'd better not talk here as we seem to be annoying Miss Lydgate.'

'Yes, she's positively *glaring* at us,' said Deirdre.

In all fairness to Miss Lydgate, it must be said that she was not glaring at them at all and was, indeed, totally unconscious of their presence. She had been making a comparative study of the vocabularies of some little-known languages and had come across a feature in one of them which reminded her of something in another. But *where* had she met it before? She plunged through the mangrove swamps of the Niger Delta, but it was not there; then up to Lake Chad, hovering around the bit that was always drying up and looking so odd on the map, then down through French Equatorial Africa to the Belgian Congo, where she lingered for a moment among the pygmies. 'Tyrell Todd? *Impossible*,' she breathed impatiently, and swept right across to the spicy coasts of Tanganyika, up through troubled Kenya and into the hills of Ethiopia. Here she stopped and murmured the poetical-sounding names of

well-known Italian ethnographers and linguists – Cerulli, Robecchi-Bricchetti, Vanutelli, Citerni – but still it evaded her. Then suddenly she took a leap across the border into the Sudan, stood up and cried out something that sounded like 'Jebel Pingpong! Well, I'll be jiggered! Come here *at once*, Father Gemini!'

Father Gemini, who had been cowering quietly out of sight in a book-lined alcove, ran across the room. The other readers, pleased to be interrupted in their studies, sat back expectantly.

Meanwhile Tom had led Deirdre into the little room where Mark and Digby had recently put the horsehair sofa. The room now contained a small coffee-table, stained with the rings of wet cups, two straight-backed chairs, a bookcase full of old foreign periodicals, and a model African village, laid out on top of a packing-case which was covered with an orange table-cloth. On the mantelpiece stood a vase of pink daisy-like flowers.

'I've found this funny little room,' Tom said. 'I was looking for the Gents and walked in here by mistake. I can't imagine what it's for.'

'Perhaps for having private conversations in,' Deirdre suggested, 'I mean for Miss Lydgate and Father Gemini and people like that.'

'Not our kind, perhaps,' said Tom. 'Shall we sit on this sofa?'

They sat down. Tom took hold of Deirdre's hand. It lay in his without moving, like a dead bird, he thought, conscious that this was just the kind of thing Catherine might have said.

'I don't think we ought to hold hands here,' said Deirdre rather anxiously.

'No, perhaps not, but we will just the same. I wanted to tell you that next week or thereabouts I'm going to get a room in the flat where Mark and Digby live.'

'Oh, but what will Catherine do?'

'Well, she'll be as she was before we met, I suppose.'

'Surely not quite that?'

'No, perhaps not quite. I meant she'll live by herself as she used to. She was always quite happy you know, she's a very solitary person, really.'

'Yes, she may have been, but now perhaps she'll be just lonely, and I couldn't bear that. Though, she did say – don't you remember – that the loneliness of men was so much worse than the loneliness of women?' Deirdre looked up at Tom, distressed and puzzled, hoping for reassurance.

Tom thought with irritation, how like Catherine to say a thing like that, for surely the loneliness of a woman abandoned by her lover is the worst of all? She probably hadn't been thinking of that and of course it *wasn't* that. *She* had driven *him* away, really, when it came to the point, and so far he hadn't even done his packing. Perhaps he wouldn't go after all. Suddenly it all seemed unbearably complicated.

Deirdre, noticing how the bright sun showed up the lines of strain and weariness round his eyes and mouth, put her hand gently on his arm and said, 'Perhaps you're right. After all Catherine isn't so very young, and she has lots of interests and her writing.'

Tom's face cleared, 'Ah, yes,' he said with an air of relief, 'she has her writing. Of course she isn't really a very *good* writer.'

'That doesn't matter,' said Deirdre with unusual firmness. 'When people write, they feel they're doing something creative and worth while and that's supposed to make up for everything else. Perhaps she doesn't really care about anything but that.'

'No, I don't think she does,' said Tom more comfortably. 'All the same, I *shall* worry about her a little.'

'Oh, naturally,' said Deirdre, feeling it a little unfair that to the worry of Tom's thesis should now be added the worry of Catherine, abandoned and perhaps lonely. 'But she's such a strong character.'

'Yes, she's certainly that,' Tom agreed.

'What did you say to her?'

'I didn't have to say much. She guessed that I might want to make a change,' he frowned over these last words, for he had not meant to commit himself when he really had no idea what he did intend to do except to move away from Catherine's flat. 'She saw us in the restaurant.'

At this point voices were heard outside the door, the loud ringing tones of Professor Mainwaring and Miss Clovis, and a soft rather fluttery woman's voice which could not be identified.

The door opened. Deirdre and Tom moved quickly away from each other.

'Now here is the little room we use for – ah, I see it is already being used for just that purpose.' Professor Mainwaring stood beaming in the doorway, his silvery beard glinting in the sun. Beside him stood Mrs. Foresight, in pink and mauve flowered crêpe-de-chine and a straw hat trimmed with sweet peas; just behind them hovered Miss Clovis, in one of her better-looking grey flannel suits.

Tom and Deirdre, feeling a little foolish, stood up.

'Two of our younger readers,' said Professor Mainwaring, turning to Mrs. Foresight. 'We felt that we needed a small room where anthropologists – and linguists too – could discuss points that cropped up in connection with their work. You would hardly believe what problems *do* crop up where two or three anthropologists are gathered together. Isn't that so, Mallow?'

Tom agreed that it was so.

'I'm sure Mrs. Foresight would be interested to know what you have been discussing,' Professor Mainwaring went on.

'Housing, mostly,' said Tom smoothly. He turned to Mrs. Foresight with his charming smile. 'When a man wants to take another wife he has to build her a separate hut, you know.'

'How very sensible,' said Mrs. Foresight, fixing him with

her round blue eyes. 'But I expect you have seen some very dreadful things *out there*,' she breathed hopefully.

'Well, I suppose they might be thought dreadful by the non-specialist,' said Tom soothingly, 'but we have to be detached, you know.'

'And no expression of disgust, astonishment or amusement must show on the face of the investigator,' recited Miss Clovis, who had once read this in an anthropologists' manual.

'I'm mainly interested in problems of local government, land tenure and that sort of thing,' said Tom, 'so I concentrate on those.'

Disappointment and relief showed themselves on Mrs. Foresight's pink babyish face. 'I'm very glad to hear it,' she said. 'I'm sure this young man wouldn't be likely to write the kind of article that that nasty Professor Fairfax wrote in the magazine you sent me, would he?' she asked, turning to Professor Mainwaring.

'Oh, dear me, no!' laughed the Professor merrily, giving his beard a sharp tweak. 'Mallow is doing valuable work which the Administration is finding most useful. *When* he publishes anything' – the quizzical look he threw at Tom took away the slight sting in his words – 'you can be sure it will be a model of dullness, *quite* unreadable, I should imagine.'

Tom gave an uncertain laugh.

'And what is this young lady doing?'

Deirdre went rather pink and murmured that she was just a student, still reading for her degree.

'And do you hope to go out and work among natives?' Mrs. Foresight asked.

'I don't know, really, I expect so.'

'A woman can be a great help out there,' said Professor Mainwaring. 'Many workers have found a wife a most useful asset, particularly if she has had the right kind of education.'

'And a man needs love and companionship wherever he is,' said Mrs. Foresight, a little reproachfully, seeming to address

Miss Clovis whom she judged to be out of sympathy with this view.

'I did not have that,' said Professor Mainwaring in a rather high tone. 'I wonder if my work has suffered from the lack of it?'

'Oh, Professor, I'm sure many women must have been fond of you!' said Mrs. Foresight in a playful, flirtatious manner. If she had been carrying a fan she would surely have tapped his arm with it.

'Well, I think I can say that I have had my share of affection,' he mused, seeming to be unconscious of his audience.

'I expect Mrs. Foresight would like to see some of the applications for the Fellowships,' said Miss Clovis rather sharply. 'Time is getting on, you know.'

'Ah, and how it is!' said Professor Mainwaring with a great gusty laugh, and, waving his hand in a friendly gesture to the young people, he escorted Mrs. Foresight and Miss Clovis out of the room.

'Excellent, my dear Esther,' he beamed, when Mrs. Foresight was washing her hands, 'to have those two in there, deep in discussion. A most happy touch, I could see that Minnie was deeply impressed. Mallow is very sound, you know,' he added, as if Tom were a fruit suitable for bottling, though it is doubtful if he would have recognized the analogy. 'Ah, my dear Minnie, now what do you say to a little luncheon? You've had a tiring morning, but I hope you haven't been disappointed with what you have seen of our work here?'

'No, indeed, I've been *most* impressed. And that charming young couple, so obviously in love, well, the girl, anyway. Perhaps women show it more than men. Romance among all these books – however much education of women there is, you can't keep it out, can you. . . .' Her blue eyes bulged sentimentally.

'Is your chauffeur waiting down below, Mrs. Foresight, or did you tell him to call back for you?' broke in Miss Clovis.

'Oh, I expect he's waiting,' said Mrs. Foresight in the vague but confident tone of one who never has to worry about getting to places or to rely on the uncertainties of public transport. 'Will you be joining us for lunch, Miss Clovis?'

'No, I am really much too busy,' said Miss Clovis, who had not been invited.

'Then perhaps we should go now,' said Mrs. Foresight, sounding relieved. She had not really taken to Miss Clovis, who seemed to her hard and unwomanly, always breaking in on what promised to be a rather delightful conversation with Professor Mainwaring with some grimly practical suggestion.

Mrs. Foresight's car, old-fashioned but of the best make and beautifully kept, was waiting in the street below. As they approached, the chauffeur stuffed the Communist newspaper he had been reading into his pocket, hurried to open the back door and, although it was a warm day, arranged a light rug over Mrs. Foresight's knees. Professor Mainwaring took his seat beside her, and dangled before her the names of a few expensive restaurants for her consideration. But in the end she chose the Ladies Annexe of his club, which was a learned and exclusive one and seemed to her to be on the threshold of those fascinating and unexplored academic circles which her late husband, with all his wealth, had never been able to penetrate.

The car moved off and went along rather slowly, as cars so often must in London. Mark and Digby, walking on the pavement, noticed Professor Mainwaring reclining against the pearl-grey upholstery, his hand on a silken cord, and with a silver vase of carnations nodding at his side.

'If he threw out a handful of coins, would you demean yourself by struggling for them in the road?' asked Digby.

'I don't suppose there would be any struggle,' said Mark. 'English people are embarrassed at that sort of thing. Everybody would just look the other way and hurry on. We should have the field to ourselves.'

CHAPTER ELEVEN

Tom's going was a distressing business, both for Catherine and for Tom himself. Catherine had never quite under, stood why it was so much more painful to see a man in tears than a woman; it couldn't only be because they were supposed to be the stronger sex. She had long ago learned that men could and did cry, but perhaps she had never recovered from the first shock of that knowledge or acquired any adequate way of dealing with the situation in the meantime. So must a mother feel when her son goes to school, she thought, and was immediately reminded of a song of childhood,

> *Going to school, the cab's at the door,*
> *Mother is waiting to kiss me once more;*
> *Father looks sad and gives me a tip,*
> *Poor little Mary is pouting her lip . . .*

So strong did this impression become that she found herself humming the tune as she walked from room to room, gathering up Tom's possessions and helping him to pack them. She could no more prevent his going now than a mother could hold her child back from school.

They had spent a sleepless and unhappy night and in the morning Tom had said, with a sideways pleading glance at her, that he didn't feel awfully well and thought he might have a temperature. Perhaps the little boy had hoped that he might awake with a rash, to be diagnosed as measles or chicken-pox, thought Catherine, hardening her heart.

'You know I haven't a thermometer,' she said, 'but if

you're *really* ill, of course you must stay in bed. I suppose we could unpack some of the things.'

'No, I suppose I must be all right really.' He glanced round the room. 'It seems to look just the same, even with my things gone, doesn't it.'

'Well, it won't look quite the same to me.'

'Oh, Catty, don't . . .'

'It will be tidier, for one thing.'

He smiled weakly. 'You're so much braver than I am. I don't believe you mind all this at all.'

'I do mind. I was very fond of you, but we can't both be in tears.'

'Aren't you still fond of me? No, I suppose I can't expect that now – and you said I'd never really understood you.'

'Oh, that doesn't really matter – people make a lot too much of it. Who understands anybody, if it comes to that?'

'We haven't many interests in common.'

Catherine laughed. 'No, I suppose we didn't sit by the fire in the evenings doing fretwork or poring over our collections of butterflies.'

'We mocked at each other's work,' said Tom rather hopelessly.

'That may be, but it surely isn't the point. You met Deirdre, that was what really mattered.'

'Oh, *that.*'

'Well, we can't go into it now. We seem to have come to a parting of the ways, whatever the reason. Now look, I've mended all your socks and everything that could be washed is done. Are you going to get a taxi? I think you'll have to. Shall I go out and find one? Everything seems to be ready now.'

Catherine hurried from the room, almost in tears, but she had managed to control herself by the time she came back to say that the taxi was waiting below.

'What will you do now?' Tom asked.

'I'm having lunch with the editor of a magazine to whom I'm hoping to sell some articles, so I must get ready soon.'

'I hope she gives you a good lunch.'

'It's a man.'

'Do men edit women's magazines – what an idea!'

'Why not? Men do know *something* about women or at least like to form their tastes for them.'

'I suppose you'll write an article called "After he's gone", and make use of all this.'

'That might be a good title – do hurry, the taxi's ticking away, you know.'

Tom hovered in the doorway still. 'I expect I'll go home for a bit later in the summer,' he said.

'Yes, do; it would be a change for you. And ring me up sometime to let me know how you are. We might have lunch together or something.'

Tom's face brightened. 'Yes, that would be nice.'

'I'll carry down your typewriter. You're not going so very far away, you know – only ten minutes' walk. Give my love to Mark and Digby, and do be careful of that geyser in the bathroom.'

Catherine did not restrain her tears when she was alone and realized the truth of the saying that one felt better for a good cry. She washed up the breakfast things and then paced through the rooms, hoping and fearing that Tom might have forgotten something or that she might find some little unconscious relic to remember him by. The wastepaper basket was full of crumpled pages, rejected bits of his thesis, and there was an old typewriter ribbon, all mangled and twisted. So he had put a new ribbon into his typewriter before leaving her, Catherine thought, touched and amused, but the old one was hardly a relic to be cherished. That would surely have been excessive sentimentality. She poked about idly among the papers and then drew out a sheet covered with large and rather childish handwriting.

129

'My own darling,' she read, 'this is going to be a silly sort of letter when I only said good-bye to you ten minutes ago, but whenever I'm not with you I feel like Scheherezade, if that makes sense, and so that's why I'm writing now.'

Poor Tom, Catherine thought, it had evidently *not* made sense to him, until he had asked her who Scheherezade was. She read through to the end of the letter with critical detachment, as if she were considering it as a piece of literature, then stood with it in her hand, not liking to crumple it up and throw it away again. She had known that men did not always keep letters as women did, but Tom was in some ways rather sentimental and she had the feeling that perhaps he had not meant to destroy it but had thrown it away by accident with his old bits of thesis. Well, there was nothing she could do about it now; it was not the kind of relic she would have cared to keep for herself, so she put it back into the wastepaper basket and then went to get ready for her luncheon.

The editor she was meeting was a good-looking fussy young man, who immediately noticed Catherine's eyelids, swollen with crying, imperfectly disguised with too much green eyeshadow. But her conversation was brittle and quite witty, and he judged that her approach would be detached and unsentimental which was the tone he aimed at in his magazine. He was pleased that she ate a good lunch, for he was fond of food and had taken trouble with the ordering of it. After they had discussed the articles she was to write, they talked about Siamese cats, cooking, and Victorian poetry.

'I've enjoyed this,' Catherine said.

'May I get you a taxi somewhere?' he asked, just like somebody in one of her stories.

'No, thank you, I shall meditate on top of a bus. I like doing that and I'm not in a hurry.'

The good lunch with cocktails and wine had given her the courage to go home, and she began to look forward to taking off her high-heeled shoes and making a good strong pot of tea.

She sat on the bus, almost contented, looking out of the windows. It passed the Law Courts and she noted with interest the little groups of people standing there, the wronged wife with a sensible-looking woman friend, the knot of relatives embittered over a disputed will. Then the bus stopped by a travel agency, its windows full of bright tempting posters. Spain, Portugal, Italy – dangerous, romantic, un-English: then Norway and Sweden – so clean and healthy: then France – which was just France, and Lourdes – a Pilgrimage by Luxury Coach. The bus moved away, leaving Catherine puzzling over this last announcement. A pilgrimage by luxury coach seemed a contradiction in terms. The bus gathered speed now, and they rushed past a church where a large poster announced what she hastily read as HOLY GHOST FATHERS – GRAND CENTENARY DANCE. But could it really have been this? Coming after the luxury pilgrimage, it was disturbing; the foundations of life seemed to be slipping. Am I imagining it, or is my mind unhinged by grief? she wondered. The bus began to crawl now, stopping at stops where nobody got on or off and waiting for the traffic lights to turn red; then it hurried again so that when she started to go down the stairs to get off it was like a perilously rocking ship and she nearly fell in her high-heeled shoes.

Nothing had happened since she went away. The rooms were tidy as she had left them. She took off her shoes and filled the kettle, then went to the window and stood looking out.

She had been there some time before she became conscious of a woman walking rather slowly along the opposite side of the street, peering at the houses as if looking for a particular number. When she saw Catherine she stopped and made as if to cross the road. Catherine drew back into the shadow of the curtain. A minute or so later her door bell rang. When she opened the door she found the woman she had seen waiting outside. She was in the middle fifties, well-dressed and good-looking, but with a worried, nervous expression and manner.

'Good afternoon,' she began. 'I wonder if you could tell me whether Mr. Mallow is in?'

'No, I'm sorry, he isn't here,' said Catherine, very much taken aback.

'Oh, I see. Well . . .' the woman hesitated.

'I wonder if *I* could help you?'

'Are you Miss Oliphant, by any chance?'

'Yes, I am. Won't you come in?'

'It was really you I wanted to see, in a way.'

'Oh, do come in, then. I was just making some tea. I dare say you'd like some?'

'Thank you, that's very kind.'

They walked up the stairs together and Catherine indicated her front door. 'My flat is in there.'

'You will wonder what I have come for,' said the woman.

'Well, yes,' Catherine smiled. 'I don't think we've ever met before, have we?'

'No.' She paused and seemed to take a deep breath. 'You see,' she declared. 'I am Tom Mallow's aunt.'

Catherine's first instinct was to burst out laughing. She wondered why there was something slightly absurd about aunts; perhaps it was because one thought of them as dear, comfortable creatures, somehow lacking in dignity and prestige.

'Oh, yes, he told me about you,' Catherine ventured.

'I am Mrs. Beddoes. I live in Belgravia,' she explained.

'Yes, of course, I should have guessed that.' Tom's other aunt, his father's eldest sister, was a spinster who lived in a hotel in South Kensington. Clearly Mrs. Beddoes was the superior one – Belgravia and the married state had raised her up.

Tea was made and Catherine produced bread-and-butter and a plate of biscuits. She had no cake, especially not at a time like *this*, she told herself. Nobody could expect it.

Mrs. Beddoes complimented her on her china. She seemed

surprised to find that it was so nice. 'Oh, dear, it's all such a pity,' she burst out. 'I suppose I shouldn't be sitting here drinking your tea.'

'I have plenty, and you must have needed a cup – it's such a hot tiring afternoon. Do have a biscuit. I hope you like Bourbons. They always remind me of exiled European royalty, and that's one of those sad but comforting thoughts that one likes to have. Do you suppose they sit around in their villas at Estoril eating Bourbon biscuits?'

Mrs. Beddoes threw Catherine a startled glance but took a biscuit.

'There's something rather good about Osborne biscuits too, don't you think,' Catherine went on. 'Dull, solid and good – the Old Queen, I suppose. *Were* they named after the royal residence, do you think?'

'I suppose they may have been,' said Mrs. Beddoes unhappily.

'But I must stop my frivolous talk,' said Catherine, relenting. 'You came to see me about something.'

'Yes, I came here with a purpose.' Mrs. Beddoes put down her cup and seemed to gather up her courage. 'My sister, Tom's mother, asked me to call on him and report on his circumstances.' She lowered her voice and added, as if she were talking to a contemporary who was in no way concerned in the matter, 'You see, we had heard that he was living in rather a poor part of London with some – er – young woman, and it did seem such a pity.'

'Yes, I suppose it would seem like that.'

'He has been a great disappointment and worry to his family, you know. Taking up such a very *odd* career – we've never had such a thing in the family before. Going out to Africa and living in such a strange way . . .'

'And living equally oddly in London,' added Catherine sympathetically. 'Believe me, I do feel for you. Perhaps that hasn't happened before in your family, either?'

'Well, of course, one does not – cannot – know about that.'
Mrs. Beddoes looked worried and Catherine remembered Tom
telling her that she had a son about his own age. 'You see,
Miss Oliphant, the whole thing is rather a surprise. You are
not at all what I expected.'

'No, I dare say not. But women who live with men without
being married to them aren't necessarily very glamorous, you
know. They can be faded and worried-looking, their hands
can be roughened with housework and stained with peeling
vegetables . . .' Catherine, looked down at her own, which
were in this state. She had tried to keep them hidden during
her luncheon with the editor, for she had not had time to
improve them or put on nail-varnish.

'Yes, we had naturally envisaged . . .' Mrs. Beddoes stopped,
either because she was surprised at herself for producing such
a curious word or because she did not like to say just what they
had envisaged.

Catherine decided that it was perhaps unfair to let her go
floundering on like this, so she refilled her cup and said in a
friendly tone, 'Well, it hardly seems to matter now. Tom
isn't living here any more. He left this morning.'

Mrs. Beddoes appeared confused, as indeed she was. Upper-
most in her mind was a feeling of natural and understandable
disappointment. The young woman seemed to be almost
respectable and there was nothing in it, or no longer anything
in it, after all. Then she noticed Catherine's swollen eyelids
and had the feeling that she was intruding on a private grief and
that it was concerned with her nephew. It was difficult to
know what to say next.

'You sent him away?' she ventured.

'Not exactly – though women always like to think that they
have taken the initiative in ending a love affair. But I may as
well be honest. I think he wanted to go.'

'My dear, I am sorry, believe me when I say that. But it was

very wrong of you, you know, to live with him without being married. Don't you realize that?'

Catherine smiled. 'I see you are thinking the very worst.'

Mrs. Beddoes seemed uncomfortable again, and took up her furs and gazed into the bright glass eyes of the little animals' heads, as if they might help her.

'Well, one does usually think something of the kind, surely,' she said, on the defensive now.

'Yes, of course women do think the worst of each other, perhaps because only they can know what they are capable of. Men are regarded as being not quite responsible for their actions. Besides, they have other and more important things on their minds. Did you know that Tom was writing a thesis, for his Ph.D.?'

'How splendid,' said Mrs. Beddoes uncomprehendingly. 'He was always a clever boy. But he's been very naughty – I don't myself think that there should be different codes of behaviour for men and women, though of course that view *was* held, and in the highest circles.'

'Yes, it does come out in some of those Edwardian memoirs,' said Catherine thoughtfully. 'But I can see that I was perhaps wrong. I'm afraid one doesn't always think whether one is doing the right thing at the time.'

There was a short silence and then Catherine went on, 'All this has been a bit like *Traviata*, don't you think? You coming to see me and begging me to give Tom up, but of course it's too late.'

'*Traviata*? Oh, I see.' Mrs. Beddoes seemed relieved and would indeed have welcomed a cosy talk about opera. Before the war they had always had a box at Covent Garden during the season. She remembered *Traviata* as one of the less boring ones. But she still had her duty to do, so she went on to ask Catherine where Tom was living now.

'He has taken a room in a flat with two other young anthropologists,' Catherine told her, 'not very far from here. It's

near the railway, not very salubrious I'm afraid, but I think he'll be able to work better there. I can give you the address, or you could telephone him, of course.'

'Oh, I don't think I shall go to see Tom now. It was you I really wanted to see.'

'Had you hoped to make me see reason?' Catherine asked in her frank way. She even wondered whether Mrs. Beddoes had been prepared to offer her money, as in an Edwardian novel, and whether she could have brought herself to accept it. She almost believed that she could.

'Well, I wanted to tell Naomi, my sister, how he was,' said Mrs. Beddoes rather lamely, 'but that seems to be unnecessary now'. She stood up and arranged her furs round her shoulders. 'I have often asked Tom to visit us but he has always made some excuse. Now, I wonder . . .' she paused for a moment, and then her tone seemed to change on to a bright social note. 'I am giving a small dance for my daughter, Lalage, you may have seen the announcement in *The Times*. Do you think I could persuade Tom to come to it – and perhaps the friends he is lodging with, if they are nice young men?'

Catherine imagined the bored distaste or derisive laughter which might greet such an invitation. She had often wondered why it was that anthropologists seemed to explore only the lower strata of their own society. Perhaps it was a kind of hidden fear that they might prove unworthy in some way, for she was sure that the experience of a débutante dance in Belgravia would be as rewarding for them as any piece of native ceremonial.

'I'm not sure if they are dancing men,' she said uncertainly, 'but they are certainly very nice. There is no harm in them.'

Mrs. Beddoes hesitated over this doubtful recommendation. Perhaps even a hostess seeking young men for a dance demands something more positive than the assurance that there is no harm in them. 'Are they tall?' she asked.

'Digby is very tall – over six feet, I should say. Mark is of medium height, perhaps a little shorter than Tom.'

'Well, that sounds ideal.' Mrs. Beddoes put on her gloves and then suddenly said in a confidential tone, 'My dear, there is this terrible difficulty of getting hold of enough suitable young men. The regular ones get so blasé and often don't turn up at all, and poor Lalage is five foot *eleven* – girls seem to be enormous these days, don't they.'

'And to think that they grew up under the Labour Government and austerity,' said Catherine.

'Yes, that *is* strange.' Mrs. Beddoes looked troubled for a moment, 'But things are all right *now*,' she added obscurely. 'Thank you, Miss Oliphant, for all your help. I shall tell Naomi how kind you have been. Perhaps I shall write a note to Tom.'

'The bus stop is a few yards down the road, or shall I get you a taxi?' Catherine asked.

'Well . . .' Mrs. Beddoes smiled apologetically. 'I think a taxi, please. I'm rather tired and it will be getting on towards the rush hour now. They tell us *not* to use public transport between 4.30 and 6.30, don't they.'

So for the second time that day Catherine saw a member of Tom's family into a taxi. The day was coming to its end, and although it had been tiring and upsetting it had at least been full and that, she supposed, was all to the good. Pain, amusement, surprise, resignation, were all woven together into a kind of fabric whose colour and texture she could hardly visualize as yet. Something with little lumps on it, she thought, knobs or knops as it said in the fashion magazines. The meeting with Tom's aunt had somehow pleased and comforted her; being without relations herself, she could, as it were, rejoice that others should have aunts, and now that there was nothing disgraceful about her relationship with Tom perhaps she might even visit his other aunt in her hotel in South Kensington.

But as evening approached she began to wish that somebody would telephone her and take her out to dinner. She thought of various men she knew but realized philosophically that it was unlikely that any of them would know of her plight and she was too proud to telephone. The best thing to do if you're lonely, she thought, is to seek out some other lonely person, but she could only think of Alaric Lydgate and somehow she did not feel that meeting him once at the garden fence was enough to justify a further advance on her side. And in any case, she told herself, she wasn't really lonely; it just felt rather strange not to have Tom there. But no more strange than when he had been away in Africa.

She lay in bed, sleepless, wondering if he were comfortably settled, but she mustn't be fussy and ring up too soon. She wished she had a 'nice book', something that would take her out of herself, but the bookshelf by her bed wasn't very encouraging, and only made her think what very strange books people gave as Confirmation presents. Obviously, she thought, noting the little leather-bound volumes, they were chosen for their size and colour. Browning, Housman's *Shropshire Lad*, the *Rubaiyat* of Omar Khayyàm – surely the gay or despairing pagan sentiments of these authors were dangerous to a young girl embarking on her religious life? The only real book of devotion she had, suitably enough from her headmistress, told her that we are strangers and pilgrims here and must endure the heart's banishment, and she felt that she knew that anyway.

CHAPTER TWELVE

Tom opened his eyes reluctantly. He had beend reaming that he was back in Africa, but when he woke up and found where he really was he turned over on his side again and lay staring at the wall, distempered a rather dirty cream, on which the sun was shining brightly. Too bright to last, he thought gloomily, and closed his eyes again. Outside a train rattled by.

The night before, Mark and Digby had thought he needed cheering up and taking out of himself; they had spent a manly evening drinking beer, whose effects are not always particularly cheering. His life had started on its new lap now; no Catherine, a little Deirdre and a great deal of work. It was not the kind of life that made him leap out of bed eagerly in the mornings. He supposed it was too much to expect Mark or Digby to make tea and bring it to him, as a woman would have done, so he eventually crept into the kitchen and started to make it himself. Mark and Digby soon joined him, the latter singing an air from *La Bohème*, because, as he put it, the light-hearted squalor of their lives reminded him irresistibly of that opera. Tom and Mark were more taciturn, not approving of music in the early morning, and being unable to sing anyway. There was plenty of milk and cornflakes, not quite enough bread and only two eggs, but they made themselves some kind of a breakfast and then left to do a good day's work in various libraries. It was vacation time now and there were no seminars or classes.

Tom had arranged that Deirdre should not visit him until he had got properly settled in, whatever that might entail, and

so it was not until nearly a week later that she saw his new room for the first time.

'Shall we meet some grim landlady on the stairs?' she asked, as they approached the house with its peeling pillars.

'No, she doesn't live on the premises, luckily. There are just the three flats occupied by students of various kinds. Ours is on the first floor.'

'No pictures of highland cattle,' she said quickly, when they were inside the narrow hall of the flat.

Tom, feeling her need for reassurance, put his arm round her shoulders. 'What have you done to your hair?' he asked. 'It looks like a chrysanthemum.'

'I had it cut. Don't you like it?'

'Yes, of course, don't look so worried.' He opened a door. 'Well, here it is, the small back room or whatever we call it.'

'It *is* rather small, but very comfortable, I should think.' Deirdre had run over to the window to hide her dismay at the general impression of meanness and shabbiness which had overwhelmed her on entering. 'And you can see the trains from the window. That's awfully continental, somehow.' Her eyes, level with his, looked appealingly at him. He, used to looking down at Catherine, found it difficult to meet her glance and turned away to fumble with some glasses and a dark-looking bottle.

'Let's have a drink,' he said.

'Oh, yes, lovely!'

Lovely was perhaps not quite the word, she realized, as she sipped the cold sour red wine. It tasted most peculiar, as if it had gone off or something, but she wasn't sure if wine *could* go off. I *must* learn to enjoy drinking, she thought rather desperately, or at least the kind of things these people seem to enjoy, beer and funny kinds of wine. For the shameful thing was that she *did* like the drinks Bernard and her brother Malcolm bought for her – gin and orange or rather sweet

dark sherry – the kind of drinks 'nice' suburban men regarded as being suitable for women, she thought scornfully.

'Catherine seems to be all right,' said Tom, relief sounding in his tone. 'Quite cheerful, in fact.'

'Oh, I'm glad. Has Mark or Digby seen her?'

'No, I rang her up this morning.'

'Why? Had you left something behind?'

He could hear the unconscious reproach in her voice and feel it in her eyes, intently fixed on him, so he said rather irritably, 'No, but I wanted to know how she was. I can't *never* hear or see anything of her again, you know.'

'Of course not – I didn't mean to be unreasonable. She's such a sweet person, I want to see her again myself, if she wants to see me.'

There was silence. Deirdre had been walking about the room, for there seemed to be nowhere to sit down except the bed which, after a quick nervous glance, she had rejected for some reason not quite clear to her.

'I haven't arranged my books properly yet, as you can see,' said Tom, indicating the confusion of the shelves and the two chairs littered with papers.

Deirdre knelt down by the shelves, holding her glass in both hands. Women so often find themselves examining a man's books, trying to find something intelligent to say about them, and even at nineteen Deirdre was beginning to get her share of it.

'I see you've got that book on Social Structure,' she said. 'It's supposed to be very new and exciting, isn't it?'

'Oh, perhaps, but I don't think we want to discuss it now, do we?' he said gently, taking the book out of her hands.

After a few pleasurable moments Tom remembered that he had resolved to have no more complications in his life until after he had finished writing his thesis, and perhaps not even then. He had not left Catherine because he intended to embark on the same kind of relationship with Deirdre, whatever

Catherine might have thought. He wondered whether it was a good thing or not to have accepted Deirdre's invitation to supper at her home this evening. Parents did not nowadays question young men about their intentions, but it was better when women were without kinship ties, like Catherine, he thought dispassionately, and then they could be rejected at will and without the likelihood of any awkward repercussions. But then, seeing that Deirdre's eyes had opened and were gazing at him with love, he was horrified at discovering such cynical cruelty in himself, he the tender-hearted, kind to animals, as Catherine always said, and sometimes even weeping at the cinema. He was very fond of Deirdre, but he pushed her away from him rather abruptly and said, 'Time we were going, isn't it?'

She was a little hurt at this sudden breaking-off, but he soon reassured her and managed to leave her with the impression that he needed understanding in some particularly subtle way, a thing she had never thought of with Bernard, who always appeared to be so dull and equable as to have nothing in him to understand.

'Do you mind the suburbs?' she asked, as they rode on the top of a bus towards her home. 'I think it's horrid here, and the people are so dreary.'

'People can be that anywhere,' he said, smiling at her, 'especially when you're young. I always found that when I lived at home.'

'But your home is a real country house,' she said.

'Yes, but falling into decay and not even old and beautiful enough to be historically interesting. My mother in the garden all day, my uncle crouching over his television set – not so very different from a suburban home, you see.'

'I suppose you always want what you haven't got,' said Deirdre, hurrying Tom past the Dulkes' house, for a quick furtive glance had revealed Mr. Dulke in his front garden apparently tying up some herbaceous plants.

'You shouldn't feel that,' he said. 'You've all the time in the world to get what you want and I hope you will get it.'

His words, with their air of chilly detachment, as if he could have no part in giving her what she wanted, saddened her, and it was almost a relief when they were swallowed up in the family circle and Malcolm was offering drinks.

'I'm *so* pleased,' said Rhoda, taking Deirdre aside. 'I've managed to persuade Mr. Lydgate to join us this evening.'

'How ever did you do it?' Deirdre asked.

'He came out into his garden this morning and I happened to be working in the herbaceous border – he was quite near the hedge, so I called out "Good morning! Isn't it a lovely day?", and then I said that the hot sun must remind him of Africa and he agreed that it did.'

'Well, I suppose he could hardly have said that it didn't.'

'No, though he did say that the African sun was even hotter and not so pleasant as this. Then I made a remark about it being nice to be able to have meals out of doors and then – well, I can't remember *exactly* how the conversation went on, but I seemed to find myself inviting him to supper this evening, and he seemed quite pleased to come. He even smiled through the leaves, I mean, I could see through a sort of gap that he was smiling, and then he came and looked over the top of the hedge, he's so tall, you see. And he's really quite good-looking when he smiles. And of course Father Tulliver is coming too, so it will be quite a party.' Rhoda paused, not so much to draw breath as to admire the arrangement of the room, the drinks set out on a little table and the big vases of mixed garden flowers at strategic points.

Deirdre's heart sank at the prospect of the evening in such an ill-assorted company, but she consoled herself by thinking that Tom might find the occasion interesting, though he did not seem to have Jean-Pierre's passion for observing the ritual of English suburban life. All the same he seemed to have fitted himself very well into his surroundings and Deirdre

could not help noticing, with a little stab of jealousy, how well he was getting on with Phyllis, her brother's fiancée.

'Doesn't Phyllis look sweet?' said Rhoda eagerly. 'That red and white dress is the one she made to go out with Malcolm on her birthday, you know. It was a Butterick pattern.'

'Yes, it's pretty,' Deirdre agreed without much enthusiasm, for Phyllis, being small and blonde with a vivacious manner, was all that Deirdre was not. What was more, she was wearing red shoes which Deirdre believed to be one of those things that men were said to like.

'Mr. Lydgate's got some terrifying African masks,' Phyllis was saying. 'I saw him wearing one in his garden one night. I nearly died, I was so frightened.'

'Ah, but they're worn to intimidate women,' said Tom in a teasing voice, 'that's the whole point.'

'Jolly good idea,' said Malcolm heartily. 'They need to be kept in their places.'

'Wherever that may be,' said Phyllis pertly.

'I'll soon show you that, my girl,' said Malcolm. He made as if to box her ears but she evaded him with a pretty gesture.

'Let me get you another drink,' said Tom gallantly. 'Now what was it that put this sparkle in your eye?'

'One of Malcolm's cocktails – in the green jug over there,' said Phyllis, preening herself like a little bird. She smiled at Deirdre in a surprised way, as if meaning to show her that Tom was really much better than she'd expected.

Deirdre found herself resenting this slightly patronizing air. Phyllis seemed to be able to bring out a side of Tom that she herself had never seen, gay and flirtatious, the last person one would imagine brooding over a thesis. Oh, blessed ignorance of anthropology, she thought rather bitterly, yet feeling that this might not be the whole answer. Bernard never *looked* at another woman, she told herself defiantly, like an outraged Edwardian dowager. In spite of everything she smiled.

144

'Sweetie, what's your private joke?' said Tom in a low voice.

'I was watching you being flirtatious,' she said happily.

'Yes, isn't it odd, I find I can still do it,' said Tom. 'I hear Alaric Lydgate is expected. Isn't that his voice in the hall?'

Alaric came into the room, looking sombre and a little uncertain of himself.

Rhoda fussed round him and then said in a loud bright voice, 'You will have to be careful what you write, Tom. Mr. Lydgate was in Africa for *eleven years*.' She gave the last words a curious and slightly drunken emphasis. It had been naughty of Malcolm to refill her glass when she wasn't looking. Especially now that Father Tulliver had come into the room, wearing a black suit of the finest and smoothest clerical material which seemed to give point to the expression 'the cloth'.

He accepted a glass of Malcolm's cocktail and then drew Rhoda aside into a place by the window, where he began talking to her in a low intimate tone. Like so many clergymen he had of necessity acquired that easy confidence in dealing with unmarried middle-aged women which is not often granted to the layman.

'It was so good of you to respond to my appeal,' he said. 'I *knew* it would not fall on deaf ears. I said to myself, "Either Miss Wellcome or Mrs. Swan will help me out".'

'I felt it was the least I could do,' said Rhoda. 'I do hope Mrs. Tulliver is making good progress.'

'Excellent, thank you. She is gaining strength every day. It was really her idea that I should put that little note in the magazine. Perhaps it would not have come well from the pulpit,' he added thoughtfully, 'but something had to be done. I hadn't a clean alb left and I'm not much of a hand at laundering,' he laughed, with the confidence of one who has never tried and does not intend to. 'You have a good drying ground at the back of the house, I suppose?'

'Yes, I shall hang the albs in the yard,' Rhoda pronounced solemnly. 'Of course we don't hang washing in the garden *itself*, it wouldn't do here. People wouldn't like it, although our neighbour Mrs. Lovell isn't always guiltless in that respect.'

'Oh, certainly, I understand that some garments might not look well in a garden, but something of an ecclesiastical nature, surely that might be condoned?'

'The Lovells are not churchpeople,' Rhoda declared. 'I doubt if they would realize that the washing was of an – er – ecclesiastical nature.' She had found the last two words rather difficult to pronounce and hoped that Father Tulliver hadn't noticed. It was a good thing, she felt, that her sister Mabel should appear at this moment and summon the party to the dining-room.

The problem of food had been difficult, for both Mabel and Rhoda had the rather old-fashioned idea that the presence of a clergyman at their table called for a bird of some kind. Cold chickens had seemed the obvious choice, but Deirdre had upset their plans by declaring one morning that you couldn't possibly give chicken to people who had lived in Africa because they ate practically nothing else there and would think it so dull. Therefore a selection of more exotic cold meats had been provided to go with Father Tulliver's chickens and the artistic salads which Rhoda had made.

'Now I suppose you Africanists won't want chicken,' said Malcolm breezily, the carving implements poised in his hands.

'What *do* people eat in Africa?' asked Mabel earnestly.

'The Hadzapi tribe will eat anything that is edible except for the hyena,' declared Alaric precisely.

'Oh, well . . .' Mabel spread out her hands in a hopeless little gesture.

'The butcher wouldn't offer you hyena, anyway,' giggled Phyllis.

'Most African tribes are very fond of meat when they can get it,' said Tom.

'Yes, and many of them relish even putrescent meat,' said Alaric solemnly.

'Do they understand the principles of cooking as we know it?' asked Rhoda.

'Oh, yes, a good many of them do,' said Alaric. 'In some very primitive societies, though, they would just fling the unskinned carcase on the fire and hope for the best.'

'Yes, like that film of the Australian aborigines we saw at the Anthropology Club,' said Deirdre. 'They flung a kangaroo on the fire and cooked it like that.'

'Now who would like some potato salad?' said Rhoda, feeling that there was something a little unappetizing about the conversation. She had imagined that the presence of what she thought of as clever people would bring about some subtle change in the usual small talk. The sentences would be like bright jugglers' balls, spinning through the air and being deftly caught and thrown up again. But she saw now that conversation could also be compared to a series of incongruous objects, scrubbing-brushes, dish-cloths, knives, being flung or hurtling rather than spinning, which were sometimes not caught at all but fell to the ground with resounding thuds. In the haze brought about by Malcolm's cocktail, she saw the little dark-skinned aborigines, swinging the kangaroo by its legs and hurling it on to the fire. Certainly she had to admit that the conversation was *different* from what it usually was and perhaps that was the best that could be expected.

'Have you published anything yet?' Alaric asked Tom abruptly.

'No, but I have a few articles nearly finished.' Tom's tone was evasive and he seemed as if he would like to change the subject.

'I suppose you'll be sending them somewhere soon,' said Alaric, and then went on to name one or two journals much respected in the anthropological world.

147

'Oh, yes,' said Tom indifferently.

'The editors will rewrite them – you must be prepared for that, they are quite unscrupulous you know. Even *I* have trouble with them sometimes.'

'I should like to read some of your articles, Mr. Lydgate,' said Rhoda. 'Do you think I should enjoy them?'

Alaric laughed shortly. 'I'm afraid one doesn't look for enjoyment in our field,' he said.

'Of course one does get a certain amount from pointing out other people's mistakes,' said Tom. 'That's a recognized sport.'

'Oh, yes,' said Alaric quite genially. 'It reminds me of the ideal hobby for retired anthropologists. Can you guess what it is?'

Nobody could.

'Apiculture,' he said, enjoying their puzzled expressions.

'Bee-keeping,' said Father Tulliver slowly. 'Well, it is healthy and interesting, profitable too, I suppose.'

'Bees in the bonnet,' said Phyllis in her bright little voice. 'Is that it?'

'You're quite right, that *is* what I meant.'

'Have you hives at the bottom of your garden, Mr. Lydgate?' asked Mabel politely. 'That would be an ideal spot.'

The sentence fell with a thud amid general laughter and then there was a pause and Father Tulliver asked Alaric a question about missions.

'Oddly enough,' he said thoughtfully, as if it were a matter of surprise to him or even some kind of oversight on somebody's part, 'I have not had the call to the Mission Field. I have felt, wrongly perhaps, though I cannot judge that, that my work lay here.'

'Oh, you couldn't leave us, Father, not when you've got everything so nice, the services and all that,' said Rhoda confusedly. 'Whatever should we do?'

'It might be just what you needed,' said Father Tulliver on a stern note. 'It might prove a testing time – to show what you were made of.'

Rhoda, thinking of the heavy wash she was about to undertake for him, felt that he was being a little unfair. Surely he could not feel that *she* had been found wanting in any way?

'Of course we come of a missionary family,' said Alaric, 'and my sister had the call, at least I suppose it was that. She went out as a missionary originally but found that she was more interested in tongues than in souls. Perhaps the devil stepped in there.'

'But surely a missionary ought to learn the language of the people he is seeking to evangelize,' protested Father Tulliver. 'I should say that the study of linguistics was an admirable thing.'

'We met your sister that afternoon when we were having tea in the garden, didn't we?' said Rhoda.

'Yes, I remember. And wasn't there another young woman with you that afternoon – with dark hair and wearing a yellow dress? Miss Oliphant, I think you said her name was.' Alaric spoke rather quickly as if he regretted having raised the subject.

'Oh, yes, Catherine Oliphant,' said Mabel. 'Deirdre, we could have asked her to come tonight. I wish I'd thought of it.'

'Well, it would have made the numbers wrong,' said Deirdre in confusion.

'We could have asked Bernard to put that right.'

Deirdre broke into nervous laughter.

'Poor old Bernard,' said Phyllis. 'Tom, you've quite put Bernard's nose out of joint, I'm afraid. But I expect you're used to doing that, what with all the glamour of darkest Africa about you.'

'I do hope you *won't* go to the Mission Field, Father,' said Rhoda, seeming to be brought back to the subject by the phrase

149

Phyllis had used. 'I really feel quite worried at the thought of it.'

'Of course we don't want Father Tulliver to go,' said Malcolm, 'but we ought not to stand in his way if he feels he ought to. You know that hymn.'

> *'O'er heathen lands afar,*
> *Thick darkness broodeth yet,'*

said Mabel.

'I expect that's why the darkness *is* so thick, because our dear Father Tulliver hasn't had a chance to dispel it,' burst out Rhoda impulsively.

How silly Rhoda is, thought Deirdre, almost as if she were interested in Father Tulliver in a flirtatious way. She was as yet too young to have learned that women of her aunt's age could still be interested in men; she would have many years to go before the rather dreadful suspicion came to her that one probably never does cease to be interested.

'Well, I expect I shall find plenty of work to do here,' said Father Tulliver, feeling that Malcolm's words were almost forcing him to hurry to the U.M.C.A. headquarters. 'And of course there is Beatrice to consider.'

'Ah, yes, poor Mrs. Tulliver. We were wondering if we could send some flowers or fruit to the nursing-home,' said Mabel.

The talk seemed to quieten down now and was sustained on a more comfortable parochial level until the end of the meal. Alaric found himself with Father Tulliver and the two older women, while the young people went into the garden.

'You should take Tom to see the river,' said Malcolm rather pointedly. 'It's really the chief attraction of the neighbourhood. I expect he'd like a walk.'

'I suppose they wanted to be alone,' said Deirdre apologetically, as she and Tom made their way towards the tow-path.

'That seems fair enough. I like your brother – he's a

capital fellow – as they say in Victorian novels,' Tom added quickly, for it was a favourite phrase of Catherine's and seemed to need explanation.

'I can't imagine you reading Victorian novels,' said Deirdre doubtfully.

'No, I don't much. And here *is* the river, just at the bottom of the road. Isn't that convenient?'

'Well, it's nice for the Boat Race, but it isn't really a very pretty stretch of river. Would you like to walk along a little way?'

'Yes, let's do that.'

They walked in silence over the thick tufty grass, Deirdre a little in front of Tom as if she were showing him the way. It was beginning to get dark now and lights were showing over the other side of the water, giving a romantic continental atmosphere.

This is the place where the young men and women walk at night and are allowed a certain amount of licence, thought Tom in his detached anthropologist's way. He pulled Deirdre towards him and almost ceremonially led her to a seat under some elderberry trees, covered with sickly-smelling creamy flowers.

'I do love you so much,' she said. 'But women aren't supposed to say that to men, are they?'

'I don't see why not.' Tom had quite often had it said to him and had never been able to see why women had this almost superstitious fear of expressing their feelings in words. It made no difference in the long run, though it could sometimes be a little disturbing in the early stages of an affair, and of course they might well consider it unwise to show their hands so early in the game.

'Because it might not be – reciprocal.' She frowned over the technical term she had used but could feel him smiling in the dark.

'I shouldn't worry about that, if I were you.'

'I suppose it's like that French saying or whatever it is, about there being one who kisses and one who leans the cheek to be kissed.'

'Let me set your mind at rest then.'

She was really very sweet, he thought, uncomplicated and honest; being with her took him back years and reminded him of Elaine, his first girl friend, whom he had known at home when he was eighteen. Catherine, being older, had already been too much of a personality in her own right, always wanting to make him conform to her idea of what he ought to be.

'I suppose we ought to go back now,' said Deirdre, sensing that he had somehow gone away from her.

'Let's stay a little longer,' he said, smoothing her rough chrysanthemum-cut hair. 'Aren't you enjoying it?'

'Oh, *yes* . . .'

The last time she had been kissed by the river was when she was with Bernard after her first meeting with Tom, she remembered. Poor Bernard, supposing he were to come along now. But it was usually in the daytime that she saw him here, coaching the sports club eight, riding his bicycle and shouting the esoteric rowing language through a megaphone.

The smell of the elder flowers reminded Tom of his childhood. There had been a bush in the garden, he supposed. Proust, he thought, that's what Catherine would say.

They walked back slowly arm-in-arm, Tom talking about his future plans.

'I shall go home at the end of August,' he said, 'and perhaps stay a few days.'

'Yes, your mother will want to see you,' said Deirdre dutifully.

'I suppose she will, but she isn't the kind of person who shows her feelings, and my brother is there all the time.'

'Which can't be quite the same,' said Deirdre warmly.

Now they were coming back to the house again and that

part of the river bank where the residents took their dogs for a short run before turning in. Two figures, followed at some distance by an old fat sealyham, came towards them. They seemed to be talking about the Test Match. Tom suddenly wished he were walking with them, making manly conversation, away from the cloying sweetness of love or, better still, at home with his typewriter, working on his thesis. For the end was in sight and it was going to be finished after all. He gave Deirdre's arm a sudden joyful squeeze and quickened pace.

'That was Mr. Lovell and his old dog and Mr. Dulke who lives opposite,' she said, hurrying too. 'I didn't want to have to stop and talk to them.'

As they turned into the road the sound of a 'cello came over the warm night air, playing a rounded melody, exquisitely satisfying.

'That's Miss Cumberledge,' Deirdre explained. 'She plays in an orchestra and you often hear her practising.'

They stood for a few moments listening, looking up at the sky and the television aerials silhouetted against it.

'Almost beautiful, aren't they,' said Tom, pointing to them. 'A symbol of the age we live in.'

'So is Mrs. Lovell putting out the breakfast cereals,' said Deirdre as they passed her neighbour's house. They could see her through the uncurtained window, laying the table, placing coloured plastic mugs on it and in the baby's high chair, and taking giant packets of cornflakes from the sideboard.

'Life goes on,' said Tom.

'Yes, I suppose it's comforting to see people going about their humdrum business,' said Deirdre. At home her mother would be laying the breakfast and later her aunt would creep down to see if she had done it correctly. And they would probably go on doing this all their lives.

CHAPTER THIRTEEN

LIFE had been going on for Catherine too, as she knew that it would. She thought of it as an old friend, or perhaps a tiresome elderly relative, pushing, knocking, clinging, but never leaving her alone, having the power to grant her moments of happiness but being very stingy with them just now. Obviously the spirit of delight in Shelley's poem, which so rarely came, was a being of another order, possibly a beautiful young man whom Catherine could not at the moment visualize. She went about seeing editors, writing stories and articles, and in the evening read her favourite depressing poets, Hardy, Matthew Arnold and the lesser Victorians; she even found the strength to embark on a course of Dostoievsky. Often she felt the lack of that cosy woman friend with whom she might spend an afternoon at a matinée, or shopping with a pleasant gossipy tea afterwards. She seemed to know more men than women and, delightful though their company was, she imagined that they were somehow less comforting than a woman would have been.

One morning she was wandering through a large store, which she liked because of its old and respectable connections, for it was the kind of place where Tom's mother might shop when she came up to town, or where Colonial administrators who had spent long years in the solitude of the bush might gather as in a refuge from the garishness of Oxford Street. It was not very surprising, therefore, that while strolling on the ground floor she should come upon a group of people sitting in basket chairs drinking coffee, and that among them should be Alaric Lydgate. She had thought of him several

times since their first meeting, for his oddness and apparent loneliness interested and attracted her. And now here he was, sitting alone, reading a journal which, to judge from its title, dealt with that part of Africa where he had spent his eleven years.

'Why, it's Mr. Lydgate!' she exclaimed, hovering by his table. Shyness was not one of her faults and she had every intention of joining him.

'Miss Oliphant.' So he had remembered her name. 'This *is* a pleasure. Won't you sit down and have some coffee with me?' A rather tentative smile was playing over the rocky Easter Island features, Catherine noticed.

More coffee was ordered and some chocolate biscuits. Catherine settled herself comfortably and took out her cigarette case.

'What are you reading?' she asked.

'Oh, an article I have written,' he said. 'There are two misprints, most annoying. But I'm sure you wouldn't be interested.' He closed up the journal and put it down on a vacant chair.

'It depends what it's about,' said Catherine honestly. 'I think you could probably help me with something I'm writing now.'

'Do you think so?' He glanced at her suspiciously, as if he were thinking of the trunks full of notes in his attic.

'Yes, I'm writing a story about somebody who's just come back from Africa. I've made him a big game hunter, that seems suitable for the type of people who will read it. Naturally I have to make him have thoughts about the country he's been in, and I was wondering if they were too wildly improbable.'

'I'm afraid I should be no judge of that,' said Alaric. 'I shouldn't like to say what thoughts might be in the mind of a big game hunter.'

'Oh, I didn't mean that exactly. You see, I have him sitting in this West Kensington hotel, remembering the noise of the

rain splashing down among the mangroves, or the laughing faces of the women as they brought in the yams, and really it's the drizzly English rain and the grey shut-in faces of the elderly ladies in the lounge – do you see the idea?'

'Only too well.' He laughed, but without much amusement.

Too near the bone, Catherine thought, for of course it was he who had given her the idea for the story about the big game hunter in the West Kensington hotel. She had at least had the grace to change the basic circumstances a little.

'And what happens in your story?' he asked politely, half smiling as if he were humouring a child.

'He meets the niece of one of the elderly ladies who comes to visit her.'

'And then?'

Catherine looked surprised, but then realized that it was most unlikely that he would be a reader of romantic fiction. 'Oh, well, that *is* the end, really,' she said. 'They go for a walk in the rain and he suddenly feels that there's something rather nice about the drizzly English rain – I haven't finished it yet, but you can see the way it will go. But would the rain splash down among the *mangroves*, and would the *women* bring in the yams? I do like to get these things right.'

'It is a pity,' he began, using his favourite review phrase, 'that others are not as accurate as you are. Contributors to the learned journals are among the worst offenders. I often find . . .'

But at this moment a voice interrupted him, calling his name, and Catherine noticed a leathery-looking man with the Ancient Mariner gleam in his eye bearing down upon Alaric. He was followed by a tweedy little woman of a mild, almost downtrodden, aspect. Alaric introduced the pair as Mortimer Jessop and his sister, Miss Jessop, who did not appear to have a Christian name and took no part in the conversation, which consisted of long reminiscences of events in Africa from Mortimer Jessop, interspersed with short comments from

156

Alaric. Catherine tried to draw Miss Jessop out in the way that she considered one woman might try to draw another, with little remarks on the weather and the display of goods in the store, but it was difficult going and after a time she gave up and listened to the men's conversation. There was a certain fascination about it although it hardly seemed to make sense.

'. . . attitude of the natives,' boomed Mortimer Jessop. 'You remember the Resident's comments on *that* one, surely? Short and to the point. To the effect that had he taken the trouble to read Crabbe's Handing-Over report he would have found that the key was precisely where he had said it was – *underneath the mat!* Government had just sent troops there – that was in '22, of course, before your time. You realize that that was why they couldn't take the railway through? Had to make a detour to avoid the territory, noble savage and all that sentimental twaddle. I know what *I* should have done.'

'Would you have taken the railway through, Mr. Jessop?' asked Catherine, looking up at him.

He seemed a little taken aback. Perhaps he was used only to his sister as an audience and had not expected any comment.

'Well, I'd have had a *bash* at it, as they say nowadays,' he said with a bark of laughter.

'I suppose we should be going now,' said Alaric with a glance at his watch.

'I hear you're working at the London Office,' said Mortimer Jessop.

'Yes, part-time. It's one of my days off,' Alaric explained.

'What do you do? Light work, I suppose – carrying trays of tea along corridors?' said Mortimer Jessop genially. 'Wouldn't do for me, I'm afraid, must be in the open air. Living in Barons Court now,' he added, as if it had some bearing on his last remark. Catherine imagined a kind of feudal spaciousness, although she knew that it was only one station beyond West Kensington.

'I really must be going now,' she said.

'Oh, so should we,' said Mortimer Jessop. 'We're lunching with our old friend Mrs. Bone and she usually does you pretty well – a bird more often than not. Well, Lydgate, it's good to have run into you again.' He made as if to go, then suddenly turned round and said to Alaric in a stage whisper, 'By the way, who *was* that dwarf I saw you with on the road in '45?'

Catherine, who had been expecting an answer on the lines of 'that was no lady, that was my wife', was surprised to hear Alaric answer rather stiffly, 'That was the Panti Ba himself.'

Mr. Jessop and his sister were then wafted away on a gust of laughter from the former.

There seemed to be nothing to say in answer to Alaric's statement. Comment was difficult, perhaps impossible, certainly for herself, Catherine felt.

'A native chief,' Alaric explained, sensing her curiosity.

'What very odd names they have,' she said, gathering her things together. 'Thank you so much for the coffee. I'm glad I came along here.'

'Yes, it has been pleasant meeting you again,' he said rather formally. 'Perhaps there may be other times?'

The question hung in the air. Catherine smiled up at him and murmured something.

'I am going to the wine department,' he said, 'to get the new list.'

'Oh, I've just got it. *Well* up to standard – I keep them to read, you see.'

'But so do I – hanging at the side of my desk,' Alaric said in a wondering tone.

'So we have something in common,' said Catherine rather primly. 'It's always a comfort to find that.'

And such a very odd little thing to have in common, she thought, as she waited on an island to cross over the road. It seemed a hopeful sign, though she was not quite sure of what. Were they perhaps to spend long evenings reading extracts from wine lists to each other? Something to look

forward to, she thought, smiling to herself in the middle of the traffic. The hot breath of the buses was puffing round her legs and still she stood there, missing her chance of getting across because she was so preoccupied and with such a ridiculous thing. Now there was a block and she found herself looking into a car, a large rather old-fashioned limousine, upholstered in pearl grey and with silver vases of sweet peas by the windows. The occupants, a fussily dressed little woman of a faded prettiness and a clergyman with a wispy beard, were deep in conversation. As the car moved on, Catherine saw the clergyman place his hand on the woman's arm.

There was something a little disquieting about this, although she could not have said why. There had been nothing unsuitable or over-familiar about the gesture – obviously he was merely emphasizing some point – and yet it seemed wrong. Catherine had never seen the people in the car before and yet she felt that she ought to know who they were. A recent conversation with Mark and Digby came back to her; they had been joking about Professor Mainwaring riding in just such a car with their benefactress, Mrs. Foresight. If this *was* Mrs. Foresight no doubt the priest beside her was her Father Confessor. There was no reason why one should not confess one's sins in a Daimler, she supposed, though it was probably unusual. The only thing was that the clergyman looked very much like the one who had been having tea in the garden with the Lydgates and Miss Clovis that afternoon when she and Tom had gone to visit Deirdre. Somehow that was a little puzzling. And yet, need it be? Why shouldn't a common interest in Africa have brought them together? It had been known to do many strange things.

CHAPTER FOURTEEN

'I WONDER if I look all right?' Mark stepped carefully backwards, so that Tom and Digby could get a better view of him.

'I can't see anything wrong,' said Digby, 'but then I'm not experienced in these matters. Tom used to move in the world of débutante dances before he saw the light and detribalized himself – ask him.'

'Oh, you'll do,' said Tom non-committally. 'The suit seems to be quite a good fit. I suppose you'll wear a white carnation?'

'Yes, I suppose so, though I should really prefer something more exotic. It seems a pity that on the few occasions when men can wear flowers they have to be so uninteresting. Think how well a spray of orchids would look.'

'My aunt will have hoped for at least two young men,' said Tom, 'so you must do what you can to make up for our absence. I think she was getting pretty desperate or she wouldn't have flung her net *quite* so wide. My cousin is so tall, poor girl. She has large golden feet, as far as I remember.'

'Golden feet?' echoed Mark apprehensively.

'Yes, I suppose she must have been wearing gold evening shoes when I last saw her.'

'Will there be much champagne?' asked Digby a little enviously.

'Oh, I think so,' said Tom. 'Apparently the room where they're going to dance and the courtyard at the back have been transformed into a sort of Portuguese fishing village – nets hanging all over the place and that sort of thing.'

'That's what you call amusing, isn't it?' said Digby. 'A sort of *trompe l'oeil*.'

'Yes, the room couldn't be left as it is,' Tom agreed. 'My aunt has asked you to dine first, hasn't she, Mark?'

'Yes, I hope that's a good sign. I was thinking that only a favoured few could be asked to a proper meal, or is it because she knows my financial state and is trying to be kind?'

'If it's that you ought not to have accepted,' said Digby. 'Even anthropologists should have their pride.'

'I told her that you were quite tall,' said Tom. 'I think that may be why. The most eligible socially and the tallest – I think you'll find those are the main criteria. Have you money for a taxi?'

'Yes, thank you. Any other hints?'

'No, I'll be seeing you tomorrow. There is the aftermath to be considered if you want to be absolutely correct.'

'Sending flowers and that kind of thing?' said Mark casually. 'Oh, I know all about that.'

'I do hope Mark will be all right,' said Digby apprehensively, after they had seen him into a taxi. 'The world can be very wicked, and I sometimes wonder whether he really has the strength of character to resist its temptations.'

'I think he ought to be quite *safe* in Belgravia,' Tom reassured him, 'though it may make him dissatisfied with his surroundings here. Let's have something to eat, shall we?'

They fried some eggs and made coffee, after which Digby retired to his room to write a seminar paper for next term. Such things are of an ephemeral nature so it is perhaps unnecessary to record its title. It consisted of a mass of information culled from books, illuminated by what Digby considered a rather startling interpretation of his own. It is the ambition of all who read a paper of whatever kind to have it recorded that 'a lively discussion followed', and Digby worked with this end in view.

Tom, on the other hand, had progressed beyond interpreting other people's material; all he had to do was to present his own in a form worthy of a Ph.D. thesis. The end had been in sight when he had been embracing Deirdre by the river and now, suddenly, it seemed, after only two hours' writing, it was finished.

He heaved a great sigh, reached for his cigarettes, only to find that he already had one in his mouth, then looked around for Catherine. But of course she was not there. He ran into the hall and dialled her number. She answered at once, and then he remembered that it was after midnight and the telephone was by her bed.

'Were you asleep?' he asked, when he had told her the news.

'Nearly, but I'm glad you rang. I was going to give you a bottle of Pouilly Fuissé, wasn't I?'

'A *what*?'

'I can never say that name twice – you know that – anyway, it's a white burgundy.'

'How are you?'

There was a slight pause and then Catherine said, 'Oh, fine, thank you.'

'We must meet soon. I'm going to visit my parents sometime, you know, so it must be before that.'

'All right, and then we could have the Pouilly Fuissé.'

'Why, have you got it now?'

'Oh, yes, I bought it some time ago, when the idea first came to me.'

'Oh, Catty . . . can't I come round and we'll drink it now?'

'I think better not – wine does keep, you know. Good night, Tom dear, I'm so glad you've finished it.'

She had hung up the receiver and just turned over and gone to sleep again, he thought resentfully, but in this he wronged her. She had to get up and make herself tea and read Dostoievsky until the first birds started to sing and it began to get light, before she could sleep again.

Tom was a little upset to think that she had already bought the wine for the little celebration she had planned; the pathos of it disturbed him and yet Catherine was such a strong self-sufficient sort of person that one couldn't really think of her as pathetic. She would see the whole thing with detachment and was probably even now planning a touching little story round the episode. All the same, he wished he hadn't known.

He stood in the hall, feeling very wide-awake and restless. Of course he should ring Deirdre. Then he remembered how late it was and imagined her mother or aunt, muffled in a dressing-gown, coming downstairs to answer the telephone, perhaps fearing that a relative had died or that Malcolm had had a motor accident. So that would have to wait till the morning. Digby was already in bed and Mark was at the dance. Tom almost wished now that he had accepted his aunt's invitation and gone to the dance too. His restlessness made it impossible for him to go to bed and sleep and he decided that a walk might do him good, so he put on his raincoat and crept out of the house. Once outside, he strode along with great energy, feeling the burden of his thesis lifted from him. Why shouldn't he go and have a look at his aunt's house, where the dance would be at its height?

Mrs. Beddoes lived in a terrace of large grand houses, all of which had once been lived in by wealthy families but which were now mostly turned into flats or even government offices. Even though Tom had, as Digby put it, seen the light and detribalized himself, he could not help feeling that there was something depressing about seeing rows of filing-cabinets in what had once been somebody's drawing-room, wooden trestle tables standing on the parquet floors, wire trays and even a thick white cup and saucer glimmering faintly in the moonlight. If we lamented the decay of the great civilizations of the past, he thought, should we not also regret the dreary levelling down of our own?

But now there was music, the throbbing rhythm of a rumba

or samba – he had forgotten these dances – and he came upon his aunt's house, a red awning and carpet laid over the pavement from the front door, and all the windows brilliantly illuminated. The dancing would be at the back and he could remember or imagine the scene – the bare shoulders of the girls in their cloudy tulle dresses, the flowers, the fishing-nets too, he supposed, the loud well-bred voices, the music, the laughter, and somewhere the tinkle of a champagne glass falling in a hundred fragments on the floor. And in the middle of it all Mark, the poor student, like a kind of male Cinderella, whirling round with a beautiful girl in his arms.

What was there to prevent him – a nephew of the house – from walking in and joining in all this gaiety? He stopped by the red carpet, trying to make up his mind. Then he looked down at his shoes, his old suède creepers with rubber soles; he couldn't dance in those. And probably his old grey flannels and leather-patched tweed jacket would look out of place, too. Was it just his clothes, then, that were keeping him out of paradise? It must be something more than that . . .'

'Now then, my lad, what are you up to?'

The gruff but not unkindly voice of a policeman interrupted Tom's meditation, making him feel that some explanation of his presence was necessary.

'My aunt's house,' he said. 'She's having a dance. I was just wondering if I should go in.'

'I shouldn't if I were you,' said the officer in a soothing tone.

'It sounds fantastic, I know,' said Tom, 'but it really *is* my aunt's house. Still, I suppose I ought to be going home.'

'That's it. You won't do any good standing here.'

Tom supposed, from the kindly, humouring note in the policeman's voice, that he must appear like some harmless lunatic found wandering at night, not even loitering with intent, he thought, a little bitterly. They wished each other good night and Tom went on his way.

Shortly afterwards, or so it seemed, he was conscious of the sunshine on his face, and Mark, still in his hired dress clothes, standing over him with a cup of tea. It was morning and the dance was over.

Mark was very full of the success he had had with the débutantes and of one in particular who had seemed anxious that they should meet again.

'I hope she's rich,' said Tom sleepily.

'Oh, yes, I found that out straight away. She and the girl friend she lives with have a flat in Curzon Street and she said she might be taking a secretarial course or doing some modelling but that Daddy didn't really want her to, only *everyone* did something nowadays . . .' he drifted out of the room.

'What hidden talents spring up in one's friends,' said Digby. 'I didn't know Mark could imitate a young girl so well. I hope he'll be able to follow up this promising start.'

'He'd better send her some flowers and follow it up quickly with an invitation to lunch at one of our drearier places. She'll find it amusing and different,' said Tom.

It was odd to think that he himself had once been on the threshold of that kind of life and that he had thrown it all away, as it were, to go out to Africa and study the ways of a so-called primitive tribe. For really, when one came to consider it, what could be more primitive than the rigid ceremonial of launching a debutante on the marriage market?

CHAPTER FIFTEEN

DURING the next few weeks some changes took place in the circle of the young anthropologists. Jean-Pierre le Rossignol, after a visit to Bournemouth to study the English on holiday, returned thankfully to France. Brandon and Melanie Pirbright set out for the field to gather material about the married life of a primitive people, giving in exchange generous information about their own, which filled the natives with delight and astonishment. Tom, after a gay evening drinking the bottle of Pouilly Fuissé with Catherine, settled down to revise his thesis and prepare it for the final typing. He saw Deirdre as often as was necessary for his well-being and happiness, which was just a little less often than she would have liked. Primrose and Vanessa set off for a holiday in Italy, while Digby and Mark gathered strength to visit their parents in Nottingham and Wolverhampton respectively.

Catherine had decided that she and Deirdre could now meet again as friends, and one morning sat waiting among the mosaic peacocks for Deirdre to join her in a simple lunch.

'Just the kind of place for two women to meet for lunch,' she said when Deirdre had arrived, 'nothing to drink and not all that much to eat – no red meat, no birds, but poached eggs and welsh rarebits, the kind of nourishment that builds the backbone of this great country of ours. And we must help ourselves, too. Need you clutch that parcel to your breast, whatever it is? I should leave it behind to mark your place.'

'Yes, perhaps I will,' said Deirdre doubtfully. 'I suppose it will be all right.'

When they returned to the table with their food she seemed

anxious about the parcel in a rather ostentatious way, so that Catherine felt that she was expected at least to make some comment and perhaps even to ask what it was.

'It's Tom's thesis,' said Deirdre in a reverent tone. 'He's just given me a copy to read. Look,' she unwrapped the paper, 'four hundred and ninety seven pages. How *does* he do it?'

'Well,' said Catherine, 'writers of fiction would tell you that one just goes on and on until one reaches page four hundred and ninety seven, but of course we don't have to write at such prodigious length and might well find it a bit of an endurance test. A thesis *must* be long. The object, you see, is to bore and stupefy the examiners to such an extent that they will *have* to accept it – only if a thesis is short enough to be read all through word for word is there any danger of failure.'

'Oh, *Catherine* . . .' Deirdre laughed a little uncertainly. 'Actually I know I shall find this very interesting,' she added, assuming the slightly patronizing tone that a specialist may when speaking to a non-specialist.

'Well, don't get scrambled egg all over it,' said Catherine, lifting the manuscript from the table. She turned a page at random. '*It would, however, be dangerous at this stage to embark on any extensive analysis . . .*' she read. 'Oh, what cowards scholars are! When you think how poets and novelists rush in with *their* analyses of the human heart and mind and soul of which they often have far less knowledge than darling Tom has of his tribe. And why do they find it so difficult to begin or start anything – they must always *commence* – have you noticed? I hoped I had cured Tom of that, but I've obviously failed.'

There was a pause, as if Catherine's words might have a deeper significance which both women recognized. I should have let him go on writing 'commence' if he wanted to, Catherine thought. I wonder if that was what drove him away in the end? It is said to be the small things that do that, the straws on the camel's back. Perhaps I should rejoice to

imagine him, free and triumphant, defiantly writing 'commence'.

'Catherine,' Deirdre began.

'Yes?'

'Who is Elaine?'

'Ah, Elaine. What makes you ask?'

'Tom was talking about her one evening when we were having dinner.'

'Poor Deirdre, was it one of those rather miserable meals, where you both look down into your glasses and trace patterns with forks and move the salts and peppers about?'

'Yes, it was a bit like that,' Deirdre smiled. 'I do *try* to understand, but Tom isn't always very easy, is he?' She went on quickly, perhaps not wishing for an answer to her question. 'I gathered Elaine was an old girl friend or something.'

'Yes, Tom's first love, and of course living in the country and not meeting many suitable people she hasn't married anyone else. She's very fond of dogs, golden retrievers I think they are.'

'Oh. Is Tom fond of dogs?' asked Deirdre rather desperately.

'Quite, I think. He would pat a dog if one happened to be conveniently near. I suppose being brought up in the country would make one fond of the *larger* animals – I mean large dogs and horses as opposed to cats and pekingeses.'

'Oh, well . . .' Deirdre gave a brave little smile.

'I shouldn't worry too much about Elaine,' said Catherine reassuringly. 'I think Tom likes the *idea* of her more than anything. There's something very sweet about the memory of one's first love – when you're a bit older you'll understand.'

Deirdre's eyes filled with tears.

'Good heavens, what *is* happening at the counter,' said Catherine brightly, 'such a fuss!'

'It seems to be Father Gemini and Miss Lydgate,' said Deirdre. 'They're linguists, you know and do a lot of work together.'

168

Catherine and Deirdre were near enough to be able to hear what was going on. Father Gemini seemed to be in some difficulty with the ordering of his meal.

'With croquette?' asked the woman behind the counter, in an almost threatening tone.

'What does she mean?' he asked.

'She is asking if you want a potato croquette with your mince,' shouted Miss Lydgate in a clear impatient tone.

'I do not know. How should I know? I do not understand this,' said Father Gemini testily. 'I do not like this place.'

'Well, go and sit down and I'll bring yours,' said Miss Lydgate roughly.

Father Gemini left the counter sulkily, seeming almost to drag his feet like a petulant child, and sat down at a table very near to Catherine and Deirdre. Eventually Miss Lydgate joined him and put food – mince on toast with carrots – before him. He looked at it suspiciously and then began to prod it with his fork before conveying some to his mouth.

Catherine wondered again as she so often did why it was that so-called 'well-bred' people had such very penetrating voices. It could not be thought, in these days, that they were accustomed to giving orders to servants. Miss Lydgate could be heard all over the room and Father Gemini matched his tone to hers. It was perhaps a good thing that Deirdre should be diverted from too much brooding over Tom and Elaine, and she and Catherine were virtually compelled to give up their own conversation and listen to that of Miss Lydgate and Father Gemini.

'Well, this is a better lunch than you'd get at St. Anthony's,' declared Miss Lydgate, naming the London house of the missionary order to which Father Gemini belonged.

'We do not trouble there about what we eat,' he replied, still rather sulkily. 'There the matters of the *spirit* are of more importance.'

'That may be, but you have to eat,' retorted Miss Lydgate

'Even the saints had to take food. Locusts and wild honey, you remember St. John the Baptist.'

'There are not locusts in Kensington,' said Father Gemini, perhaps irrelevantly.

'No, of course there aren't. What I meant was that if you're going to have food you may as well prepare it in the best way,' she said, but did not enlarge upon this point, perhaps remembering the ramshackle household arrangements of Miss Clovis and herself and possibly, even, some rather dreadful meal which Father Gemini had eaten at their table.

'I do not think you have eaten with us at St. Anthony's?' asked Father Gemini in a sarcastic tone. 'No, I do not think so. No woman has eaten there.'

'Oh, *well*,' shrugged Miss Lydgate, as if she would hardly count herself as being a woman, 'I don't see how that affects my point.'

There was silence between them for a few moments, during which they finished their mince and went on to trifle.

'I shall not be here much longer in London,' said Father Gemini at last. 'It will be good to go back again to Africa.'

'Well, you will be here until Christmas.'

'It is possible that I go before that. My plans can change themselves.'

'What do you mean? How can you afford to go out again until the money comes from America?' asked Miss Lydgate impatiently.

Father Gemini smiled secretively into his beard. 'It could come from another place. America is not the only country from which money can come. And there may be enough for me to take Father Serpentelli with me.'

Miss Lydgate snorted. 'I can imagine what results you'll get from *him*. Why, he can't even distinguish an open 'e'. Where will you get this money?' she asked, curiosity getting the better of her.

'I cannot say. I *must* not say – yet.'

170

'Oh. Then where will you go when you do get it? To the same place as before?'

'No, no – I have covered that ground most carefully. For the rest are living there *only pygmies.*' He gave the words a contemptuous emphasis. 'It would waste time to study them. I shall go to the hill tribes.'

'The hill tribes!' Miss Lydgate shouted, banging her spoon on the table. 'A few hundreds living on each hill and each group speaking a different language, *totally unrelated* to that of any of the others!' She seemed about to burst with excitement. '*Magnificent!* You know, of course, that Fairfax was there in the thirties?'

'Yes, I know it.' If he had been familiar with the expression Father Gemini would no doubt have answered 'so what?' at this point. Instead, he declared rather smugly, 'But *I* have not been there.'

'No, of course not. And Fairfax himself would be the first to admit that he was no linguist.'

'Do you think he would be the *first* to admit it?' asked Father Gemini smoothly. 'I do not think so, not the *first.*'

Catherine began to giggle and turned to Deirdre with some apt comment, but she laughed only in a half-hearted way.

'You know, I suppose,' she began tentatively, 'that Tom will be going back quite soon, after he's been to see his mother?'

'Is it really coming to that again?' said Catherine with studied vagueness. 'I hadn't realized it would be so soon.'

'He says he's going to fly,' said Deirdre. 'I shall feel so nervous.'

Catherine felt that she ought to allow Deirdre the first claim to anxiety and did not add that she herself, and probably Elaine too, would also be feeling nervous.

'He is longing to get back,' said Deirdre. 'I don't think he's really happy in England. Oh, Catherine,' she burst out,

'you don't think there's anyone out there, do you, and that *that* is why he wants to go back so much?'

'He never mentioned anyone,' said Catherine, 'and he is usually rather open about these things. I think it's just the love of his work, though, of course, the women there are very attractive. I don't think we can ever hope to know all that goes on in a man's life or even to follow him with our loving thoughts, and perhaps that's just as well. You know how you say to yourself sometimes, "I wonder what he's doing now?" You can't always know that.'

'Tom has usually been working on his thesis when he hasn't been with me,' said Deirdre, doubt clouding her face.

'Yes, writing a thesis is an excellent alibi and a good way of keeping out of mischief,' Catherine agreed. 'But one evening, when I thought he was doing just that, he was holding a young woman's hand in a restaurant.' She threw Deirdre one of her bright sardonic glances.

'Oh, Catherine, I'm sorry . . . I didn't know what to do. You see, I love him so much.'

Her words seemed to ring out among the peacocks, making Catherine wonder if they often heard or witnessed the deeper passions. The gossipy office chatter, the dreary female conversation, the quiet furtive hand-holdings, would be more what they were accustomed to, she felt.

'How am I going to bear it when he goes away?' Deirdre went on.

'Oh, people do bear these things,' said Catherine a little impatiently. 'You must get out and about with your friends more,' she added in her women's magazine tone, 'or learn a foreign language in the long winter evenings. But I was forgetting, you'll have your anthropological studies, just think how useful they'll be to Tom. In two years or less he'll be back again. The time will soon go.'

Deirdre wanted to ask Catherine if she was very unhappy because Tom had left her; she even wanted her forgiveness

for her own part in the affair, but Catherine seemed to discourage further conversation by looking at her watch and suggesting that it was time they moved.

'I hope you enjoy the thesis,' she said, 'but don't expect too much. I'm afraid you'll be disappointed if you hope to find all sorts of deliciously revealing little bits, but of course *you* won't read it for such a frivolous reason. You may even have to understand it, or pretend that you do.'

In the bus going home, Deirdre wondered if Catherine had been just the tiniest bit spiteful in her remarks about the thesis. Even the nicest people could be catty, and Catherine had been as good as jilted by Tom, when one came to think of it. It was quite possible that Catherine *wouldn't* have understood it or would at least have missed its finer points. Deirdre entered the house quietly, hoping to sneak up to her room undisturbed to begin her own reading of it.

But her aunt's voice came from the kitchen. 'Is that you, dear? Have you had tea?'

Deirdre opened the kitchen door but could not at first see Rhoda because the whole room seemed to be filled with voluminous white garments hanging from the clothes-airer and dripping on to the floor.

'What on earth have you been doing?' she asked.

'Oh, it's Father Tulliver's albs,' said Rhoda fussily. 'I washed them after lunch and now it's come on to rain. I don't know *how* I'm going to get them dry.'

'But why must *you* do them?'

'Oh, I offered to help when Mrs. Tulliver was ill, you know. It did seem as if one ought to do all one could.'

'But that was quite a long time ago. She's better now, surely?'

'Yes, she is, but I dare say she may still be feeling rather weak. An operation takes it out of you.'

'Why couldn't Father Tulliver send them to the laundry then?'

'I don't know, dear,' said Rhoda, for this disloyal thought had also occurred to her earlier, as she bent over the sink with her hands in the hot soapy water when she would normally have been sitting quietly reading her library book.

'Well, I certainly wouldn't do that for a man,' said Deirdre scornfully, forgetting or perhaps putting into a higher category the typing she had sometimes done for Tom.

'I expect you would for Tom,' said Rhoda in her coyest tone. 'Do you think it's too early for tea? I could really do with mine. Your mother is out, you know; she and Phyllis's mother have gone on a little shopping spree. There was an advertisement of some household linen bargains at Robinson and Cleaver,' she added cosily. 'Double-bed sheets, *very* much reduced, with pillow-cases to match.'

In the drawing-room Rhoda switched on a bar of the electric fire. The rain had made it rather chilly and tea always seemed to her the kind of meal that ought to be cosy.

'I suppose you and Tom will be looking around for that kind of bargain one of these days,' she said brightly.

'Will we?' said Deirdre unhelpfully.

'You'll miss him when he goes back to Africa,' went on Rhoda, taking refuge in a statement of the obvious. 'Perhaps poor Bernard will get a look-in then.'

'Whoever I go out with when Tom's gone, it certainly won't be Bernard.'

'Do you think Tom will mind if you go out with other young men?' asked Rhoda in a frank interested tone.

'He won't have to.'

'I was just wondering,' Rhoda began, emboldened by her second cup of tea, 'will you get officially engaged before he goes?'

'I should think it's most unlikely. What would be the point?'

'Well, young men and women do get engaged,' said Rhoda rather defiantly, 'look at Malcolm and Phyllis.'

174

Deirdre smiled. 'I don't think Tom and I have much in common with *them*,' she said in a superior tone, but inwardly she was wishing that they had just a little more. Enlightened though she was, Deirdre couldn't help glancing a little enviously sometimes at Phyllis's conventional engagement ring – a medium-sized sapphire with a diamond on each side – and wishing that Tom might suggest that they became engaged before he went back to Africa. Then, when he came back again, they could get married. It seemed so simple, really, but she would never admit this to her aunt. Rhoda had hoped that an aunt might win confidences denied to a mother, but in this she was disappointed. Indeed, when they had finished tea and Deirdre had gone upstairs to her room, she was left with the impression that Deirdre didn't really care whether she married Tom or not. If this were so, then poor Bernard might yet have a chance, and if not Bernard, then others. Letting her imagination play on this fancy, Rhoda could hardly fix any limit to the romantic possibilities of her niece's life.

When she had washed up the tea things, she left Father Tulliver's albs dripping sadly in the kitchen and then she too retired to her room, taking with her some mending. She stationed herself comfortably in the arm-chair by the window and proceeded to look out into Alaric Lydgate's garden.

He was in the vegetable part at the back, apparently digging up potatoes. Then Mrs. Skinner came out in her apron, holding an umbrella over her head, and began to cut some runner beans. Ordinary actions, perhaps, the getting of vegetables for the evening meal, but, like Deirdre's reluctance to talk about her feelings for Tom, it seemed as if they must have some strange significance.

When they had gone back into the house, Rhoda turned away from the window and switched on her portable wireless set. The news seemed dull and ordinary by comparison.

CHAPTER SIXTEEN

Tom arrived at the railway station of the Shropshire market town at the unpromising hour of half past one in the afternoon. There had been no restaurant car on the train and he had forgotten to provide himself with sandwiches. He hurried off the platform, anxious to avoid meeting anyone who remembered him from youth or childhood and with whom he might have to embark on the difficult business of explaining exactly what it was that he was doing now.

'Good afternoon, Master Tom,' said the ticket collector. 'It isn't often we have the pleasure of seeing you – you've been in foreign parts, I hear?'

'Yes, in Africa.'

'In the army, I suppose.'

'Well, not exactly.' Tom smiled, thinking of the great inquisitive army of anthropologists, the seekers after knowledge. 'I've been studying the – er – customs of an African tribe.'

The man's face brightened. 'Ah, I've heard about some of them,' he ventured. 'You chose a good day to come, you did, what with the carnival and flower show this afternoon.'

'Oh, of course. It's always on a Thursday, isn't it.'

The arrival of other travellers enabled him to escape, and he set out to walk through the 'town' to the house where his mother and brother lived. Thursday was early closing day, which was why the carnival and flower show were always held then. Some of the shops had their blinds down, and Tom could see himself reflected in the dark surfaces, a shabby trudging figure, carrying a brief-case and canvas bag. He

resented this, and tried not to catch any more glimpses of himself. In the centre of the town there were some signs of what might have been described as festivity. Lines of coloured flags strung across the main street hung limply in the hot afternoon air, interspersed with notices welcoming visitors to the town. Char-a-bancs, or coaches as they were now called, were drawn up in the car-park, and troupes of children dressed in fairy, Chinese and pirate costumes, were to be seen getting out. When he came to the town's park, Tom noticed the big marquee where the flowers and vegetables would be exhibited.

The scene reminded him of the African festivals he used to attend, observing meticulously how this or that old custom of which he had read had died out and been replaced by some new and 'significant' feature, avoiding in his descriptions the least suggestion of vivid or picturesque language, and flattening out the whole thing until it sounded rather less interesting than a flower show and carnival in a small English market town.

Mallow Park, for the house bore the name of the family who had lived in it for several hundred years, lay a little way out of the town on a slight eminence above it. It was a red Victorian house, with a small Georgian bit hidden away somewhere but now almost engulfed by later 'improvements'. There was a long drive leading up to it, bordered on each side by dark shrubberies, now excessively luxuriant after the summer rains.

Tom's brother, Giles, was standing on the terrace. He was a conventionally good-looking young man of twenty-seven, dressed in an old but good tweed suit.

'Well, Tom,' was his greeting, 'so you've come at last.'

'Yes, my thesis is finished now.'

Giles could not be expected to appreciate the significance of this announcement and he certainly gave no sign that he had, merely remarking that if Tom had let them know what time he was coming he would have brought the shooting-brake

down to the station to meet him. 'I suppose you left your luggage there?' he added.

'This is all I have,' said Tom, indicating the canvas bag he was carrying. 'We travel light in the bush. Where's mother?'

'In the garden. We're all going to the flower show in a minute. I suppose you'll come?'

'Oh, yes. I'll just go and find her.'

If the shrubberies and lawns seemed overgrown and neglected, the large vegetable garden was well kept, for Mrs. Mallow had a stall in the local market and sold the produce at it, like some African woman petty trader, Tom thought. He expected to find her among the beans or peering at something in a frame. But when he came upon her she was standing very still, looking into the distance. The massive grey-clad figure with its rather small head stood out like a great Henry Moore sculpture in a London park. She showed no emotion at seeing her son, merely inclining her stony cheek for him to kiss. Tom was her favourite son and she loved him deeply, indulging his whims and thinking by that to bind him more closely to her. But it was Giles who had stayed behind. Now she worked hard in the garden and found comfort in the things of the earth, even in digging, for she was a strong active woman and the hand that Tom took was rough and not very clean.

'Well, Tom,' she said, 'so you got the nine-ten from Paddington?'

'Yes.'

She remembered this train from the old days when she used to go to town, but it did not occur to her that he would have had nothing to eat. Tom had also forgotten it by this time.

'I'm showing begonias and carnations as well as vegetables this year,' she said, as they walked back to the house together. 'And what have you been doing? Your aunt tells me that you have been living with a young woman in Camden Town but that you have now abandoned her – is that so?'

'Well, yes, in a way.'

'Surely you must know whether you have or not?' asked Mrs. Mallow sharply.

'I suppose I don't like the word "abandoned"', Tom admitted. 'We parted by mutual consent. It was leading nowhere.'

'Where did you expect it to lead?'

'We didn't really think of that when we started. It seemed pleasant and convenient . . .' he broke off, conscious of the inadequacy of the words he was using to describe his relationship with Catherine. 'I think I was in love with her in a curious way and perhaps still am. Then there was Deirdre, a young girl of nineteen . . .'

Mrs. Mallow gave a snort of laughter. 'Oh, there are always young girls of nineteen,' she said. 'Giles is to marry Felicity,' she continued in a different tone. 'We are all very pleased.'

'Felicity? Oh, of course, Elaine's youngest sister. I should think that will be very suitable. I wish *I* could have done what was expected of me. If I had married Elaine . . .' he began, but Giles had come towards them and was urging them to hurry.

'Mother is to open the flower show,' he said. 'The usual story – they'd hoped to get some actress or television star, but in the end have to fall back on what we can provide. We've only twenty minutes before it begins. Surely you aren't going like that, are you, mother?' he went on in an exasperated tone.

'I shall wear a hat, I suppose,' said Mrs. Mallow, 'my grey one. It is hanging in the hall.'

They were standing now in the little room which Giles used as a kind of study and from which the business of the estate, such as it was, was conducted. As he looked about him, Tom realized how little it had changed since his father's time. The old horsehair-covered chair with the stuffing coming out of the seat was still unmended. The desk was

stuffed with bills, receipts and forms dating back many years. Giles's game-book lay open, recording in his sprawling schoolboy hand that he had shot so many pheasants, partridges and pigeons at various dates. The same stuffed hares' heads, foxes' brushes and crooked sporting prints looked down from the walls. Tom felt as if he were observing some aspect of a culture as alien to him as any he had seen in Africa. He imagined how Catherine would have enjoyed it, her bright eyes darting here and there, missing no detail. He wished now that he could have brought her to see his home.

'Mother, there is earth on your hands,' continued Giles in the same exasperated tone. 'Surely you are going to wash, at least?'

Mrs. Mallow glanced down at her hands indifferently. 'Yes, I suppose I must,' she admitted. 'Where is your uncle? Is he ready to come with us, if he is coming?'

'I'll go and see,' said Tom.

'You'll find him in the morning-room,' said Giles.

Tom found his uncle sitting in semi-darkness, looking at some sporting event on the television set, which had the central position in the room like a kind of altar. Green plush curtains had been dragged across the windows, shutting out all but a chink of sunlight which filtered incongruously through on to the elderly man with his military bearing and white walrus moustache.

'Hullo, uncle,' said Tom cheerfully. 'Aren't you coming with us to the flower show?'

'Tom, my dear boy. When did you arrive? I think I shall *not* accompany you. Hearing Naomi make a speech is not my idea of an afternoon's entertainment,' he chuckled. 'And besides, I don't want to miss the women's programme at three o'clock. This week we are to be shown the best cuts of meat to buy, most instructive. Of course it is for young housewives, really, newly-weds, I suppose you might call them, who haven't had experience of these things.'

Tom left the room feeling rather sad. He had the impression that his uncle was a kind of prisoner, or a sacrifice laid before the altar of the television set which demanded a constant tribute of victims.

'Hervey is not coming?' asked Mrs. Mallow as Tom rejoined them. 'I didn't think he would. We'd better get a move on.'

Giles now began to criticize Tom's appearance; apparently his blue corduroy jacket and grey flannels were not suitable for the occasion. 'You must remember,' he said, 'that many eyes will be upon you. We are still the leading family here whatever else may have changed.'

Mrs. Mallow had found a shooting-stick in the antlered umbrella stand. 'You could carry this,' she suggested.

'The insignia of rank,' said Tom, 'but not a particularly distinctive one. Only the chief is permitted to wear a necklace of leopards' teeth.'

'Well, it does make you look slightly better,' said Giles seriously. 'We shall be seeing Felicity and Elaine, of course. Delia is away. You remember Elaine, don't you?'

They were driving in the shooting-brake now, down the road along which Tom had walked less than an hour before.

'Yes, I remember her,' said Tom. 'I must congratulate you on your engagement to Felicity. Do you feel you can afford to marry?'

'Well, they have money of their own, those girls,' Giles reminded him. 'Not that that really makes any difference to one's feelings, but in this case it's certainly a help. We shall be able to get a good many things done. Mother and uncle will move to the lodge, but mother will keep the garden, of course.'

'I hope the lodge has a suitable site for the television set,' said Tom.

'Oh, yes, there is a good enough little room,' said Mrs.

181

Mallow casually. 'Now here we are, and the mayor is waiting to receive us. Perhaps you will find this little ceremony of interest, Tom,' she added dryly.

They entered the large marquee. It was very hot and smelled of roses and warm canvas and humanity. There was a buzz of conversation which died away when Mrs. Mallow and her entourage appeared on a little dais at one end. Tom and Giles stood down below, not listening to their mother's speech, which was rambling and confused, obviously not prepared at all. But as she was a member of the leading family in the neighbourhood and well known to her audience it did not matter what she said.

Tom looked around to see whether anybody he knew was there, but the faces all seemed indistinct, the men ruddy and healthy or pale and worried according to their occupations, the women young or elderly all wearing light-coloured summer dresses and straw hats trimmed with various kinds of artificial flowers and fruits. Somewhere, at a lower level, there would be children, but Tom was not interested in them. Surely, he thought, Elaine and her sister Felicity would stand out in some way among this crowd, or had we really reached the point where all women looked alike, regardless of where they bought their clothes?

'Well, Tom,' said a voice, giving him what seemed to be the stock greeting here, 'don't you recognize me?'

'*Elaine!*' He took her hand in his and held it for a long time. 'I was looking for you.'

She was, he noticed, dressed just like everybody else in a flowered silk dress with a white hat and gloves, but her pearl necklace and small stud ear-rings were probably real. She was a fair rather plump girl, the same age as Tom, with freckles and what are usually described as 'candid' grey eyes.

They were standing by a table where some fruit was displayed, little dishes of raspberries and plums arranged on leaves. The roof of the marquee cast a greenish light on to

their faces, giving an air of magic and unreality to the occasion, as if they were under water or in a forest.

'You haven't been home for such a long time,' she said, but without reproach in her tone.

'No. Just a week-end here and there, but I think you were away the last time.'

'I wrote to you for your birthday last year – did you get it?'

'Oh, yes, thank you.' He remembered now, such a very long letter, full of the daily trivia which can be so fascinating or so tedious according to the feelings of the recipient towards the writer.

'You didn't answer, so I wondered. I expect you were busy.'

'Yes, there was the election of a new chief and trouble among the plantation workers, and we were cut off by the rains for six weeks – oh, and various other things.'

'You always have such grand excuses, much grander than anybody else's,' she smiled. 'You didn't really need the "various other things", did you, Tom?'

He marvelled, as he had done before, at the sharpness of even the nicest women. All except Deirdre, but she would learn, he supposed.

'Well, anyway, it's very nice to see you now,' he said. 'Could we have tea together? I didn't have any lunch, now that I come to think of it.'

'Oh, Tom!' She was at once concerned and led him to the tea tent where she insisted on giving him all her share of the sandwiches and cakes provided. Somewhere a band was playing, its brassiness softened by distance into a pleasant background noise. 'There's the dance tonight,' she said. 'Are you coming?'

'Yes, I'd forgotten – there's always a dance, isn't there, at the King Edward Rooms, I suppose?'

'Of course! How could it be anywhere else?' She paused and then said, 'Did you know, I imagine you did, that we're going to be related?'

'Yes, Felicity and Giles. It seems a very good thing.'

'Obviously . . .' she looked down at the tablecloth. 'I heard you were attached too.'

'I? Don't you believe it,' said Tom heartily. 'I'm wedded to my work.'

Elaine finished her cup of tea and they got up to look at the begonias, too big and too brilliantly coloured to be regarded as flowers but seeming for that very reason to demand exclamations of wonder and disbelief. Mrs. Mallow's exhibit had won a first prize.

'Is it as big as a dinner-plate – that yellow one?' asked Tom. 'That's what one hears people saying.'

Elaine laughed and looked up at him.

'Could we slip off to a pub?' he asked. 'They'll be open now.'

'Not a *pub*,' she said doubtfully. 'I couldn't really, Mummy wouldn't like it, not *here*. If it were somewhere where I wasn't known it would be different. But perhaps we can have a drink together at the dance tonight?'

'Yes, of course, and lots of dances, I hope.'

When he got home Tom was surprised to find his dress clothes hanging in the wardrobe in his old room, as if they had been waiting for this moment when he would come back and wear them. He hardly recognized himself in the long looking-glass at the top of the stairs, and decided that he looked easily as distinguished as Mark had done on another similar occasion. Of course his hair needed cutting, as Giles pointed out, but the detribalized must have some distinctive mark of their condition.

The King Edward Rooms were full of childhood and adolescent memories for him. The large glowing head and shoulders portrait of the monarch had beamed down on him at children's parties and at his first grown-up dance. The stags' heads with their melting eyes had seen the beginning of his romance with Elaine, the palms and the little gilt chairs

ranged round the room must surely be those of his early youth; only the banked hydrangeas and gladioli would be different, and the people older and perhaps sadder, conscious that a new generation were now the young and gay.

He danced once or twice with Felicity, his future sister-in-law, but mostly with Elaine, who seemed the perfect dancing partner and companion, her conversation conventional and gentle, so that he almost found himself praising the floor and the band and asking her what shows she had seen or whether she had read any good books lately. But when they were walking in the gardens one of them, or perhaps both, began a sentence with 'Do you remember . . .', that powerful insidious phrase which can upset the most carefully formal conversation. So there they were, remembering their rides together, the long walks, the dances, the first shy and somehow comic attempts at love. Once, Elaine reminded him and he had quite forgotten it, he had quoted a poem to her, something terribly sad, but she couldn't remember what it had been. Catherine would have been able to guess it, he thought, Housman or something out of *Poems of Today*, probably something very obvious, but it had gone now. He found himself mourning the young man of those days, who went for long country walks and quoted poetry. Now he went into Regent's Park and talked about his thesis. He wondered if the change was for the better.

Elaine accepted his good-night kiss with a calmness which disappointed him after their intimate conversation in the gardens. But he could not know how she had trained herself not to think of him and to go on with her country activities, the dogs, the garden, the women's institute, the church work, as if they were her whole life. The birthday letter, written on an impulse, showed that she had not quite achieved the friendly indifference she aimed at, and Tom's sudden reappearance would disturb her for some time to come. The circumstances of her daily life, less usual now than fifty or a hundred

years ago, were not conducive to an easy forgetting. While Delia and Felicity had been trained for careers, Elaine had been the one to stay at home. She might, if she had come upon them, have copied out Anne Elliot's words, especially as she was the same age as Miss Austen's heroine: 'We certainly do not forget you so soon as you forget us. It is, perhaps, our fate rather than our merit. We cannot help ourselves. We live at home, quiet, confined, and our feelings prey upon us. You are forced on exertion. You have always business of some sort or other to take you back into the world immediately, and continual occupation and change soon weaken impressions.' But Elaine was not much of a reader; she would have said that she had no time, which was perhaps just as well, even if she missed the consolation and pain of coming upon her feelings expressed for her in such moving words.

A few days later Tom, in a confused and not altogether happy mood, returned to London. When he got to Paddington he rang up Catherine and they went and had rather too many drinks at one of their old haunts. He told her all about meeting Elaine again, but she seemed, rather to his surprise, not to be very sympathetic. He had imagined that she would be the one person who would understand his bewilderment and be able to advise him what he ought to do. Instead, she made frivolous remarks about Elaine's dogs and that seemed to lead her on to Deirdre, and was he going to marry her or go back to Africa or what? He could only reply, rather crossly, that he wasn't going to marry anybody at the moment, and that she knew perfectly well that he was going back to Africa as soon as he could make the necessary arrangements.

'Your people wait for you,' said Catherine. 'How soothing it will be to get away from all this complexity of personal relationships to the simplicity of a primitive tribe, whose only complications are in their kinship structure and rules of land tenure, which you can observe with the anthropologist's calm detachment.'

CHAPTER SEVENTEEN

Tom's departure for Africa was an experience that those of his friends who shared it with him would not willingly have undergone a second time. He went about looking haggard and flustered, seeming unable to decide what he wanted to take with him or how his heavy luggage which he could not take on the plane was to be sent.

'I suppose this is good practice for us,' said Digby mildly as he hammered nails into a crate.

'I thought there were firms that did this kind of thing,' said Mark irritably. 'When *I* go I shall see that things are better organized. I can't imagine why he's left everything to the last minute like this. And why must he go back in such a hurry, anyway?'

'I suppose it's the shock of getting his thesis finished when it seemed that he never would,' said Digby. 'And then the visit home, that apparently upset him in some way. He saw himself excluded from his family and all the useful things they were doing, perhaps he hadn't realized before how completely he had alienated himself.'

'Yes, even in sophisticated societies a man needs to feel the security of the kinship bond.'

'Has it occurred to you that there is some likeness between Tom and Prof. Mainwaring?' Digby went on. 'In their circumstances, I mean. Both have broken away from a rather high-class background.'

'But there the similarity ends, I should think. I don't imagine that Felix had such trouble with his girl friends – if they were that – as Tom is having now.' Mark leaned back

on his heels, seeming to bask in his friend's troubles. 'There was the girl at home, reminding him of what might have been. Then Catherine, abandoned and deserted, a continual reproach to him. And now Deirdre, who has flung herself at him – how difficult it sometimes is to resist the admiration of a young girl!' He sighed reminiscently.

'I'm sure Deirdre did no such thing,' said Digby angrily.

'Well, be that as it may, to quote Fairfax, Tom feels that only in Africa is he really appreciated. There he can do the work for which he is *really* fitted and which nobody else could possibly do, namely, the investigation into the role of the mother's brother in marriage ceremonies.'

'You sound almost bitter.'

'Perhaps I am, a little. Where are *we* going to get money to go into the field? Tom seems to have no difficulty.'

'No, but perhaps we can't really consider ourselves on a level with him.'

'You mean this myth about Tom's brilliance? What signs have you seen of it?'

'Oh, well, one doesn't expect to see *signs* of a thing like that, does one?'

'I should have thought that one might have discerned the faintest glimmer of his genius by now.'

'Certainly his conversation isn't brilliant, perhaps even ours is a little better than his,' said Digby uncertainly. 'And I thought that paper he read in the seminar last term was – well – *confused*,' he added, plunging further into disloyalty.

Mark took him up eagerly on this point and they went into a rather technical discussion at the end of which they had the satisfaction of proving, at least to themselves, that Tom, far from being brilliant, was in some ways positively stupid and not always even 'sound'.

'Almost a *diffusionist*,' said Mark, his eyes sparkling with malice.

'Oh, *come*,' said Digby in a shocked tone. Feeling that they

had perhaps gone a little too far, he changed the subject. 'You've heard the latest about the Foresight Fellowships, I suppose?'

'Yes, I was there when Fairfax was talking about them. The candidates to be invited down for a week-end at Prof. Mainwaring's country seat in November – it seems an odd arrangement but I suppose it will be a good thing to get it settled. There are two grants to be made, aren't there?'

'Yes, I think so.'

At this moment the bell rang. Digby hurried to answer it and found Catherine on the doorstep, a pile of neatly laundered shirts and shorts in her arms.

'Would you believe it,' she said. 'Tom discovered all these things in a trunk with his notes and as there wasn't time to send them to the laundry he rang me up, so here they are.'

'Won't you come in?'

'No, I think not. Is Tom there?'

'Yes, I think he's getting changed into some respectable clothes; he seems to be going out somewhere.'

'Ah, yes, to have a last evening with Deirdre, I expect,' said Catherine in a matter-of-fact tone. 'I can imagine what that will be like. I'm coming to the air terminal to see him off tomorrow, by the way, so I'll see you there.'

'I suppose a last evening with Deirdre might not be quite tne same as one with Catherine,' said Mark thoughtfully, 'so I wonder if Catherine really can imagine it.'

'Writers like to think that they can imagine everything,' suggested Digby, 'or do you think that Catherine has now reached the age when she has had so many partings and last evenings that she really does know all that can possibly happen?'

'How dull the life of an experienced woman must be, if everything has happened before,' said Mark. 'They do say, don't they, that hell hath no fury like a woman scorned.' He smiled his malicious little smile. 'It could be that.'

189

'Oh, I don't think there was any fury about her. She looked rather flushed, certainly, but that was probably because she'd been bending over the ironing-board – ironing is hot work, you know,' said Digby sensibly. 'I suppose I'd better take these things to Tom.'

He found him taking a swig of brandy out of a small flask. 'Going on a journey always makes me feel sick and nervous,' he explained rather apologetically, 'and one needs strengthening to face the good-byes.'

Digby made no comment but put the laundry down on the bed and left the room. A few moments later he heard Tom hurrying out of the house. He imagined him meeting Deirdre in a restaurant, making light gay conversation, perhaps getting a little drunk, then kissing her good night and coming home reasonably early, a little relieved that the last evening was over.

He seemed hardly to have settled down to his evening's reading when he heard Tom's key in the lock, and then looked up to find him standing in the room, blinking in the unaccustomed bright light.

'Don't worry,' said Digby heartily, 'I'll look after her for you.'

Tom smiled wryly. 'I must finish my packing,' he said.

'Let's hope it will be a nice day tomorrow,' said Digby, conscious that he was being banal but feeling that any other kind of talk would be too difficult.

He awoke next morning feeling rather smug as if he alone had been responsible for the brightness of the day.

'This sunshine will make everyone feel better,' he declared, as he and Mark cooked breakfast in the kitchen.

'Digby, what is this coming out in you, this hearty manner in the early morning?' said Mark irritably. 'I feel it should be nipped in the bud.'

'I was thinking of Deirdre and Catherine, really. It won't affect us. Do you think the air terminal is more romantic

than a railway station?' Digby asked, as they approached the looming grey bulk of the building.

'Yes, I suppose so, because one imagines longer and more fantastic journeys, and there is the possibility that the plane might crash,' said Mark in a detached tone. 'And people are going to the uttermost ends of the earth, perhaps for years.'

'I shouldn't stress that aspect of it before Catherine and Deirdre,' said Digby. 'It might upset them.'

'I almost wish they weren't coming,' said Tom. 'I really prefer to slip away quietly without anyone knowing it.' He was a little distracted with last-minute things left undone, and was still wearing his raincoat and carrying his brief-case; it would be some hours yet before he could discard these characteristic insignia of his calling. 'Oh, look, there they are.'

'They seemed to have arrived together,' said Mark. 'Both staking a claim at the last minute. Well, my dears, I hope you are feeling equal to this,' he greeted them.

Deirdre, who had been feeling for some days past as if she had been dealt a heavy blow in the pit of the stomach, had been unable to eat breakfast at all. Catherine had managed toast and even a boiled egg – not of course a *fried* egg – of which she felt slightly ashamed, but she told herself that Tom's going back was different for her this time, and that it was fitting that it should be distinguished from the other times, even if only by the eating of a larger breakfast.

'We were wondering which was the more romantic, this building or a great railway terminus,' said Digby to Catherine, 'and we decided that this was.'

'Yes, in a way, but it's all more streamlined and hygienic, isn't it. Almost like the difference between a cremation and an old-fashioned funeral.' said Catherine, talking rather fast and drawing Mark and Digby away so that Tom and Deirdre could have a little time together. 'But we musn't make it too gloomy for Tom. After all he is *glad* to be going back.'

'You look tired,' said Deirdre, saying to Tom the words she had imagined herself saying, for indeed he did look tired.

'And did *you* sleep well?' he asked almost formally.

'Oh, no. I didn't know birds started to sing so early, even at this time of year.' She had woken at dawn crying, and the memory of it now constricted her throat so that she could hardly speak, and had to turn her face away from him. He took her hand, but unobtrusively as if he did not want Catherine to see.

'We've time for a cup of coffee,' said Digby sensibly. 'That might be a good idea.'

They sat drinking and talking until a disembodied female voice announced that the passengers for that particular flight should take their places in the bus to go to the airport.

Tom's travelling companions – a number of smartly dressed African business men, a dried-up-looking elderly man and woman and a few other more nondescript persons – were already climbing into the bus. Except for the Africans, there was really nothing unusual or remarkable about any of them. But at the last minute, just as Tom himself was about to get in, a party of four black-clad priests came hurrying towards the bus.

'Now be sure and tell Father O'Halloran and Father Kinsella that I was asking for them,' called out a strong Irish voice belonging to another priest who was seeing them off.

'We will too,' said one of them.

'And you have the *Limerick Times* with the account of the hurling? That way I'll be after saving the postage,' he chuckled. 'A grand match it was, a *grand* match, do you be sure and tell Father Kinsella . . .'

'Well, old boy,' said Digby, grasping Tom by the hand and feeling as if he were acting the part of an Englishman seeing off a friend, 'all the best.'

Mark shook hands too. Then Catherine stretched up and kissed Tom lightly on the cheek but he seized her in his arms

and embraced her more warmly. He then did the same to Deirdre, seeming to make no difference between them.

Surely he ought to have made some distinction? thought Mark in his detached way. And does one kiss girls in public like that? Only if one comes from Tom's stratum of society; ours is so much more inhibited when it comes to questions of love and sex.

'Look,' said Catherine in her brightest tone, 'Tom is sitting by one of the priests. I feel he'll be all right now.'

They all waved and the bus drove away. Digby and Mark would then have gone home, but the women wanted to watch it out of sight so they all stood there rather stiffly as if they were at some kind of military ceremony.

'He hasn't really gone yet,' said Deirdre in a stifled voice, 'not *really* gone, that's what makes it worse.'

'No, I suppose there's about an hour and a half before he will actually rise into the air,' said Mark.

'But in a way he will have gone the moment he left us,' Deirdre persisted. 'His thoughts will be fixed on the future and we shall be the past.'

'Only where he is concerned,' said Digby. 'We are still ourselves, you know.'

He had taken her arm and was attending to her with great kindness and solicitude. Catherine was glad to see this and made no attempt to take upon herself the role of comforter, which is often regarded as a kind of female monopoly though it can be admirably filled by the right kind of man.

'Good-bye, Catherine,' said Deirdre absently. 'We must meet some time for lunch or you must come home to tea or supper.'

'I'd love to,' said Catherine, seeing the greyness of these future meals through Deirdre's eyes. She did not particularly want to be left alone with Mark and for him to feel under any obligation to buy her a drink or a meal and was relieved when

he excused himself, saying that he was lunching with the girl he had met at Tom's aunt's dance.

Catherine got on to the first bus that came and let it take her where it would. Her thoughts seemed to be in three layers. On the top layer she was saying over to herself like a chant two lines of verse which often, though for no apparent reason, came into her mind at moments of stress or emotional upheaval:

What was he doing, the great god Pan,
Down in the reeds by the river . . .

It was a jingle, perhaps with some long forgotten comic significance, but it persisted, over and over again like a bluebottle buzzing in a closed room. The middle layer was a preoccupation with a series of beauty articles she was writing for one of her magazines. Having dealt with the problem of acquiring a good sun tan and then bleaching away its last traces, she was now thinking of winter beauty treatments, getting the arms and shoulders nice for New Year parties, softening those rough elbows. Try sitting with your elbows cupped in halves of lemon, she thought derisively, advice she would never have dreamed of following herself. And on the shoulders try cucumber peel, one of grandmother's recipes for whitening the skin. Underneath all this, in the bottom layer of her thoughts, was a dark and confused sadness about Tom which she did not attempt to bring out and analyse.

She got off the bus and entered a large restaurant with a noble foyer thronged with people, none of them seeming to know which direction they were going in. They wandered, bewildered, rudderless, in need not only of someone to tell them which of the many separate cafés would supply their immediate material wants, but of a guide to the deeper or higher things of life. While a glance at the menus displayed or a word with an attendant would supply the former, who was to fulfil the latter? The anthropologist, laying bare the

structure of society, or the writer of romantic fiction, covering it up? Perhaps neither, Catherine thought. And why should she assume that these people, temporarily confused and wandering, were in greater need of guidance than she was herself?

She passed counters laden with chocolates and dishes of brilliant hors-d'œuvres, and walked out of another door. What was he doing, the great god Pan . . . and still Tom wouldn't quite have left the country. She ought to be in some church, praying for his safety.

In common with many people who are not regular church-goers, Catherine sometimes felt the need to enter a church at special times, but she did not know of any in this area and wandered for quite a long time before she came upon one that seemed 'suitable'. Unsuitable ones she regarded as those with a bright welcoming message outside and presumably a light and unsympathetic interior. The one she eventually chose seemed to her just right, with its mysterious dimness pierced by a red light hanging before an altar in a side chapel, and its lingering fragrance of incense. She thought it must be a Roman Catholic church, especially as there was a little table with candles on it, some of which had already been lit, standing in front of a statue. Attached to the table was a box with a slit in it, presumably for money. But what did one pay? she wondered. She looked in her purse and found a shilling, which seemed about right, then placed a candle in one of the little holders and lit it. At first the flame was very feeble but then suddenly it seemed to shoot up and burn brightly. Obviously this was a good omen, though she was not sure of what. She knelt for a moment in one of the pews, making up prayers in the rather stilted language she remembered from childhood. Was it necessary always to address God as 'Thou' and to use such archaic grammatical forms? she wondered, deeply conscious of her ignorance in these matters. Perhaps she had come to a stage in her life when she

should begin going to church and then she might learn. After a while it seemed easier just to sit and let some kind of peace flow over her and she did this for some minutes, until she heard a movement outside the door. She stood up quickly and made her way out, fearful of being pounced upon by a dark swift-moving figure in cassock and biretta, who might ask her what she was doing there. But the voices, when they came, were women's voices, and the snatch of conversation she heard was not really very alarming, showing as it did the universal concern of women for men.

'. . . will wear himself out. If only he would let Father Amis take the early Mass sometimes. The trouble is that one can do so *little* oneself, one feels so helpless.'

Two middle-aged women came out of a door, one of them carrying a small electric bowl fire. They glanced at Catherine with friendly but restrained curiosity.

'Can we help you at all?' asked one of them pleasantly. 'Father Summerhayes will be here soon, if you want to see him.'

'Oh, no, thank you,' said Catherine quickly. 'I was only just . . .' she had been going to say 'looking round' as if she were in a shop but stopped herself in time. What *had* she been doing? Lighting a candle for Tom or for herself? Anyway, nothing that these good women would be able to help her with.

'The church is always open for private prayer,' said the other woman. 'We did have to lock it at one time because a valuable carpet was stolen, but now we arrange for somebody to be here so that it can be open all the time.'

'Well, thank you, I shall remember that,' said Catherine, managing a suitable sentence. Then, smiling at them, she hurried out of the door, nearly colliding in her haste with a dark swift-moving figure in cassock and biretta.

'Hullo, Miss Dewsbury!' he called out. 'Still keeping up the good work?'

He had gone before Catherine could disillusion him. She walked away, smiling to herself, amused and disconcerted to feel that she could so easily be mistaken for a church worker. Was there a place for her there, perhaps? She imagined herself worrying over Father Summerhayes, who had not, from her brief glimpse of him, looked at all worn out. But of course there would be more to it than that, even she knew something of what it would involve and she did not feel she could face it yet. Like one of the saints – she couldn't remember which it had been – but it seemed an irreverent comparison and she pushed it quickly away.

CHAPTER EIGHTEEN

IT was a cold sparkling Saturday morning in early November when Professor Mainwaring and Miss Clovis stood in the morning-room of his house in the country, watching the candidates for the Foresight research grants coming up the drive.

'Well, they have surmounted the first obstacle,' declared Professor Mainwaring, smiling and tweaking at his beard.

'And what was that?' asked Miss Clovis, trying to remember whether there was a water jump in the lane or savage dogs to be overcome at the gates.

'They have come on the train I told them to take,' he chuckled.

'*That* can't have been very difficult. It doesn't show much intelligence on their part to have caught the train.'

'Ah, perhaps not, but there was a catch in it. Only the *front* portion of the train comes here. The rear portion goes in *quite another direction*!' His voice ended up on its highest note and he stood rubbing his hands. 'I deliberately omitted to give them that information.'

'Then I suppose the ticket collector must have told them when he punched their tickets.'

'You think so?' Professor Mainwaring sounded disappointed. 'But I have known many – and anthropologists among them – who have taken the wrong turning, as it were.'

The drive was long and straight, so that the four candidates, Mark and Digby with the two young women Primrose Cutbush and Vanessa Eaves, had been visible for some time.

Professor Mainwaring looked at the pretty French clock on

the mantelpiece. 'It seems as if they have walked from the station, and that's the best part of a mile, carrying their luggage, too. How very little they have brought,' he commented. 'The ladies are carrying their own – that is a good sign. I should not feel inclined to offer a research grant to a lady who expected a man to bear her burdens for her. In my young days it was different, of course; things are so very much changed now. I should hardly have been surprised to see the young ladies carrying the young *men's* luggage. I see that they are wearing their raincoats.' He moved across the room and tapped at a small barometer. 'Well, perhaps they are wise. There may be some rain and they have come prepared.'

'They have no overcoats, that's why they are wearing raincoats,' said Miss Clovis sharply, noting that Felix was evidently in one of his rather tiresome rambling moods this morning. It was certainly cold enough to be wearing overcoats; could it be that they were unable to afford them? She had also seen that Digby Fox was wearing what looked like hand-knitted gloves and the sight had disturbed her with its pathos.

'This is a week-end they will remember,' declared the Professor. 'I think a glass of sherry in here, first, and then luncheon. Henry will announce it, of course. They will appreciate that little piece of ceremonial.'

'We are getting very near now,' said Mark. 'I can see Esther and Felix standing at a window watching us.'

'Isn't the house romantic-looking,' said Vanessa. 'A noble *pile*, the term really seems to be justified here.'

'It's much too big for one person to live in,' said Primrose. 'It could be turned into a school or a home for unmarried mothers.'

'What things you think of, dear,' said Mark, giggling.

'I think it's hideous,' said Digby bluntly. 'Those red gothic turrets and lancet windows or whatever they are.' He wished that Deirdre could have come too, but she was as yet too young to apply for a research grant. In the weeks that

had passed since Tom's going, he had seen her as often as he judged to be politic, guessing that she would not appreciate too much of his company at this stage. He had sometimes observed her from a distance, sitting alone in the college canteen, reading a blue air letter which could only be from Tom. Sometimes the letter looked as if it were falling apart at the folds, which made him think that she must be reading the same letter over and over again and wonder whether Tom wasn't writing to her as often as he should. He longed to ask her and to comfort her and even to rush out to Africa with a horse-whip should it be necessary. He was experiencing that difficult stage of love which seems to consist only of patient waiting, but his nature was better suited to it than some would have been.

'Do we ring the bell?' asked Primrose bluntly. 'Or will they come running out to meet us?'

'I suppose we pull this,' said Mark. 'Look, it's a friar's head and you pull out the tongue.'

'What a quaint idea!' said Vanessa. 'Did dear old Felix think of that himself, I wonder? No, I suppose the house is older than he is. What a loud pealing! I wonder who will come?'

The door opened and a manservant, hardly old or dignified enough to be called a butler, stood before them.

'Good morning. Will you kindly tell your master that the Foresight candidates have arrived?' said Vanessa, assuming a grand manner.

'The Professor is in the morning-room,' said the manservant. 'Perhaps you would care to wait here a moment.'

They stood in the hall looking about them. The monastic motives were repeated here, with more friars' heads appearing in unexpected places, as bell-pulls and handles to the carved gothic doors.

'Is all this supposed to have any significance?' muttered Mark. 'I wonder if it gives any indication of the kind of hospitality we may expect?'

'Ah, so you have all come,' Professor Mainwaring emerged from a door, rubbing his hands. 'Henry will take your luggage to your rooms, which you shall see after luncheon. Now here is the cloakroom, no doubt you would like a wash after your long journey.'

Mark and Digby, who were not in the habit of washing their hands more than they considered absolutely necessary, which was not very often, and did not need the cloakroom for any other purpose, declined his offer, but the girls took advantage of it.

'Let us leave the ladies to *powder their noses*, then; I believe that is the correct expression,' chuckled the Professor. 'They should be able to find their way to the morning-room to join us in a glass of sherry-wine. The sound of our laughter will, I hope, point the way if they are at all doubtful.'

Mark and Digby followed him shrugging their shoulders and tapping their foreheads with significant gestures. The Prof. was evidently in what they regarded as one of his ga-ga moods today.

'Good morning,' said Miss Clovis, rising from her seat by the fire. 'Now do come and get warm. I'm afraid you must be cold after your journey.' A glance at Digby's hands had told her that they were red with cold in spite of the knitted gloves, and he looked as if he might be getting chilblains.

'Now, what has Henry seen fit to bring us?' mused Professor Mainwaring, retiring to a side table and lifting various decanters, like a priest at an altar, thought Mark dispassionately. 'The Tio Pepe – I wonder if you would find that too dry? – or the Amontillado? And what is this? Ah, yes, ginger wine, a non-alcoholic cordial, very warming to the vitals, I believe.'

'I should prefer the Tio Pepe,' said Mark boldly. 'I prefer a dry sherry.'

'I should like Amontillado, please,' said Digby, thinking he had better be different. There was, as far as he could see,

no clue as to which they were supposed to choose. It was like one of those questionnaires which Catherine sometimes made up for her magazines, where you received marks for your answers and the total indicated the type of man you should marry or whether you were really well-groomed or would make a good wife.

It did occur to him that perhaps they ought to have chosen the ginger wine, as Primrose, who disliked alcohol, had done. Vanessa was very feminine and undecided and in the end asked the Professor to choose for her, which seemed to please him very much. But Digby felt that he and Mark could hardly have adopted this course.

'Miss Clovis and I have been drinking – ah –' he examined his glass and went on in a surprised tone, '*gin*. I forget now why that was.'

'I don't like sherry very much,' said Miss Clovis brusquely.

'Yes, that was it. You prefer "mother's ruin", as they call it.' He went into laughter in which the young people joined a little doubtfully. It did not seem quite right to be joking about Miss Clovis.

At that moment the booming of a gong was heard and Henry appeared in the doorway. 'Luncheon is served,' he announced gravely.

'There need be no formality about going in to luncheon,' declared Professor Mainwaring. 'Perhaps Miss Clovis and I should lead the way to the table simply because we know where it is to be found.'

Digby appeared almost to choke as he drained the last drop of his sherry. Mark gave him a hearty thump on the back which hardly improved matters.

The dining-room was papered in deep crimson. On the walls were two or three oil-paintings which looked as if they might have been valuable, mainly because they were so very dark and old-looking; it was just possible to see that they were

still-lifes of dead pheasants, hares, lobsters, and other raw materials of the kitchen. The round table was laid with a heavy white double damask cloth and well-cared-for silver and glass. An Edwardian epergne, filled with out-of-season fruits, stood in the centre.

'Now I wonder what Mrs. Bush has provided for us today,' said Professor Mainwaring in a confident tone. 'Ah, soup, that is a good beginning. And I see that we have Barbara to wait on us. She is good enough to come up from the village when I have guests.'

A tall awkward-looking girl with red hands began to serve the soup.

'My mother had a maid called Barbara,' said the Professor in a thoughtful tone.

There was a polite expectant silence round the table.

'She had a song of willow,' he continued, perhaps surprisingly, but Mark managed to catch the allusion, though he hardly knew what he was expected to do with it.

'Othello,' he muttered.

A haunch of venison was brought on to a side table.

'During the last war,' the Professor went on, 'we had American troops stationed here in the village.'

Barbara put a hand up to her mouth to stifle a giggle.

'Well, perhaps I had better not continue my story here,' he broke off regretfully. 'Now, have you everything you want?' Roast potatoes and brussels sprouts had been served with the venison, also red currant jelly and a thick dark gravy tasting of port wine.

Let's get on with the eating and not talk so much, thought Digby desperately. He and Mark had found almost nothing in the kitchen for breakfast that morning, and his hunger was formidable.

'I wonder what you will think of this wine?' asked Professor Mainwaring genially, as Henry came round with a bottle. 'I should be interested to have your opinion of it.'

I bet you would, thought Mark, and yet the old man did not appear to be speaking sarcastically.

'Very full-bodied,' he murmured.

Digby did not venture an opinion, but Vanessa said that it tasted like the smell of incense.

'Are you a Catholic, then, Miss Eaves?' asked Miss Clovis sharply.

'Oh, no, I'm not anything, but I adore Catholic churches, don't you?' said Vanessa, turning her head in Professor Mainwaring's direction so that her long jade ear-rings swung in a rather provocative way.

'We have not asked for details of the candidates' religious views on the application forms,' he said thoughtfully. 'It might have been interesting if we had. It is perhaps a mistake to concentrate exclusively on academic achievements. In my young days it was rather different, though the light had been seen in certain quarters. It took courage, I can tell you, not perhaps of the very highest order, but courage nonetheless, to proclaim oneself a Rationalist. Now, it seems more courageous to be a Baptist or a Methodist. There is something *chic*, is there not, about Roman and Anglo-Catholicism?'

'High church services are more interesting,' Digby ventured. 'The ritual is more colourful.'

'Do you believe in the celibacy of the clergy?' rapped out Miss Clovis suddenly.

'I don't know. I'm afraid I've never really thought about it,' said Digby.

'Well, then, what about the celibacy of the anthropologist in the field?'

'Oh, surely a man needs a companion out there,' said Digby warmly.

'A woman can be such a great help in his work,' said Vanessa in her soft tones, 'and men do need loving, after all.' She seemed to enfold Professor Mainwaring, as well as Mark and Digby, in a glance from her melting eyes.

'Then you don't regard the anthropologist as a dedicated being very much like a priest?' went on Miss Clovis.

The young men did not answer immediately, for although they regarded themselves in their role of anthropologists as superior to most other men and certainly to priests, they did not consider that it was necessary for them to forego any of the pleasures enjoyed by these lesser men.

'After all, there're some things a man's just *gotta* have,' said Mark, in imitation of his American colleague Brandon J. Pirbright.

'I believe that to be a fallacy,' declared Professor Mainwaring. 'It is like the idea that one should drink more alcohol in the tropics, which is quite erroneous. Indeed, the less you drink there the better you will be.'

This pronouncement seemed to plunge the young men into a gloomy silence. Deprived of love and of drink, a spell of fieldwork seemed less delightful.

'I don't think anthropologists should be married. There might be the complication of children and all that,' said Primrose, rather red in the face.

'Of course the *great* ones have been in some way dedicated beings,' mused the Professor. He then went on to name one or two who had been and rather more who, in his opinion, had not, whose names it would be invidious to mention here.

'I always think Mr. Mallow is in some way dedicated to his work,' declared Miss Clovis. 'He has that look about him. I was very much afraid that he was going to marry Miss Swan, but I see that it has come to nothing. Of course I am all for bringing people together where it is likely to be of lasting benefit to anthropology, but in this case I felt the girl was really much too young.'

'A fanatical light shines in his eyes when he speaks of the mother's brother,' said Mark, who was becoming a little tipsy.

An apple tart and a dish of mince pies were brought to the table.

'Shall we say then that we are aspiring rather than dedicated beings?' said the Professor, seeming to sum up. 'You remember Pope's line, *And little less than angel, would be more* – of course his argument is not altogether appropriate here and it would take too long to go into it now, though I am sure we could have a most interesting and fruitful discussion. Now what would your plans for fieldwork be, should you be awarded a grant?' he asked, suddenly almost businesslike. 'Shall we go round the table? Miss Eaves?'

The candidates were by this time considerably mellowed by the food and drink, so that they were able to expand and even embroider the bare schemes they had thought out. It seemed as if each one was going to benefit some primitive people so enormously that it would be difficult to decide who was *not* to be awarded a grant. The mysteries of secret societies were to be unveiled, so that grievances could be set right and the task of the harassed Administration lightened an hundredfold; primitive agricultural methods, after a careful study of the indigenous social systems and rules of land tenure, were to be revolutionized, so that the desert should indeed blossom like the rose; the position of women was to be so vastly improved that they could take their place as equal citizens with men to the benefit of all. And finally, reports and articles were to flow forth for the glory of pure knowledge and the swelling of the learned journals.

Professor Mainwaring listened with attention, but it did seem to Digby, who was the last to speak, that by the time his turn came the old man was beginning to grow a little sleepy. Once his eyes seemed to close and his head to droop forward on to his chest.

'I suppose we shall have coffee in the smoking-room?' asked Miss Clovis sharply, for Henry was hovering near, awaiting instructions.

'What was that? Coffee?' The silver beard jerked up 'By all means, wherever you like. I shall retire to my study now.'

'He will have a rest,' said Miss Clovis confidentially, as she poured the coffee, spilling it in the saucers. 'I expect you would like to explore the grounds. I have one or two things to see to so I shan't come with you.'

'Do you think that manservant has been mocking us?' asked Digby as they strolled by an ornamental lily pond. 'And what has he done with our luggage? I hope nobody has unpacked for us. I believe that used to be the custom in some houses before the war.'

'I hope not,' giggled Vanessa. 'I can guess what newspaper Primrose will have wrapped her bedroom slippers in.'

'*The Times* is best for wrapping things,' said Mark seriously. 'The sheets are larger and more durable. There seems to be a moral there.'

'All that talk about celibacy was rather unnerving for you boys,' said Vanessa. 'Strange, isn't it, that Felix has never married, and he's still so attractive. I wonder if *I* could make him happy? There's only about fifty years' difference in our ages, less really.'

'Seventy weds twenty,' said Mark. 'You can imagine the headlines.'

'Do you think Clovis is after him?' asked Digby. 'Or even old Minnie Foresight?'

They discussed these possibilities for some time in a rather frivolous and unsuitable manner and then, as it was getting near the time when they might expect tea and the air was becoming too chilly to make walking enjoyable any more, they went back to the house. They found Miss Clovis waiting in the morning-room, Professor Mainwaring still apparently 'resting'. Tea was brought and Miss Clovis, unused to the rather elaborate apparatus which it seemed to entail here, asked if one of the young women would like to

pour out. But in the end it was Digby, slow, but careful and efficient, who managed the complications of the silver teapot and the kettle with a little flame underneath it.

'We don't change for dinner here,' said Miss Clovis. 'I don't suppose you have brought anything with you to change into,' she added, remembering the smallness of their luggage

'I have a clean shirt,' said Mark jokingly, 'but perhaps it won't be necessary to put it on? Do you think Professor Mainwaring would expect it?'

'Oh, no, he is taking you as you are,' said Miss Clovis rather obscurely. 'And in any case, the dining-room is not particularly well lit. I shall see you anon,' she added with a touch of gaiety.

Dinner was as elaborate as luncheon had been, and the candidates almost wondered whether they were being put through an ordeal by eating and drinking. When the meal was over they went to have coffee in the drawing-room which they had not yet seen. It was a nobly proportioned room and the walls were hung with more oil-paintings whose dense brownish texture, made it seem, like those in the dining-room, that they might be of some value. Some were portraits, presumably of the Professor's ancestors, though no immediate likenesses were discernible.

One was especially interesting and seemed to have some direct bearing on the art or science of anthropology. It was of a gentleman in eighteenth-century dress, attended by a turbanned negro servant. The man held a skull in his hands and was gazing down at it thoughtfully. In the murky background two or three dim forms, men or even apes, could just be seen leaning against a ruined column.

'What a lovely romantic picture!' exclaimed Vanessa, striking an attitude in front of it. 'How I wish I could be right inside it.'

'My dear, I wonder if you would really like that,' said Professor Mainwaring benevolently. 'The man in the picture,

Robert Wyverne Mainwaring, was addicted to fits of deep melancholy, you know it was a fashionable cult at the end of the eighteenth century – and I fear he would have been a most unpleasing companion. Who reads those great poets – Wharton, Blair and Young – now?' he suddenly rapped out.

'I'm afraid we don't have much time for reading poetry,' said Digby with a slight air of priggishness.

'A pity, but I suppose it is a sign of the times. I see that you are examining my books,' he added, speaking to Mark.

'I suppose the anthropological books are in your study?'

'Anthropological books?' chuckled the Professor. 'You won't find any in this house. I have given them all to the Foresight Research Centre.'

'But surely . . .' Digby was too shocked to finish his sentence.

'I am an old man now, I can do very well without them. They are not the kind of reading to see me into my grave.'

'But what *do* you read?' asked Mark.

'Well, there are other books. I find myself turning to Shakespeare and the Bible – those classic desert island choices – there is a good deal of reading in them. And at the moment I am quite engrossed in Anthony a Wood's *Athenae Oxoniensis* – do you know it?'

'Oh, it is not a book for young people,' said Miss Clovis quickly. 'Wood's obsession with mortality wouldn't be at all their cup of tea and one wouldn't wish it to be.'

'Ah, *tea*!' said the Professor, giving her an almost roguish look.

'Of course we do read Shakespeare and the Bible sometimes,' said Digby, feeling that they had given an impression of cultural narrowness which it might be well to dispel. 'It's only that one finds it difficult to fit in all the wider reading one would like to do.'

'And Miss Cutbush has read a good deal of Marx,' said Vanessa rather spitefully.

'And now, what about some music?' said Professor Main-waring, going over towards the piano. 'We are told that it has charms to soothe a savage breast and that seems very suitable, does it not. Perhaps you would care to do some jigsaw puzzles while you are listening. Now here is one of the Grand Canal at Venice – "over four hundred pieces, fully interlocking",' he read from the box. 'That should keep your hands and brains occupied while you are listening to the music.'

'How lovely – we went to Venice on our holiday this year,' said Vanessa.

'Then you will find the puzzle easier. Travel is a great medium of education, as we know.'

'Do you play the piano, Professor?' asked Digby.

'Well, perhaps I don't, really, but I have the illusion that I do. You see, this is a pianola.' He took some music rolls out of a box and consulted the titles. 'Now, I wonder what would be suitable for this evening? Miss Clovis, what do you think?'

'Oh, I'm quite indifferent. You know I can't tell one piece from another.'

The young people settled themselves round a table with the jigsaw puzzle. Digby, characteristically, took up a handful of pieces of sky and began trying to fit them together, leaving the more interesting sections of gondolas, water and buildings to Mark and the girls.

Professor Mainwaring put a roll into the pianola and began peddling vigorously. An Edwardian musical comedy tune, no doubt a favourite of his youth, rang out. As he peddled he hummed and occasionally sang a snatch in a light tenor voice. One tune followed another, but all were of the same kind – *Two little girls in blue, I wouldn't leave my little wooden hut, The optimist and the pessimist*, and others.

'Quite a vivid picture of Felix's salad days,' mumured Mark 'Can you imagine him haunting the stage door of the Gaiety or Daly's?'

'No wonder he didn't publish much in those days,' said Digby.

'How handsome he must have looked in evening dress,' sighed Vanessa.

'It seems a contradiction in his character,' said Primrose, 'to think of him leading that kind of life and then going to Africa to study a tribe. I wonder what made him do it?'

'Perhaps an unhappy love affair,' mused Vanessa.

'But young anthropologists now are quite gay when they can afford to be,' said Mark, remembering his triumphs at the dance. 'I don't see anything unusual in that. It's this crippling lack of money.'

'Yes, Felix would have private means,' said Digby sadly.

'Well, that is done away with now,' said Primrose rather hotly.

'Hush, Miss Clovis might hear,' warned Digby.

They were startled by the shrill sound of the telephone ringing somewhere outside the room. Nobody made any attempt to answer it, but after a moment Henry appeared in the doorway.

'It's a call for Miss Clovis,' he said.

Miss Clovis went out of the room.

> *'Oh, oh, Antonio,*
> *He's gone away.*
> *Left me alonio,*
> *All on my ownio . . .'*

sang the Professor. 'Delightful! And *Floradora* – do you know that? It seems to me that young people are not as light-hearted as they used to be,' he went on, making them wonder if he had overheard their conversation. 'I wonder why that is?'

'Two wars, motor-cars, and newer and more frightful bombs being invented all the time,' said Mark. 'One feels there is something not quite right in being gay. A gloomy

evening in the cheap seats at the pictures, but no stage door afterwards or drinking champagne out of slippers. Did you ever do that, Professor Mainwaring?' he inquired, boldly, but at the same time with an air of deference.

'Ah, those days,' said the Professor, seeming to evade the question. 'What is it, Esther?' he asked, as Miss Clovis came back into the room. 'Not bad news I hope? You look somewhat *distraite.*'

'Felix, I must have a word with you in private,' said Miss Clovis, who certainly seemed to be both agitated and angry.

'Very well, then.' He rose from the pianola and followed her out of the room.

A buzz of conversation broke out and there was much speculation as to the news Miss Clovis could have received. It was difficult to guess what event would be likely to produce such an effect upon her; even the death of a near relative or friend was thought to be unlikely to upset her very much, so lacking in the ordinary human emotions did they judge her to be.

'Perhaps the Folly has been burnt down, or a thief has broken in and stolen the horsehair couch,' suggested Mark.

'Or it may be something to do with Miss Lydgate's brother,' said Digby. 'Do you think he has eloped with his housekeeper?'

Voices were heard again outside the door, more in anger than in sorrow, and a few broken sentences could be distinguished. '. . . a *disgusting* thing!' 'We shall not forget *this* . . .' But they did not throw much light on what had happened.

'We hope it was not bad news?' asked Mark politely, hoping for some information.

Miss Clovis gave a characteristic snort, but Professor Mainwaring said in a soothing tone, 'Oh, it is not so much, really. It may not turn out to be so bad after all. Now who would like a nightcap? Whisky or a hot milk drink? I'm sure you have all had a tiring day and will be glad to get to

bed. Leave the jigsaw on the table, you may be able to finish it tomorrow.'

Upstairs there was a good deal of conversation and laughter before the candidates finally retired for the night.

'I wonder if there is any special arrangement of rooms,' said Mark, when he and Digby had said good night to the girls, 'like an Edwardian house-party. You know what went on there.'

'I don't,' said Digby sourly. 'You seem very much up in high life these days. Personally I'm tired.'

'I wonder how we made out this evening?' said Mark thoughtfully, 'It wasn't easy, was it. I'm sorry I didn't have an opportunity to put my neo-Malinowski plan for field research across in more detail, but I hope he got the gist of it.'

'Well, spare me the recital of it for another time,' yawned Digby. 'Look, biscuits by the bed, rather a good idea, and some light novels by female authors. I shall have a nice read. I wonder what time breakfast is?'

'Nine o'clock, I should think. Good night!'

They were soon comfortably asleep, but downstairs Professor Mainwaring and Miss Clovis talked until a late hour. 'What is to be done?' they asked at intervals, but they went to bed without having solved the problem in any way.

CHAPTER NINETEEN

'GOOD morning! Have you everything you want? Mrs. Bush usually provides a good selection of breakfast dishes when I have guests, so I hope you were able to find something you liked.' Professor Mainwaring paced up and down the dining-room, stroking his beard. It was half past nine on Sunday morning and a fine day. There was no trace of anxiety in his manner, from which it might be presumed that the news of the night before, whatever it had been, had not left any very deep impression. 'Miss Clovis keeps to her room,' he went on. 'She sent a message that she would breakfast there.'

'I hope she isn't ill?' asked Mark, politely but with a note of hope.

'Oh, no, just feeling a little tired, I think. I hope you all slept well?'

'Oh, excellently, thank you,' said Vanessa. 'It was lovely to hear owls in the trees. I felt really in the country.'

'It would have been appropriate if I could have arranged lions for you,' said Professor Mainwaring. 'My ancestor whose portrait you were admiring last night had a private *menagerie*' – he pronounced the word in the French way which gave it an exotic and slightly shocking air – 'I believe the roars of the beasts could be heard for miles. Of course when you are in the field you may hear them there.'

'I should think we are more likely to hear the roar of the high-powered motor-car of one of the urbanized anthropologists,' said Mark. 'At least in West Africa. New travel books

will have titles like *Through Yorubaland in a Cadillac* rather than the good old *First Footsteps* kind of thing.'

'Yes, it is perhaps to be regretted,' said the Professor. 'Now, who is for church this morning?' he asked with startling briskness. Without waiting for an answer, he went on, 'Or would you prefer a walk in the woods? You remember your Wordsworth, of course,

> *One impulse from a vernal wood,*
> *Will teach you more of man,*
> *Of moral evil and of good,*
> *Than all the sages can*'.

Now indeed they were in a dilemma. They were none of them regular churchgoers though they would certainly have attended the service to please Professor Mainwaring. But the fact that he had offered them an alternative confused them. What did he expect them to do?

'Of course this wouldn't be a *vernal* wood,' said Mark, temporizing, 'though presumably one could get the same benefit from a wood in autumn.'

'It would be against my principles to go into a church,' said Primrose bluntly. 'So I'd rather go for a walk.'

'I sometimes go at home with my mother,' said Digby. 'Is the church here an ancient one?'

'No, it is rather ugly,' declared the Professor. 'It was built by an ancestor of mine in a style similar to this house, which was rebuilt, as you have probably guessed, about a hundred years ago. The old church was pulled down at the same time. My ancestor had his own ideas about architecture and ornament. Still, I imagine the prayers of the worshippers might be of better quality in an ugly building. They would be less likely to be distracted by their surroundings.'

This seemed a rather unusual view, for it is generally held that beauty and antiquity create the best atmosphere for worship, but nobody felt disposed to argue the point. In the

end, Digby and Vanessa went to the morning service, while Mark and Primrose walked in the woods. It was not known how Professor Mainwaring and Miss Clovis spent their Sunday morning, but they appeared before lunch for drinks in the morning-room. The churchgoers felt a sense of virtue, for the singing had been hearty and the sermon short but good; the walkers had perhaps gained less spiritually, but their skins glowed from the fresh air and they felt ready for their lunch. Miss Clovis seemed rather subdued and pale. She drank two glasses of gin with steady concentration.

They sat down at the table for the last big meal of their stay, for it had been arranged that they should leave after an early cup of tea.

After the soup a pair of ducklings was brought on to a side table and Professor Mainwaring rose to carve them.

'I hope you all like the meat of brown-fleshed birds?' he asked.

'Oh, yes, thank you, I prefer it to chicken,' said Vanessa, and the others made suitable murmurs.

'I expect you are wondering why I asked you here for this week-end, instead of interviewing you more formally with my good colleagues Professor Fairfax and Dr. Vere,' the Professor went on.

'It has been very pleasant for us,' said Digby.

'Yes, and I feel that I know you all better now. Each one of you has appeared in his true colours, has emerged as a definite personality. You, my dear,' he turned to Primrose, 'are a brave young lady with Bolshevist views. I think you will go about trying to do good.'

Mark stifled a laugh.

'And you, Mr. Penfold,' continued the Professor turning to him, 'are a promising young man who will go far. I see you in a wealthy setting, a connoisseur of fine living, perhaps not as an anthropologist at all,' he mused, as if trying to reconcile a contradiction in terms here.

'I can't quite see myself taking a dozen of this excellent claret into the bush,' said Mark lightly, but inwardly he was cast down, for it seemed that he was not to be awarded one of the grants.

'And you,' he turned now to Vanessa, 'are an impressionable young lady, who will look for the romance of life. Perhaps you would find it difficult to take the detached view necessary for successful fieldwork.'

'Oh, dear,' Vanessa cried out, 'that means I haven't got a grant, then.'

Digby awaited his turn with a certain amount of complacency. It looked as if it was going to be Primrose and himself. All the same, he thought Mark's character reading much more interesting than his own which Professor Mainwaring was now giving out.

'I think you are a worthy young man,' he declared. 'You will not, perhaps, set the Thames on fire, or even the Niger or Zambezi,' he added with a chuckle, 'but you are very conscientious and will probably make an excellent husband and father.'

Mark shot a malicious glance at Digby, who was annoyed to feel himself blushing.

'I wonder how many of you have read Shakespeare's *Timon of Athens*?' asked the Professor. 'Not one of the *great* plays, but there are some fine passages in it, and it may be appropriate here . . .'

'Felix, this is intolerable – you will have to tell them. You can't keep them in suspense any longer,' Miss Clovis burst out.

'Could not *you* tell them, my dear Esther? It might come better from a woman.'

'I? Certainly I will tell them.' She paused and took a gulp of wine, then began speaking in short gruff sentences. 'It is this. There is *no* money. And there are no research grants. Father Gemini has *stolen* it. We heard last night.'

Nobody knew what to say.

'Oh, dear,' Digby ventured, feeling that the feebleness of his utterance accorded well with the character he had just been given.

'Sire, this is grievous news,' said Mark, the shock making him flippant.

The girls did not say anything at first, but after a while Vanessa asked what Father Gemini had to do with it and how could he have 'stolen' the money.

'Somehow, perhaps we shall never know how,' said Miss Clovis, 'he persuaded Mrs. Foresight to let him have the money she had promised to us for a research project of his own. Gertrude – Miss Lydgate – telephoned me last night to tell me. I am not sure that she herself is entirely guiltless, though I cannot believe that she can have been a party to such a dastardly plan,' she concluded dramatically.

'Then Mrs. Foresight had not actually given the money?' asked Mark.

'Well, no,' Miss Clovis sounded flustered, 'but she had promised it. Isn't that so, Felix?'

'Yes, certainly she had promised it,' he said in a casual, almost uninterested tone. 'Now, I wonder if you can see why I am reminded of *Timon of Athens*? You have forgotten the play? Let me refresh your memory of the banquet scene. When the dishes are uncovered they are found to contain nothing but warm water!'

'Well, that certainly doesn't apply here,' said Digby, magnanimously, he felt.

'Afterwards,' continued Professor Mainwaring, 'Timon retires to a cave, but I don't think I can carry the parallel as far as that. I am very sorry that this has happened. Naturally I shall do all I can to see that you get grants for field research from somewhere, though really,' he mused, 'I often wonder whether the whole business of going out into the field to study a primitive tribe isn't vastly overrated. Heat, discomfort,

illness, frustration . . . and at the end of it all – what?' He faced his hearers almost challenging them to answer him, but his sentence fell into silence. 'And now,' he went on, 'I shall retire to my – er – *cave*, there to meditate on the machinations of Minnie – Mrs. Foresight,' he added quickly. 'Henry will order a taxi to take you to the station as I have no motor-car of my own.'

The young people stood up rather sheepishly, then Vanessa went forward and shook his hand, thanking him for his hospitality; the others followed her example. Miss Clovis stayed with them and they had coffee together in the smoking-room.

'I can't help feeling that the Jesuits are behind this,' she said.

'But Father Gemini isn't a Jesuit, is he?' asked Mark.

Miss Clovis snorted. 'No, he isn't. The Jesuits are men of *intellect*, even their enemies must allow that. But he is known to have visited one of their establishments several times this year. I can imagine the plotting that went on there. Father Gemini is weak – he would be as wax in their hands. And Mrs. Foresight has taken him for a drive in her motor-car on more than one occasion. Who can tell what may have passed between them then?'

'It might have been interesting to have heard their conversation,' said Digby mildly.

'*Interesting!* I should think so indeed!'

'If I may venture a criticism,' said Mark. 'I think it would have been better if Professor Mainwaring had been sure of the money before he attempted to award the grants.'

'I feel rather sorry for him,' said Vanessa warmly. 'This whole thing must have been a blow to his prestige. I think you can see by his rather odd behaviour that he is feeling it very deeply.'

'Oh, he will do another tour in the United States,' said Miss Clovis. 'He has not yet lost the power of persuading elderly

ladies to part with their money.' There was a touch of contempt in her tone.

'It is a power we should all like to have,' said Mark. 'I wonder if a young man would have any chance of acquiring it?'

'Oh, you will go far, Mr. Penfold,' said Miss Clovis. 'That is obvious.'

'But in what direction?' asked Digby.

'We none of us know at the moment,' said Mark. 'I suppose we'd better see to our packing.'

'I hope this unfortunate affair doesn't mean that I shan't be seeing you at the research centre,' said Miss Clovis as they waited by the taxi.

'Oh, no, we shan't hold it against you,' said Mark almost insolently, but he might perhaps be excused for feeling that their relationship had undergone some subtle change which justified the tone.

'I think Miss Clovis was very upset,' said Digby, when they were in the train. 'After all it was rather a dreadful thing to happen – it will take some living down. Can't you just see Fairfax and Vere, yes and Todd and Apfelbaum too, rubbing their hands with glee, jumping for joy in the Antipodes? It will give *us* a kind of power, too. I think our status will be definitely improved now.'

'The whole system is wrong,' said Primrose indignantly. 'This being dependent on wealthy individuals for the money to do essential work.'

'A brave young lady with Bolshevist views,' chanted Mark, in mocking imitation of Professor Mainwaring's manner. He put his arms around her and attempted to kiss her, but she pushed him away and a good-natured struggle followed. Now that they were free from the strain of the week-end their conversation and behaviour became frivolous, almost licentious, and it was perhaps fortunate that the train was not crowded and they had a carriage to themselves.

Digby did a passable imitation of Miss Clovis breaking the news; they concocted a plot to kidnap Professor Mainwaring and imprison him in a cave, and were just deciding which of the learned societies would be likely to provide the highest ransom when they arrived at Victoria Station.

Their high spirits continued throughout their evening meal which they had all together in a Corner House, but eventually they flagged and went their separate ways, Vanessa to her home in Kensington, Primrose to her lodgings in West Hampstead, Mark and Digby to their flat in Camden Town.

'I think,' said Digby with a self-consciously casual air, 'I'll just ring up Deirdre and tell her what's happened. I hope it isn't too late – I shouldn't like to disturb the household.'

Rhoda answered the telephone. Deirdre was upstairs in her room, writing, or trying to compose, a letter to Tom. She was beginning to experience the difficulties of correspondence with a person for whom one feels infatuation rather than love or friendship. When she had finished telling him her rather meagre bits of news there seemed little else to say. She loved him, she missed him, she still felt like Scheherezade trying to keep his love and interest, but she could not go on saying these things. She even found herself wondering what Catherine would have said, but then Catherine was a writer of fiction and might look upon a letter as a piece of literature composed by herself to suit a particular person, rather than a spontaneous outpouring of the feelings. Deirdre had her own ideas, for who has not, of how to write a love letter, but Tom was the first person on whom she had ever practised the art, and somehow he did not seem to fit with the person who should receive the kind of letters she could write. His own were full of a variety of news which she could barely comment on intelligently, let alone equal – political intrigues, elections, local gossip – but once he wrote 'Do you remember that evening we went walking by the river and sat on the seat by the elderberry bushes? The smell of them reminded me of

childhood – a moment out of Proust.' Deirdre had not remembered the flowers particularly, only that she had declared her love for the first time and he had seemed to accept it. Must I then read Proust? she asked herself despairingly, seeing the twelve blue volumes with red labels in Catherine's bookshelves, for she was not much of a reader at the best of times.

Her aunt's tap on the door and subsequent appearance in the room were almost a relief, though she looked annoyed at the interruption.

'Telephone for you, dear, a *man's* voice,' Rhoda could not resist adding, for it was not Bernard and she was curious to know who could be telephoning her niece at this late hour.

Deirdre approached the instrument suspiciously but her manner warmed when she heard Digby's voice. They had a very long conversation which Rhoda was able to hear through the drawing-room door which she had left ajar. Deirdre sounded indignant and tender by turns and said that she would meet whoever it was for lunch next day.

'I wonder if Tom would like that,' said Rhoda to her sister, who was mending one of Malcolm's shirts and listening to a religious talk on the Light Programme.

'What? Deirdre having lunch with another young man? But why shouldn't she?' asked Mabel in her usual mild tone 'After all, they aren't engaged, you know.'

'That was Digby Fox,' said Deirdre coming into the room 'Isn't it a shame, there's no money for the Foresight research grants after all. Father Gemini has pinched it for his linguistic research.'

'What, that little priest who is a friend of Miss Lydgate's?' asked Mabel. 'Fancy that! Such a funny-looking little man, too.'

'Digby Fox is a friend of Tom's isn't he?' asked Rhoda, adjusting the situation to her own satisfaction.

'Yes, and a friend of mine, too,' said Deirdre. 'I must go

and tell Tom about this – I was just in the middle of writing to him.'

She still had a half sheet of air-letter to fill up and the news Digby had told her brought her nicely to the end of it. There was hardly even room for an affectionate ending. She read the letter through, kissed it, and then sealed it up. It would be nice having lunch with Digby tomorrow, she thought; it was the first time since Tom had gone away that she had consciously looked forward to anything.

Digby came away from the telephone smiling and humming a little indefinite tune. He saw himself, perhaps as Professor Mainwaring had described him, worthy, painstaking and biding his time. Perhaps it would be like the tortoise and the hare – Tom, with his narrow aristocratic face and brilliant grey eyes, and Digby – he paused to look at himself in the glass above the umbrella-stand – mousy fair hair, blue eyes, good teeth . . .

'Do you realize,' said Mark coming out of the kitchen, 'that we have absolutely *nothing* for breakfast tomorrow morning?'

'No, I didn't,' said Digby absently.

'We ate what there was yesterday, and haven't had a chance to do any shopping,' Mark explained. 'I think I shall ring up Catherine, she may be able to help us. Perhaps she'll invite us round for a glass of beer.'

But Catherine's telephone went on ringing in her empty flat while she sat drinking bitter with Alaric Lydgate in a nearby public house. She had taken the bold step – which she would hardly have advised her magazine readers to imitate – of inviting him round for Sunday evening supper, knowing what a depressing meal this can be for anyone who lives alone. Afterwards she had thought he might like to visit the local, and so here they sat at a little round wet table and Catherine listened to Alaric talking about the trunks of notes he had up in his attic.

'Tom Mallow didn't approach me about them,' he said, 'and if he had, I should have felt bound to refuse him access to them until I had written up the material myself.'

Catherine was too tactful to inform him that Tom hadn't thought the notes would be of any use to him. 'Yes, I can appreciate that', she said. 'But . . .' she looked up at him, her eyes rather wide and soft-looking with hardly a trace of their usual sardonic merriment, 'do you *have* to write up the material? I mean,' she went on, 'wouldn't it be rather a bother to have to do it?'

Her suggestion was so outrageous that he could think of absolutely nothing to say. Ever since he could remember, almost, he had been going to 'write up his material'. He felt as if the ground were slipping away from under his feet and it was quite an effort to stand up and walk to the bar for some more drinks.

When he came back Catherine noticed that he carried two double whiskies. Oh, dear, she thought, he looks terribly Easter Island, or even like Mr. Rochester in *Jane Eyre*.

'And what is going on in your head now?' he asked, a little sarcastic.

'I was thinking,' said Catherine slowly, 'that it isn't only we poor women who can find consolation in literature. Men can have the comfort of imagining themselves like Heathcliff or Mr. Rochester. I wonder if they often do?'

'What rubbish you talk,' he said brusquely. But suddenly the sun broke through on the grim surface of the carved rock and he smiled.

'But what should I *do* with all my notes if I didn't write them up?' he asked.

'Oh, we'd soon think of something,' said Catherine gaily.

CHAPTER TWENTY

THE first meeting between Miss Clovis and Miss Lydgate after the fatal week-end was a stormy one. Things were said on both sides which might be regretted afterwards, and both felt the perverse satisfaction which is to be got from saying things of precisely that kind. It is very seldom that we can tell our friends *exactly* what we think of them; for some the occasion never presents itself, and they are perhaps the poorer for not having experienced the exultation of flinging the buried resentment and the usually irrelevant insult at a dear friend.

Afterwards they were both exhausted and hungry. They went together to the kitchen and, with hands still shaking, Miss Lydgate attempted to open a tin of pilchards. Miss Clovis took over from her with rough affection.

'I'm sorry, Gertrude,' she declared. 'I can see now that this was none of your doing.'

Miss Lydgate was bending over the bread-bin to get out the loaf. 'Let's have a strong cup of Nescafé,' she said, 'we both need it. I can't help feeling,' she went on as she filled the kettle, 'that I might have been a little more intelligent, though. That day when we were having lunch, he *hinted* in that sly way of his – you know how he does – that he might be getting funds from somewhere. Perhaps I should have *known*.'

'But if you *had* known, what could you have done?'

'I could have warned you and Felix. I could have spared you the strain of the week-end.'

'Well, the young things had some good meals, better than they usually get, I'm sure. That is something to the good.'

'Gemini – twins – there is something two-faced even about his name,' declared Miss Lydgate in a disgusted tone.

They sat down at the table, both rather subdued.

'I suppose this has been a purging, a catharsis,' said Miss Clovis. 'It has had the effect on us that a Greek tragedy might have. We are drained and exhausted of all feeling now.'

'This means the end of our linguistic collaboration. And I know what I shall do.' Miss Lydgate laid down her knife and fork and thumped the table. 'We were writing an article together, but it was not finished. *I shall withold my material on the Gana verb,*' she declared harshly, 'without that the whole thing will fall to pieces, but *he shall not have it*!'

Miss Clovis paused, then said, 'Yes, Gertrude, I can understand your feeling like that and I am grateful for your loyalty. But you are too great a scholar to be able to carry it through. That material on the Gana verb is too important to be withheld and it must be published in conjuction with Father Gemini's researches.'

'Yes, I see what you mean. It is greater than any of us and through it we must somehow rise above our petty squabbles.'

'That's it. *Floreat scientia!*' cried Miss Clovis.

They rose from the table making no attempt to do anything with the dishes, for it was not their custom to.

'I am worried about Alaric,' said Miss Lydgate. 'I telephoned him last night and he was not in. Mrs. Skinner didn't seem to know where he had gone.'

'I suppose he didn't tell her – he may not have thought it necessary.'

'But she told me that he was in the house when she went out to evening service at the chapel and when she came back he had gone without leaving any message. She didn't know what to do about the meal.'

'Well, he is a grown man,' said Miss Clovis with a bark of laughter. 'I'd always imagined he might break out sometime.'

'You don't think it could be anything like that, do you?'

Miss Lydgate looked worried. 'I am fifteen years older than he is and have always felt responsible for him. Mother always used to say that he was weak.'

'He may just have gone out to the cinema,' said Miss Clovis reassuringly, 'but if you're anxious let's pay him a surprise visit. He will surely be back now, twenty-four *hours* later.'

'Yes, let's do that. We'll go on the bus.'

As they got out of the bus and walked along the road, they heard a number of explosions, some in the distance, others startlingly near, and once the night sky was illuminated by a rocket which broke in a shower of green and golden stars. There was a smell of gunpowder in the cool frosty air.

'Why, it's Guy Fawkes night,' said Miss Clovis, 'what fun!'

'I hardly think that Alaric will be celebrating it in any way,' said Miss Lydgate, as they walked up the path to his front door.

'I don't know about that,' said Miss Clovis, peering round the side of the house. 'It looks almost as if he has a bonfire in the garden, unless it's next door.'

They rang the bell but nobody came for some time. Then Mrs. Skinner opened the door. She looked even more worried than usual and the large flower ear-rings she wore contrasted incongruously with her pinched anxious little face.

'Oh, Miss Lydgate,' she cried, 'Mr. Lydgate is in the garden, and Miss Oliphant is there.'

'Miss Oliphant? Who is Miss Oliphant?'

'We met her that Sunday afternoon,' Miss Clovis began to explain, but Miss Lydgate was already striding through the hall and out of the back door. 'Alaric!' she called. 'What are you doing?'

There was no answer so they ventured further into the garden, then stopped in the middle of the lawn to gasp at the sight that met their eyes. A large bonfire of sticks and garden

rubbish was blazing beyond the vegetable patch. Two figures, a tall man and a small woman, were poking at it vigorously with long sticks, pausing from time to time to throw on to it bundles of paper which they were taking from a tin trunk which stood on the ground nearby.

'Alaric, *what are you doing?*' Miss Lydgate's voice had now risen to a screech.

'Why, hullo, Gertrude,' he said, 'we're having a bonfire.'

'Yes,' said Catherine, her face shining in the firelight, 'Alaric had so much junk up in his attic and Guy Fawkes night seemed just the time to get rid of some of it.'

She is calling him Alaric, thought Gertrude irrelevantly.

'But these are your notes,' screamed Miss Clovis, snatching a half-burned sheet from the edge of the fire. '"They did not know when their ancestors left the place of the big rock nor why, nor could they say how long they had been in their present habitat . . ."' she read, then threw it back with an impatient gesture. 'Kinship tables!' she shrieked. 'You cannot let *these* go!' She snatched at another sheet, covered with little circles and triangles, but Alaric restrained her and poked it further into the fire with his stick.

'Esther, it's no good,' he said. 'I shall never write it up now. If Catherine hadn't encouraged me, I don't think it would ever have occurred to me that I could be free of this burden for ever.'

'Miss Oliphant, you are a wicked woman!' cried Miss Clovis, making as if to strike her.

'The bonfire was my idea,' said Alaric, 'and now we are all going to have some mulled wine.'

'What, even Mrs. Skinner?' asked Miss Lydgate, again with seeming irrelevance, but the idea of drinking with Mrs. Skinner was certainly a startling one.

'Yes, she will be joining us.' He threw another bundle from the trunk on to the fire. Some of it, eaten by white ants, fell away like a shower of confetti.

'Oh, *pretty*!' Catherine cried.

'But what will you do now?' demanded Miss Lydgate.

'I don't really know. I shall be free to do whatever I want to. I shall still review books, of course, but I could even write a novel, I suppose.'

There was a shocked silence.

'He has the most wonderful material,' Catherine said.

Mrs. Skinner appeared on the lawn. 'The wine is ready,' she announced uneasily.

'Then let's go in and drink it,' said Alaric. 'We can come out again afterwards to see how the bonfire is getting on.'

It was 'afterwards' that Rhoda, stationed at her uncurtained window in the darkness, saw them, dancing, or so she thought, round the fire. She imagined, though she could not really see clearly enough to be certain, that some were wearing masks. One figure, a small person, it might have been Catherine or even Mrs. Skinner, appeared to be wrapped in some kind of native cloth or blanket.

Rhoda had been out to supper at the vicarage earlier in the evening, so had not seen the beginning of the bonfire, only this strange 'orgy', for really it did seem to be almost that.

'Didn't you see them earlier?' she asked her sister accusingly.'

'Well, no, I was getting supper, and I can't see their garden from my room.'

'You should have gone into mine.'

'But how could I have known that anything was going on?' asked Mabel a little peevishly. 'Malcolm brought Phyllis in to supper and there was quite a lot to do.'

'I don't know what to make of it,' said Rhoda. 'I thought perhaps Deirdre might be with them, seeing Catherine there made me feel it.'

'Oh, Deirdre is across at the Lovells' helping them with their fireworks. She went after tea.'

'Oh, I see.' Rhoda appeared to hesitate as if wondering

where her duty lay. 'Perhaps I'll go across to the Lovells', then,' she said.

Next door she found the firework party in full swing. Mr. Lovell was enjoying himself enormously, sending up rockets and setting off the more elaborate pieces. It was perhaps a grief to him that his little boys, Roy and Peter, did not seem to share his enthusiasm, but he soon forgot his disappointment in his own enjoyment. The boys cowered at a safe distance, occasionally lighting a sparkler and watching it burn with a kind of fearful delight. Jenny was terrified and clung to Deirdre who, remembering her own childish fear of fireworks and dread of Guy Fawkes night, comforted the little girl and tried to draw her attention to the beauties of the scene. Mrs. Lovell was in the house with Snowball, the old sealyham, who was allowed to be frightened because it had been given out on the wireless that pets should be kept indoors. He sat complacently in his usual chair by the fire, covering it with his stiff white hairs.

'I don't know *what's* going on at Mr. Lydgate's,' said Rhoda, stumbling across the lawn. 'They're burning papers on a bonfire and dancing round it. It seems so ' – she hesitated for a word – '*unsuitable*', she brought out. 'We don't usually have things like that happening here, do we?'

'High time we did!' said Mr. Lovell jovially. 'Come on now, the last one. Who's going to set it off? Roy? Peter?'

The boys hung back. 'Oh, well, then I suppose I must do it myself. Look out, everybody!'

Cries of mingled delight, terror and relief were heard as the last rocket swished up into the sky. It broke in a shower of gold and silver stars.

Mr. Lovell then invited them into the house for refreshments, and they drank cocoa and ate sandwiches in the cold bare sitting-room, full of shabby Scandinavian furniture. As the dog was sitting in the only comfortable chair, they were obliged to crouch round the fire and soon took their leave,

for Mrs. Lovell had to put the children to bed and Mr. Lovell to take Snowball for his evening walk.

'Look, the party seems to be breaking up,' said Rhoda eagerly, for voices could be heard in Mr. Lydgate's front garden and when they came a little nearer it was possible to see Miss Clovis and Miss Lydgate by the front door. Catherine was somewhere in the shadows by a laurel bush and when the others had gone came over to talk to Deirdre.

'What news of Tom?' she asked.

'Oh, I've just written to him,' said Deirdre. 'It's difficult to know how he really is. He seems busy,' she added doubtfully.

'Don't I know those letters!' said Catherine. 'So terrifyingly occupied with such momentous things. But darling Tom, we wouldn't really have him any different, would we?'

Deirdre did not much like the 'we' but could hardly do less than agree with her.

'Don't forget that you must send Christmas greetings horribly early,' said Catherine. 'Almost now, I believe.'

'Yes, I know,' said Deirdre a little stiffly.

'Tom always sends such curious cards, scenes of African life, that only make him seem even farther away and they always arrive *weeks* before Christmas.'

Catherine did not know, indeed how could she, that before Tom could post his Christmas cards, he would be lying dead, accidentally shot in a political riot, in which he had become involved more out of curiosity than passionate conviction.

The harassed young administrative officer, who had been in charge of the proceedings, had quite enough to worry him without the added anxiety of protecting anthropologists who meddled in politics. But he had liked Tom Mallow – they had often had an evening's drinking together – and it was he who found the Christmas cards, stamped and ready to be posted, lying on the table in Tom's hut. He had thrown them away, feeling that his friends would only be distressed to receive

them now. There had also been an unfinished letter on the table – obviously to a girl – and he had not known what to do with that. He remembered that Mallow had once brought out a photograph of a girl sitting on a seat in a garden with two dogs – retrievers, he thought – lying at her feet. But later, when he was gathering up some more papers, he had come across letters from two different girls. Which was the one with the dogs, then? And had she been his girl friend or the only one he happened to have a photograph of? Well, it was none of his business, and perhaps it was better not to meddle in things that might become too complicated. So he bundled up the letter with the notes on kinship and land tenure and sent the whole lot back to Mallow's family in England.

CHAPTER TWENTY-ONE

MARK and Digby received the news from Professor Fairfax, who, perhaps because of his nervousness, had seemed almost facetious, as if Tom had been caught out in some childish prank.

'Anthropologists don't usually die in the field,' Mark pointed out. 'It's hardly surprising that Fairfax didn't rise to the occasion. He may do better the next time it happens.'

They talked together in their usual way, for they did not know how otherwise to express their feelings or even yet what their feelings were. Digby thought first of Deirdre and the effect that Tom's death might have on her; Mark of the 'unexpended balance' of Tom's field grant and who was likely to get it.

'The money can't die with him,' he pointed out sensibly. 'Obviously it will be given to somebody else – why not you?'

'But why me particularly?'

'I may not be needing it myself. I've been meaning to tell you sometime that I may be giving up anthropology,' said Mark quickly. 'Susan's father talks of offering me a position in his firm.'

'Well, perhaps you're the most fitted of all of us to wear the bowler hat and carry the rolled umbrella,' said Digby. He spoke lightly but inwardly he was shocked to think of Mark deserting like this, leaving their life of struggle and poverty for the prospect of ease and luxury. It was as if a monk should forsake his cloister to embrace the riches of the world.

'What about Catherine?' he said suddenly. 'Will anybody

have told her? Perhaps we should try to comfort her.' He did not mention the comforting of Deirdre, feeling that Mark's presence would be unnecessary here.

It was the middle of the afternoon when they went to her flat. She came to the door, her hair rough and wild, and with no make-up on her face, and offered them beer from a quart bottle which had been opened but not corked up again. It tasted flat and sour. A teapot and cup stood on the table and there was a sheet of paper in her typewriter. Mark craned his head round to read what she had been writing; it seemed to be an article about how to give an 'inexpensive' cocktail party.

'Yes, darling, "inexpensive" or *cheap*, really,' said Catherine brightly. 'Don't get the *best* French vermouth and put more and more ice with the drinks so that as time goes on people will be drinking coloured melted ice-water and they won't even know! And if they suspect, then they're horrid people and not the kind you'd want to have at your party anyway. Writing is such a *comfort*, isn't it, that's what people always say – it really does take you out of yourself. I sometimes feel it lets you more into yourself, though, and really the very *worst* part.'

'Catty, dear, we're so very sorry,' said Digby helplessly. 'We came to see if there was anything . . .'

'Bless you both, but what can anyone do? It seems a noble way to die, doesn't it, fighting for an oppressed people's freedom against the tyranny of British rule? You can see now that it was all really justified, the breaking-away from his upbringing, the great house, the public school . . . the last time he went home he was so upset – he thought he had done the wrong thing, leaving it all.'

'But surely it wasn't quite that, was it?' said Mark a little impatiently. 'He got involved in this crowd purely by accident. I don't think he intended to set himself up in opposition to anyone or anything, he just happened to be there, as any other anthropologist might have been.'

'Any *other* anthropologist!' said Catherine scornfully. 'The others would all have been hiding in their huts behind their files of notes. You were always jealous of him, all of you, because you knew you could never hope to equal him in anything . . .' she burst into tears and ran from the room. They heard her go into her bedroom and then leave the house, slamming the front door after her. Digby hurried to the window and saw her jump on to a bus which was just leaving the stop.

'I suppose she knows where she's going,' he said uneasily. 'Perhaps she'll just go for a ride till she's calmed down. It was a pity you had to argue with her, we should just have humoured her, whatever she said.'

'But it's going to be so tiresome if Tom is going to be built up into a kind of Lawrence of Arabia figure,' said Mark. 'I didn't mean to be unkind, but it seemed so very far from the truth.'

'I wonder if your regard for truth will be helpful to you in your business career,' said Digby sarcastically. 'It might even be a hindrance.'

They began to bicker in a senseless way and then left the flat. Digby had telephoned Deirdre to meet him and began anxiously to rehearse what he was going to say to her. Mark went back to his room rather sulkily. He was sorry about Tom but in his experience it was only elderly and distant relatives who died. All this, as he put it to himself, was a bit much. By going to such extremes Tom had gone too far.

On the bus Catherine had time to calm down and even to feel sorry that she had spoken so sharply to Mark. She sank now into a kind of peace and began to think about Tom. But she found herself remembering not the things they had shared but the things that had kept them apart, and mixed with spontaneous grief for him was a more selfish and personal sorrow at the failures in their relationship which had been her fault. How annoying she must sometimes have been with her

235

wild fancies and her quotations! She remembered the first and only time they had walked along this suburban road together, the house called 'Nirvana' and the stone lions with their blunted paws and noses. The gardens were bare and wintry now, the little front lawns dull and rough-looking; bulbs would be pushing up under the earth but she could not see them yet. Inside the houses all was cosiness and security. In one, a woman bent down over a fire and toasted crumpets; Catherine imagined them charred at the edges but deliciously dripping with butter. In another, a child sat at a table with a green baize cloth, drawing in brightly coloured chalks. Some rooms already had their curtains drawn and she could only guess at the scenes inside. When she had nearly reached the Swans' house she happened to glance across the road and was in time to see a movement of the rust-coloured curtains and old Mrs. Dulke's head come peering out between them.

'Catherine! How nice to see you!' Rhoda came to the door in answer to her ring. 'You're just in time for tea.'

Obviously, then, they didn't know about Tom.

'Is Deirdre in?' Catherine asked, after she had acknowledged Rhoda's welcome in a suitable way.

'Well, no, she's just gone out – I'm surprised you didn't see her on your way from the bus-stop. You can only just have missed her. One of her boy friends rang up and wanted her to meet him for tea.' Rhoda's tone was full of satisfaction.

'Do you know who it was?'

'Let me see, now . . . really, she seems to know so many boys and of course she doesn't always tell her aunt or even her mother who she's going out with, but I did just happen to hear her on the telephone, and I *think* it was Digby, that nice tall fair young man.'

'I'm glad she is with him,' Catherine said, 'I'm afraid we have had a piece of tragic news – Tom has been killed in Africa.'

'Oh, *no* . . . how terrible! By natives?'

Catherine saw past Rhoda's shocked face into her thoughts, the shouting mob of black bodies brandishing spears, or the sly arrow, tipped with poison for which there was no known antidote, fired from an overhanging jungle tree.

'No, there was apparently some rioting at the time of the elections and the police had to open fire. Tom was mixed up in the crowd. It was an accident, of course – they couldn't have seen him.'

'But, surely, a white man among all those natives . . .' Rhoda protested, and again Catherine saw her picture of Tom, the British anthropologist in immaculate white shorts and topee, note-book and pencil in hand.

'I'm afraid it wouldn't be quite like that,' she said. 'He was probably wearing a native robe – he often used to.'

'Oh, what a mistake!' Rhoda burst out. 'No good can come of lowering oneself like that.'

'Well, he used to say it was more comfortable,' said Catherine lamely, feeling that they were getting off the point.

They had been standing in the hall, but now Rhoda led Catherine into the drawing-room. There was some light tinkling music on the wireless and the sound of it, together with the bright fire, chintz-covered chairs and sofa, and Mabel Swan sitting with her feet up on a pouffe reading the latest work of a best-selling female novelist, gave Catherine a feeling of safety and comfort, for she had seen no domestic interior that day but the desolation of her own flat. She was glad to sit for some minutes making small talk with Mabel while Rhoda went out to make the tea. Mabel had evidently been dozing over her book so Catherine said nothing about Tom. It was not until Rhoda came back into the room that the news was broken to her.

Rhoda adopted a firm manner as if fearing that Mabel might become hysterical. 'You mustn't cry, dear,' she said to her sister, who showed no signs of doing so. 'We must be strong for Deirdre's sake.'

'He was a nice young man,' said Mabel vaguely. 'I can't say that he made much more impression on me than that. He seemed just like Malcolm or Bernard, but to Deirdre he was something special.' She sat with her hands round her teacup as if to draw warmth from it. 'He was her first love and that isn't easily forgotten.'

'There will be other young men in her life,' said Rhoda sensibly. 'We must encourage her not to brood too much.'

'You must allow Deirdre her grief,' said Mabel almost sharply. 'You don't know what it is to lose somebody you love.'

'You've no right to say that, of course I do . . .' Rhoda's voice trembled and she began to refill the teacups in an agitated way.

Catherine noticed her confusion and wondered if she were trying to justify herself, to think of some kind of compensation for the shame of not having lost lover or husband, but only parents and others who had died at their natural and proper time. If women could not expect to savour all the experiences that life could offer, perhaps they did want the sad ones – not necessarily to have loved or been loved, but at least to have lost, she thought simply and without cynicism. She felt sorry for Rhoda and tried to turn the conversation away from Tom.

Shortly afterwards Malcolm came in with his flat brief-case and evening paper and the news was broken to him. He stood awkwardly in the doorway, not knowing what to say, darting embarrassed glances at Catherine. Then he went away and came back with a decanter of sherry and some glasses.

'This may make us feel better,' he said apologetically.

'I suppose it would be quite hot in Africa now,' said Mabel uneasily, 'though I suppose it's always hot there, really.'

'Yes, the harmattan begins about now.'

'What is that?' Rhoda asked, a strained look of interest on her face.

'A hot dusty wind, isn't it?' Malcolm offered.

'I suppose the funeral will be *out there*,' said Rhoda. 'They could hardly ...'

'No, I expect there's an English cemetery or something,' said Catherine. 'Like Keats and Shelley in Rome, or Fielding in Lisbon. Yet Richard Burton is buried in Mortlake.' She paused, then went on quickly, 'Many Englishmen have died in Africa, you know, explorers and pioneers. Mostly they died of fevers or were killed by natives. Of course people manage to keep much healthier now, though there are still lots of unpleasant diseases people can get, Tom used to tell me. A little worm that races about all over your body and the only time you can catch it is when it goes careering across your eye-balls ...'

Rhoda threw a distressed glance at her sister. If only she had not mentioned the funeral, but she had a horror of silence at the best of times and this was surely one of the worst.

'You'll stay and have supper, won't you, dear?' she said, putting her hand on Catherine's.

'Thank you, I'd like to very much.'

Rhoda went out to the kitchen and Mabel followed.

'We could have some soup and open those lambs' tongues,' Rhoda said. 'Or the jar of chicken breasts. Or there's the cold beef. Do you think Deirdre will bring Digby in to supper with her?'

'I don't suppose she or Catherine will feel like eating,' said Mabel, 'and I'm not hungry myself, are you?'

'No, but the men must be fed,' said Rhoda firmly, holding on to the idea as something stable and comforting. Perhaps in some ways Martha's was the better part, she thought, as she bustled round the kitchen. Certainly there was satisfaction to be had from being able to do something practical in a time of sadness. 'Do you think we should ring up Father Tulliver?' she asked.

'Well, I hardly think so,' said Mabel. 'I don't know

Catherine's religious views, but she is talking rather wildly and one doesn't know how she might receive him.'

'No, and it's choir practice tonight, anyway,' said Rhoda sounding relieved.

'Oh, there's the front door,' said Mabel. 'Deirdre must have come back.'

Deirdre and Digby stood blinking under the hall light. Digby was so tall that his head knocked against the imitation lantern and set it swinging. Deirdre seemed to cling to him and at supper hardly took her eyes off him. She was too bewildered with the confusion of having lost one love and apparently found another all at once to be able to say very much.

Catherine was quite gay and Malcolm did his best, so that it was almost like one of the little supper parties Rhoda loved to arrange. This nice Digby did seem to be devoted to Deirdre. Tom or Digby, what did it really matter to her, as an aunt?

Later it was arranged that Catherine should stay the night, and she sat up in bed in the spare bedroom, wearing one of Mabel's nightdresses which was so much too long for her that she could wrap her feet in it. Deirdre stood by the bed or walked about the room, apparently trying to find words to say something.

'Oh, Catherine, I can talk to *you*,' she burst out at last. 'I know you won't be too shocked when I say that I can't really *feel* anything about Tom. Perhaps I'm stunned and the feelings will come later, but I think I used them all up when he went away. *That* was like a kind of death – people say parting is, don't they – and I was so worn out with crying then and being miserable and now I can't seem to feel *anything*. It seems so dreadful . . .' she covered her face with her hands and began to cry.

'I shouldn't be too upset about that,' said Catherine. She felt she ought to say something about Tom not wishing her

to be sad, the kind of things people say with such confidence about the dead as if they knew their feelings better than when they had been alive. But sometimes, she thought, grief was all one had to give them and even then one was conscious of the poverty of one's feelings as if there were some lack in oneself that prevented one from suffering as deeply, as splendidly almost, as people did in the works of sensitive female novelists.

'I'm only twenty, after all,' said Deirdre, 'and though I did love Tom terribly, of course, I just don't feel like a tragic figure and I'm sure Mother and Rhoda will expect me to be.'

'No, they won't,' said Catherine soothingly. 'They'll be glad that you've got Digby to comfort you.'

'Oh, yes, *Digby* . . .' The thought of him started Deirdre crying again but after a while she controlled herself and said, 'Do you remember when we were having lunch you said something about Elaine, about the memory of one's first love being very sweet?'

'Yes, I remember. And one's second love is perhaps even more sweet, but in a different way. And last love is supposed to be the best of all,' said Catherine almost merrily.

'I suppose you know when it *is* the last,' said Deirdre rather hopelessly.

'People say that you do,' Catherine reassured her. 'And now we'd better try to get some sleep, hadn't we?'

Deirdre went to her own room and Catherine got out of bed and stood by the window for some time, looking into the darkness of Alaric Lydgate's garden. Was there some movement there – did a masked figure on stilts move swiftly along the hedge – was that the low hum of a bull-roarer or only the wind in the apple trees? The Swans had asked her to stay with them for a little while and she thought that she might enjoy it, entering into the comfortable kind of life which she had only seen from the outside. She would be able to keep an eye on Alaric too, for she felt somehow responsible for him

since the evening when they had burned his notes. Like so many men, he needed a woman stronger than himself, for behind the harsh cragginess of the Easter Island façade cowered the small boy, uncertain of himself.

She grew cold at last and crept back into bed. She did not think she would be able to sleep so she settled herself down to read the books on the bedside table, mostly paper-backed thrillers and novels and a selection of poetry. Tom hadn't liked poetry, except Housman when he had been at school, but he used to let her recite or read it just as he would endure the extracts from the wine lists. She skimmed through the book from the beginning until she came to Vaughan, where she read,

> *He that hath found some fledg'd bird's nest, may know*
> *At first sight if the bird be flown;*
> *But what fair Well, or Grove he sings in now,*
> *That is to him unknown.*

She remembered the church she had gone into and the candle she had lit for Tom, then the meeting with the two pleasant-faced women and the clergyman who had mistaken her for somebody else. Did *they* know, she wondered?

CHAPTER TWENTY-TWO

ONE morning a few weeks later, Miss Clovis and Miss Lydgate sat at breakfast, reading their letters.

Miss Lydgate opened an envelope, snorted contemptuously, and flung down on the table a sheet of foolscap paper which Miss Clovis then took up. On it had been duplicated, rather badly and smudgily, a kind of circular letter, which began, 'Dear Colleague, I wonder if you are interested in the origins of the word *hyaena*?' Then followed a string of sentences in English and various African languages.

'The hyaenas have stolen the beer-strainers of the bad sons of the good women,' read Miss Lydgate in a derisive tone. '*Really!*'

Miss Clovis was not sure whether her friend's scorn was directed at some point in the sentence itself which, though certainly a little unusual and stilted, did not seem to her any more so than many others she had read in grammars of African languages, or whether it was the signature at the end of the letter – 'Egidio Gemini' – which had so enraged her.

'It seems to be rather badly done,' she commented, examining the paper more closely. 'I believe there is a kind of fluid you can get to cover up mistakes in the stencil. Evidently the fathers do not know of it, but of course they live out of the world.'

'I can just see them,' said Miss Lydgate angrily, 'turning the handle of the machine, wiping their inky hands on their cassocks, in the damp basement of that great barn in Kensington – well, *North* Kensington to be more accurate and, as we know, that is not really Kensington at all.'

'Well, *are* you interested in the origins of the word hyaena?' Miss Clovis asked.

'That's neither here nor there. If that's the way they're going to squander Mrs. Foresight's money, I think it's absolutely disgraceful.'

'Now listen to this,' said Miss Clovis soothingly, 'such a nice letter from Everard Bone, who's just back from the field; he asks whether anybody has thought of collecting together a volume of essays to celebrate Felix's seventieth birthday which will soon be upon us.'

'Festschrift for Felix!' boomed Miss Lydgate. 'What a splendid idea! We must cook up something really good.'

They left the table busy with ideas about the birthday tribute, turning over the names of those who should be asked to contribute and, almost as important, those who should not. Everard Bone would perhaps edit it himself; Miss Clovis would 'do the work', as she put it, rounding up and bullying the contributors and harrying the printers; Everard's wife Mildred would of course do the typing. Perhaps they could even think out an arresting title, the sort of thing that might make people buy it, in the hope that it was something new instead of a ragout of scraps which the contributors had had lying around for years and never done anything about. Of course it was possible that they might get *some* new or exciting stuff. Gertrude's work on the post-prandial fricatives, or whatever it was, would be most stimulating, Esther thought.

She arrived at the research centre later than usual and, glancing in at the readers in the library, noticed a good many new faces among them. So they come and go, she thought, perhaps a little tritely, hoping for much and sometimes receiving a little, or expecting nothing and getting more than they bargained for . . . she smiled and nodded vaguely at the two lumpish undergraduates, the dapper little priest and the three young women who had looked up at her entrance.

Then she moved on to the little room next door wondering if anybody had made use of the hat-stand there.

Inside, sitting rather far apart on the horsehair sofa, were Digby Fox and Deirdre Swan. They looked up a little guiltily as they said good morning.

'Ah, you find it quieter to work in here, do you?' Miss Clovis beamed. 'I am so glad that you are to have poor Tom Mallow's grant,' she added, turning to Digby. 'I feel that you really deserve it.' He was a nice young man and he had helped to move the horsehair sofa, she remembered. 'Is it true,' she asked, lowering her tone so that it was almost hushed, 'that your friend has forsaken anthropology and gone into *business*?'

'Yes, I'm afraid Mark's deserted us. It was rather a blow to me, really. He is going to work in the office of his future father-in-law in Leadenhall Street.'

'*Leadenhall Street!*' hissed Miss Clovis. 'The very sound of it is dreadful. And yet one is reminded even there of the African custom of the suitor giving service to the father of the girl he wishes to marry, but *Leadenhall* Street' – she seemed unable to leave the name alone – 'that's rather different from raising the mounds for the yams.'

'Yes, it certainly is,' said Digby rather feebly.

'And you, my dear,' Miss Clovis turned towards Deirdre, meaning to say something and then realizing that perhaps nothing was necessary. But had she not once, and not so very long ago, either, been discovered on this very sofa with poor Tom Mallow? Perhaps it would be better to have it moved back into her own room after all. Her thoughts flew to the lumpish young men in the libarary, they looked strong and willing, indeed, if she asked them to do it they could hardly refuse . . . But then one of those disconcerting waves of sentimentality which she had surprised in herself lately came over her and she thought, no, let the sofa remain where it is and if the young things want to hold hands, why shouldn't

they? After feeling a pang of sadness for Tom Mallow, who seemed to have been so quickly replaced, she remembered something she had once read about the beliefs of a certain African tribe. It described how the dead survive only as long as people think of them. When they are forgotten they die a second time and then reappear in the form of small mushroom-shaped anthills in the bush. This time they are thought to be really dead. She began to wonder how long she herself would be kept alive, under these conditions, Gertrude would remember her, perhaps . . .

'Ah, Esther, my dear, there you are!' Professor Mainwaring stood before her, wearing a rich-looking overcoat with an astrakhan collar. 'I have a piece of good news for you.'

'Really? I wonder what it can be.'

'I think I am going to be able to get some money for research grants. And where do you think I am going to get it from?'

'I can't imagine,' said Miss Clovis rather shortly.

'You could easily guess, but it is really *so* obvious that perhaps you won't be able to.'

'Oh, I don't know. Sweden? China? Brazil?'

'No, you are quite wrong. The United States of America!' he said gleefully. 'So simple, isn't it. I wonder we didn't think of it before.'

'Well, didn't we? I'm sure *I* did, but all the money seemed to have been snapped up by other bodies.'

'But they didn't know about Mrs. van Heep! She seemed *most* interested in our work. Cornelia,' he said thoughtfully, 'that is her name, beautiful, isn't it.'

'It's better than Minnie, certainly.'

'Ah, poor Minnie. You knew, of course, about our painful meeting? I am afraid I had to talk to her rather severely. You see, my dear Esther, Minnie is too full of what is known as *simple* goodness, and goodness is so much better when it is not simple. Can you imagine it, she really thought that as

Father Gemini was doing research in Africa too it wouldn't really matter who had the money – that it would come to the same thing in the end. I tried to make her understand how wrong she was, poor Minnie. I wonder if I succeeded?'

'Oh, I should think so,' said Miss Clovis shortly. 'And now, Felix, I really must get on with my – er – work.'

'And I shall go to meet Cornelia for luncheon. She returns to the United States next week.'

'Well, be sure and get the money before she goes.'

'Yes, I shall do that. *This* time I shall bring it away with me in a little bag!' He left the room in high good humour, hurried down into the street and hailed a taxi.

CHAPTER TWENTY-THREE

CATHERINE stayed nearly a fortnight at the Swans' house, during which she was cosseted and cared for and almost knew what it was like to be one of a family. In that short time she experienced all the cosiness and irritation which can come from living with thoroughly nice people with whom one has nothing in common. She enjoyed breakfast in bed, shopping, reading books from the library after lunch, listening to the wireless and knitting in the evenings. Sometimes it was a morning in the West End followed by lunch and a matinée, with the comfortable rattle of the tea-tray being passed over the knees in the dark as the third act began. But after a while she began to feel restless, like a trapped bird who might be safe and happy in a cage but must go out into the cruel world because it is the natural thing. She began to long for her flat and her typewriter and her odd solitary life. All sorts of ideas for stories and articles were bubbling up inside her and she could hardly wait to get back to work.

'Of course you must go, dear,' said Mabel, 'you will want to get back to your flat, though we have so much enjoyed having you here. You could always write upstairs in your room, you know. We shouldn't mind that a bit.'

Catherine imagined herself sitting up at the little desk in the spare room with the gas-fire on and everybody moving with rather ostentatious quiet on the stairs. Her eyes would be sure to light on the dressing-table, with its blue linen duchesse set embroidered with crinoline ladies and she knew that that would upset her.

'We were thinking of asking Mr. Lydgate in to supper

tomorrow evening,' said Rhoda hopefully. 'And if Deirdre asks Digby and Malcolm brings Phyllis it could be quite a nice little party.'

'Oh, yes,' Catherine agreed enthusiastically, for she did enjoy the supper parties and the preparation that went with them. But yesterday, over the garden hedge, Alaric had asked her to come out to the pub with him at a quarter to one and she had been forced to say that she couldn't very well because they always had lunch at one, and she couldn't come in late and smelling of beer. His face had gone rather Easter Island and he had turned away as if he had thought she didn't really *want* to come. She felt she could re-establish the right sort of contact only if she were free and living by herself.

'I shall often come and see you,' she told Mabel and Rhoda when she took her leave of them. 'But of course I must get back to my own squalor, really – you understand, don't you?'

They said that they did, but afterwards Rhoda remarked to Mabel that she couldn't understand why Catherine always referred to her living conditions in such strange terms. Surely it was just as easy to have things nice as not to, and Catherine did seem to be such a home-loving girl.

So Catherine returned to her flat and found her sitting-room just as she had left it, with the sheet of paper still in her type-writer and the cup and teapot still on the table, all untouched since the day she had heard of Tom's death. For she had been back only once to get some clothes and had done no more than open the door of her sitting-room and shut it again.

But now she set to work vigorously, turning on the wireless as she swept and dusted. It was Brahms, really 'noble' music which seemed to raise her work into a higher sphere, so that she found herself wondering if there were not something after all in the phrase 'dignity of labour' in which even women could share. When she had finished her cleaning she went over to the Cypriot restaurant and bought a bottle of red wine to drink with her evening meal. She cooked herself an oily

dish full of garlic, of the kind she had not eaten for a fortnight. Later, as she looked at herself in the glass in the bathroom, she noticed that her teeth were blackened by the wine, like Queen Elizabeth's were said to have been, she thought.

The next morning she was at her typewriter, wrestling with the 'inexpensive' cocktail party, when the telephone rang. It was a brisk 'good-class' woman's voice, the kind that might be accustomed to giving orders at Harrods or Fortnums.

'You don't know me,' it said, 'but I'm Josephine Coningsby, Tom Mallow's sister. My aunt, Mrs. Beddoes, gave me your address, I believe you've met her.'

'Yes, certainly, we . . .' Catherine's sentence tailed off, for it was difficult to know how to describe that curious meeting the day Tom had left her.

'Well, look,' said the voice briskly. 'I was thinking it would be nice if we could all meet together for lunch or something.'

'All? I don't quite see, I'm afraid.'

'Oh, I meant you and me and Elaine and this other girl – Deirdre I think her name is – could you get hold of her? I thought we could have a sort of talk about Tom, you know.'

'Oh, yes, that would be so – *right*, I think,' said Catherine falteringly, for everything today seemed to defy description. 'When shall we meet?'

A day was fixed and the place, which was to be Josephine's club somewhere near St. James's Street. Catherine looked forward to the occasion with a certain amount of apprehension, her lively fancy leaping forward and picturing all sorts of awkwardnesses and embarrassments. She had a long telephone conversation with Deirdre, whose chief worry had been about her clothes. Would black or grey – colours which she never wore – be expected, or would her tweed coat do? And must she buy a hat? Catherine did not think it would matter very much how they dressed since it would be most

unlikely that they would attain the standard set by Josephine and Elaine.

When Catherine and Deirdre entered the lounge of the club, Catherine's suppositions were proved correct, for they had hardly set foot on the soft carpet before two women, both wearing well-cut grey suits, small hats and pearls, and carrying fur wraps, stood up and advanced towards them. It was perhaps humiliating, Catherine felt, that she and Deirdre should be so easily recognized, hatless, in loose tweed coats and flat shoes. Deirdre had scraped back her loose and flowing hair into a kind of tail and darkened her eyebrows so much that she looked quite fierce. Catherine was just herself, but had made an effort to be neater than usual.

Introductions were made and they all sat down rather nervously. Elaine was the fairer of the two and looked younger. Josephine, Catherine noticed with a shock of surprise, once you got past the neat formality of her clothes was exactly like Tom. She had his wide-open grey eyes, delicate nose and sweet smile, but lacked Tom's gentle rather diffident manner. The effect was strangely disturbing.

'Well, now, what about a sherry?' said Josephine briskly, as if there were no other drink. 'A medium dry for everyone?'

The drinks came and were gratefully seized upon. It was difficult, perhaps impossible, to name a toast, so each woman took a rather furtive sip and then set down her glass.

'I thought it was a good idea for us to meet together like this,' said Josephine, as if beginning to fear that it might not be after all.

'Yes, we were all fond of Tom,' said Catherine, rising to the occasion. 'I suppose in a way we represent all the different aspects of his life.'

'Yes. I have known him the longest, of course,' said Josephine, 'but Elaine has known him since childhood too. We all went to children's parties together, just imagine it.' She smiled Tom's smile.

'He always hated them,' said Elaine gently. 'He was so shy.'

'I knew him for less than a year,' Deirdre broke in abruptly. 'I was sitting in the anthropology department one morning and he came in wearing his old blue corduroy jacket, and we went out and had a drink . . .' her voice faltered and she turned her head away.

'Shall we go in to lunch now?' said Josephine. 'The dining-room is through this way.'

They got up and walked slowly, in a kind of procession, into a large well-proportioned room, whose walls were hung with oil-paintings of middle-aged and elderly women. Catherine wondered who they were, for she was not clear as to the function of the club, the particular kind of tie that bound its members together. It must, she thought, be something to do with the Empire or politics, and must surely be rather more than the wearing of good clothes and furs and real pearls and accounts at the best London shops.

'Who were these women?' she asked brightly. 'What did they do?'

'Do?' Josephine seemed puzzled. 'I'm not sure that they *did* anything particular, they were just people who belonged in the past, the more distinguished members, I suppose.'

'Did they ride to hounds, perhaps?' Catherine asked.

'Perhaps they did,' said Elaine with her pleasant smile. 'It could be that. You see, this is a club for country women up in London. My mother used to belong.'

'Now, what shall we eat?' Josephine was studying the menu.

Another was placed before Catherine who read down the list of dishes in a daze, seeing only in a kind of horror that braised heart was five shillings.

'I'm not really very hungry,' Deirdre murmured.

'But it's a cold day and we ought to have a good meal,' said Elaine sensibly. 'I should think soup to begin with and then perhaps roast lamb or boiled chicken.'

The others accepted her suggestions gratefully, glad to have the choice made for them.

'The District Officer has very kindly sent all Tom's papers back by boat,' said Josephine, 'but they haven't actually arrived yet. Elaine and I were wondering whether you or Deirdre would like to have them. Of course we shouldn't really know what to do with them or even understand what they were,' she said comfortably. 'It seems a pity that we should have them if there's anything of value to anthropology in them.'

'You could send them to Miss Clovis,' Deirdre suggested. 'She would know what to do with them or who would be able to make use of them. Or perhaps Professor Fairfax might be better.'

'You wouldn't like to have them yourself?'

'Oh, no, please, I . . .' Deirdre stammered in confusion, overcome with dismay at the picture of herself and Digby starting their life together with the burden of poor Tom's field notes upon them.

'Of course I could get Harrods to store them,' said Josephine practically. 'I believe there are seven or eight large wooden chests. To think of Tom writing all that!' she laughed.

'Some of them probably contain carvings and sculpture,' said Catherine.

'You mean African carvings?' said Josephine. 'Well, I suppose that would be very crude stuff wouldn't it, not the kind of thing one would want to have in one's house?'

'Oh, some of them are positively *rude*!' said Catherine, temporarily forgetting herself. 'Of course they wouldn't go very well in some rooms,' she added quickly. 'I believe you have some lovely dogs,' she went on, turning to Elaine. 'Tom often spoke about them.'

'Yes, my golden retrievers, they are rather sweet. Tom told us that you wrote stories and were a very good cook,' said Elaine simply.

Catherine wondered if that was all Elaine knew. She hoped that she had perhaps been spared the full knowledge of what their relationship had been, but she felt that even had she known all she might have understood and forgiven.

'Tom's grave is in the cemetery out there,' said Josephine rather gruffly, 'and we shall have a tablet put up in the church at home. We thought you and Deirdre might like to know. It will be something quite simple, of course.'

'Thank you,' said Catherine, wondering why people always said things like 'quite simple, of course'. Presumably they had not in the seventeenth and eighteenth centuries, and she felt now that she would have liked Tom's memorial tablet to have weeping cherubs and a wealth of beautifully tortured marble surrounding it. As it was, she supposed it would be a flat piece of stone or brass with dull simple lettering, possibly outlined in red; the kind of thing for which some rather cowardly diocesan official could grant a faculty without any fear of criticism.

After coffee and some more general conversation it seemed to be time for them to go their separate ways.

'I'm going to see my aunt in Belgravia,' said Josephine. 'My cousin has just managed to get herself engaged – in her first season, too. Good show, isn't it.'

'Oh *yes*,' said Catherine sincerely. 'Your aunt seemed anxious because she was so tall.'

'Well, Guards' officers are the answer to that,' laughed Josephine. Then she became serious and, drawing Catherine aside, said in a low voice, 'I don't suppose anybody told you, I suppose nobody would, really, but a half-written letter to Elaine was found on the table in Tom's hut. The District Officer sent it with some small personal things. It was a nice chatty letter, you know, but at least she is able to know that he was thinking of her so very shortly before the end.'

'Yes, that is nice, I'm very glad,' said Catherine. She was feeling tired now and wanted to get away.

'That's what I feel. You see she has always loved Tom, there has never been anybody else.'

'Apparently there has never been anybody else,' said Catherine to Deirdre as they walked away from the club. 'You can imagine it somehow, can't you, that sweet girl, and really so unsuitable for Tom. Oh, *look*,' she exclaimed, for they were passing a pavement artist who was drawing dogs' heads, 'those dogs! You can see it all, can't you, so solid and brown and faithful. What *I* wanted to ask was if Josephine ever visited the *other* aunt, the one who lives in a hotel in South Kensington. I have a feeling she's rather old and neglected and pathetic somehow.'

'Catherine, are you all right, would you like to go and have a cup of tea somewhere?' asked Deirdre solicitously.

'Yes, let's have a cup of tea, but first I must find a coin for the dog-man.'

'You won't be lonely, will you?' Deirdre asked. 'You can always come and stay with us, you know.'

'Thank you, Deirdre, but I never mind being alone. And my life isn't quite over yet, you know,' said Catherine a little fretfully. For a moment she almost fancied that life, that tiresome elderly relative, had tweaked at her sleeve in a playful manner. 'I shall come and see you, of course, and I shall probably visit next door, too.'

'You mean Mr. Lydgate? I suppose he is rather intriguing, in a way.'

'It will be an interest, and it will take me out of myself to study somebody equally peculiar.'

'You sound so very detached. Won't it be any more than that?'

'Who knows!' Catherine called out in a gay tone as they parted outside the teashop.

Deirdre remembered these words when, some time later, she went up to her aunt's room to ask her for something and

found Rhoda and Mabel at the window. Rhoda was giving what appeared to be a running commentary on Alaric Lydgate's doings in his garden.

'All the masks out on the lawn,' she said, 'and now – oh, my goodness – he's got a great big shield and two spears and some moth-eaten old feather thing, I can't quite see what it is. I should think those things attract the moth terribly and will be all the better for a good airing. Now he's gone into the house again.'

'But he's come out again and with Catherine too,' said Mabel.

'Oh, yes, and he's got a knife in his hand. They're going right to the bottom of the garden. Now he seems to be cutting something and Catherine is helping him – what *can* they be doing? Why, now she's standing up and her arms are full of rhubarb! What a strange girl she is – first burning all those papers on the bonfire and now this. What odd turns life does take!' And how much more comfortable it sometimes was to observe it from a distance, to look down from an upper window, as it were, as the anthropologists did.

'We could have given her some rhubarb,' said Mabel mildly. 'We have plenty. She needn't have troubled Mr. Lydgate.'

'Oh, I don't suppose he would regard it as being any trouble,' said Rhoda. 'Besides, it might not be quite the same thing, having it from our garden.'

This last point, she felt with some complacency, was of a subtlety that perhaps only an unmarried woman could fully appreciate. But oh dear, she thought, if ever Catherine and Alaric should marry, what a difficult and peculiar couple they would make!